BALLYHOO

A COASTAL CRIME THRILLER

CAROLINE CLEMENS

FOUR OAKS
PUBLISHING

FOUR OAKS
PUBLISHING

SARASOTA. FLORIDA

This book is a work of fiction. Names, characters, places, and incidents are either the product of the author's imagination or are used fictitiously, and any resemblance to actual persons, living or dead, business establishments, events, or locales is entirely coincidental.

BALLYHOO

Cover art © Deranged Doctor Designs
Interior layout/typesetting by NightOwlFreelance.com

Paperback ISBN-13: 979-8-9895852-9-8

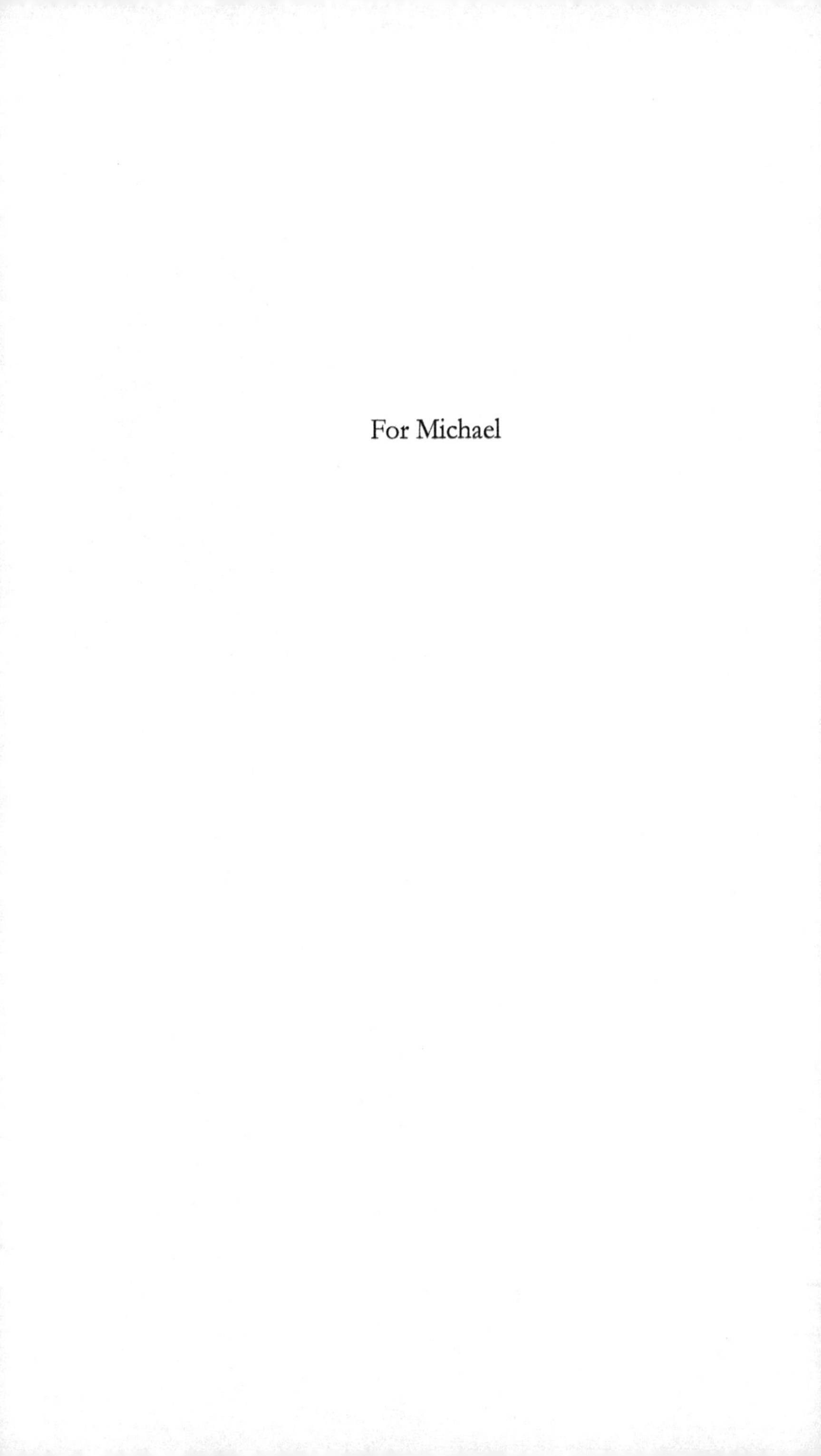

For Michael

"The sweetest smiles hold the darkest secrets..."
— *Sara Shepard, Flawless*

Contents

Contents

BALLYHOO

CHAPTER 1

"**I** know who you are! Here put the baggy in your hand, then move it under the bar top." The large older woman with medium-length, golden blonde hair instructed the young student sitting next to her at the bar across from the beach. The young female had tried to shake her hand after she recognized the woman from her internet picture. No need to be rude about it, thought the drug seeker.

"Now order me a coke to go, pay me fifty. Use your hand with the baggy to get it out of your purse after dropping the drugs in your purse. There are cameras in this joint." Mary settled in her seat wondering why she was even doing this small-time clown scene. She knew she could get busted. Her husband did and went to jail for a lengthy stay. She just needed to make a few extra bucks for her visit to the grandkids up north. "I'm glad you found this corner."

"Sure." She complied with her demands. All she wanted was some pills to get through exam week. Her friend told her about the speed pills that helped you to concentrate and get even better grades. She thought she'd try it out even though she never took drugs. "I thought the price was twenty-five."

"My price is fifty at first, then I will gift you the second time. Okay?"

"All right."

The bartender came around and asked for their drink orders. "I'll have a black cherry Truly and she needs a coke to go," she said fixing her gaze upon the newcomer. She put her hand in her purse, fumbled around placing the baggy down deep, then pulled out a fifty she had taken from her mother's purse and paid the woman.

"Thank you. You are doing fine. Smile. Your study pills are in there. I have heard they work super well!"

Silence.

After all what does an older woman and a young student have in common? Maybe she is a cop thought the young girl. No. Her friend gave her the tip. Her hand had shaken a bit getting the money out and a tingling sensation across her chest made her almost get up and leave. What was she doing? The drinks arrived. She pulled out a ten-dollar bill to pay. The bartender picked up the money and the old lady picked up her drink and left. Over. Done. Relief.

The band started up and the young student, about to graduate, decided why not begin tonight's study session. One week to go. She reached in her purse, fiddled with the baggy and pulled out one pill. She had heard they last like ten hours or so. The thought of one week to go put a smile on her face as she slipped the small pill in her mouth then chased it with the drink in front of her. She would order some food to go, stay up all night and ace her exams tomorrow thanks to this speed pill.

Sipping on her drink, waiting on her to go order, the

young student felt lightheaded. She felt tingly and her arms seemed to not do what she wanted them to do. Then the figures, other people at the bar became blurry. She flagged the waiter for a glass of water. She wanted to lay her head down and take a nap. And so, she did. Minutes later when her food came, she fell off the barstool to the ground hitting her head possibly cracking her skull. Observers looked and saw a very pale girl laying on the ground. Two customers got up to check her breathing to see if she was okay or needed help. One popped up and yelled, "call 911."

The scene held many bystanders sitting around the bar as a couple folks got to work. The paramedics slipped in minutes later and quickly assessed the situation. Initially, an oxygen mask was placed, then subverted to a closed mask which allowed forced bagged air to enter her lungs while cardiopulmonary resuscitation was instituted after vital signs failed to show active life. Things appeared dire in such short notice. They slipped her on a stretcher, miraculously performing continuous CPR, starting an intravenous source for medications and fluids. Then they cleared the area to defibrillate her heart. A decision was made to make haste for the emergency vehicle. Once in the vehicle a dose of epi was given via the IV source and observation of outcome was seen on the small monitor. No response. An emergency attendant intubated her quickly. The emergency vehicle sped away with sirens blazing and continuous emergency measures being deployed. The whole thing stirred up chills in numerous persons enjoying cocktails beachside that early evening in May. They all hoped she would be okay.

Because she was so young the paramedics needed to

understand what they were dealing with, one of them opened her purse to get an idea of maybe what she had taken. Usually, the very young just do not keel over sitting at a bar. He found the baggy looked at them and could see the color of the pill. One pill and a cocktail were not going to knock her on the ground. What is up he thought? He would have to send these off quickly if they were to save her life. And that was not going well right now. Her predicament seemed to lack story. One minute here having a drink, talking and the next on the floor. The bartender gave his description on the scene. Emergency cardiac drips were started for her heart. If they did not get her back soon, they would have to do a direct epi shot to the heart as the defibrillator was having no luck at all in restoring a heartbeat. He notified the emergency room the circumstances and estimated time of arrival. Then he called the chief of police to notify her parents, or family after looking at her license. The police chief told him he would send an officer to the hospital to identify the drug. Chief of police also put an officer on detail to review the bars surveillance video.

Off to the hospital they rushed. The bridge was notified to stay down. Hospital route time was six minutes. The emergency room prepared for her arrival. Unfortunately, they were use to overdoses and heart attacks near the small resort town.

Rachel walked the trail around the lake at her favorite park out by the highway. Trees were interspersed throughout the state park. Large oaks with their meandering branches held Spanish moss swaying from the gentle breezes. The place brought tranquility to one's soul. It was a place to forget the business of the day. She forgot about her patients and focused on her. What did she want to do with her one big life? She thought about her date tonight. It would be nice to catch up with a guy she knew back at the end of high school almost fifteen years ago. She was 33 and had not dated in a while. She had almost forgotten about her classmates and the many good times they had before graduating. Now that social media was everywhere, as they did not have it when they were in school, she could look up old friend's guys included. Rachel saw his profile on Instagram, hovered over it, then decided to follow him. He followed back and asked her out. She wondered what he would think about her being someone's mother. Her sister died but before it happened asked her if she would raise her only child. And, of course, she said yes through tearing eyes. Her heart ached for both of them. She checked her phone and still had 30 minutes before her new son needed to be picked up from after school.

Rachel walked around a second time. She sat down on one of the benches near the edge of the lake under a tree for shade. She watched a man, and apparently, his sons and daughter, throw a net and catch bait fish. They worked the shore. He knew what he was doing like maybe he fished for a living she realized. The picture was surreal. The sun glimmered across the small lake or pond and reeds hung close to shore, while birds flew around and ducks swam amongst the growth causing ripples to stream as far as one could see. The man looked up at her and smiled before he moved to a new location. Maybe they were from Mexico. She saw the wife. She surmised they were doing what they knew to do. It looked skillful and measured. She also wondered if he knew there was an alligator that lived in this pond. But, of course, he would know that. He put his capture in a bucket and kept moving. Time for her to move on too. She got up and walked to her new truck, a Jeep Gladiator. She loved the color, Snazzleberry Pearl, and had treated herself after working hard at two jobs with a truck! It had a vintage look with an elegant appeal. Patrick went to a friend's house for after school time due to getting out early. He saw her and ran to the truck.

"Aunt Rachel, I had so much fun!" He exclaimed almost out of breath.

"You did? Without me?"

"Yes."

"Why are you out of breath? Been running?"

He told her all about the games they had been playing and checking each other's running times. She smiled at him and told him her plans. Would he be okay tonight hanging out with another neighbor?

"Yes. Mam. What a day. I can handle it, for sure." He replied.

Rachel turned up the music just a little as she did not feel like talking now. Her mind was drifting and she drove to her two-bedroom apartment north of Cortez near the beach. She lived right next door to the Mexican restaurant where she worked a second job. She did that for fun and extra money. A neighbor of hers had a 14-year-old son and Patrick could stay with him tonight while Rachel had a date.

Once at the hospital personnel pulled the stretcher quickly into the ER and continued, seamlessly, life saving measures. Two officers arrived shortly thereafter; one took the pill for tests while the other stayed to meet with the family. Hopefully someone was coming. Another officer back at the station pulled up the bars surveillance video which had been sent to them and began to review it. He thought he recognized the older woman and told the chief. Chief told him to go question her at her residence. Good police work happens quickly and all things seemed to be going in the right direction except for one item. The young girl did not look like she was going to make it. It would be a miracle if she survived. Her heart had not started back up on its own. But they kept at it, now it had been over an hour.

The officer sped over to Mary Peters house. He knew where she lived as they use to canvas her neighborhood in the past trying to intervene in drug deals. It was not a bad neighborhood; it was just known to have lots of activity. Her husband was jailed five years ago for armed robbery of a bank and manufacturing meth. She had nothing to do with that as they were separated and living apart at the time. He knocked on her door. Mary had just gotten home after selling some harmless prescriptives to a student. Harmless is what she told herself because everyone has these in their cabinets anyway. Why the girl did not get them from a friend she did not know? But, hey, she made fifty bucks off her friends' friend.

"Mary?"

"Yes, officer. What can I do for you today?" She actually wondered why he was here. Maybe she was speeding or had an expired tag.

"I need your help. It is serious." He paused. He wanted to see if she would get rattled. She did not. She probably had no idea.

"Sure. You know I would help you with anything."

"I am not accusing you of anything. We got a young girl in the hospital ER, overdosed or something, and it is looking grim. She is not breathing and her heart stopped."

"Oh, no."

"Thing is you are on tape talking with her about a half hour ago at the bar in Cortez near the beach. You follow?"

"Officer. I follow."

"I am not here to arrest you. I need the name of the drug she took and where you got it from. We will worry about consequences later. I mean that."

"Shit. Are you kidding me? She must have taken something else. I gave her five speed pills, the kind for studying all night, you know for ADHD." Mary put her hand to her head to help her think better. "My friend has a friend who cleaned out her cabinet-at least that is what she told me. Do you think it was laced with something?"

"I am thinking something like that. How many more of those do you have?"

"Tons. Like she gave me about ten bottles with sixty each. I stood to make six hundred bucks a bottle for people who like to study. Damn." Mary shook her head. She had to go sit down.

"Mary, this is serious. Give me the rest of the pills and any others. We have got to investigate this. I think it might be fentanyl but we haven't had any down here in Florida yet." The officer got her to comply and told her the chief would oversee this case. He told her to say a prayer for the young victim. She nodded.

"Officer, let me know when she comes around. I want to know."

He said he would and that the chief would be in touch. He also instructed her to be quiet about the friend of the friend. Do not alert them before we investigate. He told her thanks.

"I will not. I will be right here. I thought I was helping. People sell these all the time, closest thing to meth but not as bad."

CHAPTER 2

Rachel pulled in to her place at the beach. She couldn't have been more excited to rent this place last year after she began a part time job as a server in the Mexican restaurant next door, Wicked Casa. Working four ten-hour shifts at the hospital using her college nursing skills provided her good money but the server job was just fun. She liked serving margaritas, Tex-Mex food, chips, and salsa to vacationers. Glancing over at the beach and watching the sunset with string lights around the tables mirrored the smiles and laughter from her guests. It could not be better and she was making bank! She brought in as much from the tables in eight hours as she made at the hospital. Sometimes she thought maybe she should ask for a raise.

She turned the car off. She would worry about these troubles later. She had another person to worry about now. It was a pleasure but it was babysitting twenty-four seven. Sometimes she forgot about him like she gently slapped her face to wake herself up. She hadn't been his mother for twelve years and it would take time. She caught herself either over worrying or just his presence completely slipping her mind. She did not feel like a mother yet, maybe that would come fairly soon.

"I will make you guys a frozen pizza. Does that sound good?"

"Perfect. Do you have pepperoni?"

"Of course, my favorite, besides pineapple and bacon."

"I will try that sometime. If you like it maybe I will too." Patrick responded. She liked that last comment.

"Okay. I am putting it in the oven while I shower. It will be here for you guys." Rachel hurried. She played some music from her YouTube channel. She heard a version of Jolene, an old Dolly song which sounded different. After her shower she poured a glass of wine and replayed the song. Something about it reminded her of an old love, maybe the one that got away. It was sad, reflective, stirring. She paused over her Pinterest account scrolling until she saw a vintage wedding gown on what could be her twin. Pretty. Nice. Marriage. Maybe that is something she should try. She scrolled away and saw a beach scene and special drinks. She finished looking about the time the song was over.

Tonight, though, would not be sad. Rachel was thirty-three with highlighted brunette hair and brown eyes. Her skin was flawless-she knew she was lucky in that regard. She tanned a few times a week and living here over on the beach she was getting dark this summer. Somehow, she maintained a health kick of fruits galore and salads topped with chicken or steak. Her swimming and scuba diving kept her fit and walks on the beach toned her legs. With her sixth sense, driving abilities and internet skills she sometimes told herself to get a job with an undercover unit. Afterall, at the end of high school, she and Seth, who she was meeting tonight, helped his dad, the chief of police work with the CIA to do a drug bust involving several business men and a pharmacist. The work was right out of the Miami Vice squad playbook. Rachel laughed; she had not been scared at all … until it was all over. She decided scary shit like that was not for her so instead she went to nursing school and used her empath and math skills to care for patients who needed highly skilled care. She was good at it too. Seth went into the service to get the bad guys, followed by a degree in something and then into the three letter agencies to get more bad guys. But now what? What were they both doing post high school? The question of what's life all about bothered her? The two of them would have plenty to talk about tonight.

Rachel pulled the pepperoni pizza out of the oven and let it cool for a few minutes. She went to her room and removed her robe. Looking through her clothes she found a fitted sundress, not too short or revealing. She wanted to feel casual and yet, well, a bit sexy. She fixed her hair up and away from her face and put on minimal makeup, added a few silver pieces of jewelry and went to cut the pizza for the guys.

She heard them in Patrick's room and gave them her spiel: no strangers allowed in, don't leave the premises and only go to Henry's place two doors down. Did they understand?

"Yes, we do. We will be right here playing video games!"

"Promise?"

"Promise. Do not worry, Aunt Rachel. I like it here and I want you to have a fun night. On your date."

"Thanks. I will. I will be home by one am."

"Bye."

"Bye. Pizza is ready. Night."

She left and drove down the road to Cortez. She had not been there in a while. The night was young and the air warm with a slight ocean breeze. She anticipated a wonderful evening.

The day was falling fast and one must arrive at their destination if they wished to watch the sunset. She knew she had about twenty minutes when she parked behind the hotel and crossed the street to the Driftwood Deck. She walked upstairs and went to the bar looking around. She had seen his IG photo and figured it wouldn't be too hard. Her burgundy and navy dress with white accents was perfect for tonight, sleeveless on one side and a low back showed off her tanned skin. The silver necklace had creatures from the sea banged out delicately and draped across her upper chest. She fiddled with the sand dollar and decided to order a drink. He must not be here yet.

"I'll have a white wine, please." She asked the bartender once she had his attention.

"You made it for the sunset, Rachel." A man standing next to her said softly near her ear. When she turned, she saw an unshaven and bearded man with long hair she did not recognize. He wore numerous studs of earrings in his left ear and a hoop on his right. She took a sip of her wine almost ignoring him. She should be nice and at least agree with him.

"I did. How do you know my name? Do I know you?"

"I suppose you do not really know me. It's been a while, quite a long while," he explained.

She took a better look at him. She stared into his eyes and then glanced over his body on down to his sandaled feet.

If he put a scarf around his head he could be a pirate, or better yet, a gypsy. He was tanned with wavy dark-blonde and long, very long hair. She saw steel blue eyes waiting for her approval. He stood a hand taller. It could not be. Wow. Had it been this long? He was so changed. She imagined she looked the same. Did she?

"Seth."

"Yes. It is me."

"You should update your Instagram photo. I would not have recognized you. How are you?"

"You look amazing! I mean that. Time has been good to you."

"Are you working up at Disney, or something, maybe acting in a play?"

"No, no and no. Let us get a table. I cannot wait to hear everything about you and watch the sunset together." He clinked her glass and they set out for a table to view the sunset.

"Let's do that."

"If you do not mind there's another level, which isn't finished yet, but the bartender lets me go all the way up. It is right here." He opened a door and let her in then both climbed up some stairs. She followed him all the way up to a private deck which held about four chairs. For Rachel it felt like she entered the first phase of a dare. Dare she go upstairs with a man she once knew?

"Beautiful." And it really was breathtaking. She and her pirate date sitting down above the bar in exclusivity. Her silver pieces sparkled like fireworks as in sparklers catching the setting sun and its glimmer of hope for another day.

"Yes. Beautiful." But for Seth the beauty was three feet from him. He wanted to reach out and touch her. Seth was a former Marine, spy detective, CIA and untouchable. He was not in love and had not been for over a decade. It took him by surprise when she followed his profile. It was all quite simple. He followed back and asked her out.

Seth was thirty-seven years old and working under cover for four years. His business was mostly drugs, money, intel, and some security issues. The big guys were worried about our interior, the comings and goings, especially with the internet. The internet was not his expertise, he had a couple of young guys handling that for him. He liked the one on one and following certain individuals, learning about their strengths and then the weaknesses, which allowed him access.

Rachel pulled out her phone and took a couple of sunset shots. She drank her wine and looked at her date still not comfortable with the look. "What do you want to talk about first? The old days or the new days?" She smiled at him.

"Let's go for the new days like we are starting fresh."

"I agree. What a good idea. You go first. What are you up to?"

The chairs they were sitting on had been side by side. Now he pulled his around and faced her with the sunset to his backside. Three stories high they were all alone with some faint music below and distant conversations. "Rachel, my get up is a disguise. I've been under cover for four years now, working my way into drug runners and cartel like groups here in America."

"No fucking way." She stared hard, waiting for him to laugh. He did not. He is serious.

"Just like that little stint we did in high school when they had us help with the sting."

"Yeah. But we weren't undercover and it was one day, one afternoon of pretending we were stoners."

"You remember? Good." He already told her way more than he had planned. She just brought it out in him. The truth. "Tell me what you are doing?"

"Okay. I'm a mother of a twelve-year-old, a cardiac nurse and I work at a Mexican restaurant for fun, and money. Also, I am still in shape. I dive, drive and have internet expertise. Swim too."

"You would make a fine partner. Want in?" What was he thinking? He could not believe those words flew out of his mouth. He did not look at her. He could not.

She was shocked. Did he just ask her to work with him undercover the first ten minutes into this date? "Well."

"That's a deep subject."

"I need a refill on my drink."

"What will you have? I will order. He will bring it up."

"Something stronger for this intense conversation. Order for me."

He uses his phone and texts the bartender to bring two Jameson and ginger ales to the rooftop. His phone dings back and reads "coming up right away." Seth had to make this arrangement especially for this date. He did not know how this was going to pan out and needed to safeguard himself and her.

"Tell me about your boy?"

CHAPTER 3

"Oh, he is adorable. His name is Patrick and he loves the computer. He lost his mother, my sister a few months ago. She asked me to be his mom and I said I would. It was all so sad. But life goes on and here I am on my first date in ages and I have a child I sometimes forget I have. I am adjusting."

"I am impressed you took that on. But I know you really had no choice. Still, lots of responsibility. So, kudos." Seth is impressed. He quiets for a few moments taking it in what it would be like to be a father.

"You know they teach you and you react back. It is natural like that. I am not saying it's easy, it's that it's not overly difficult. I heard you are supposed to love them and discipline them. I like to call it guidance and direction. I have been told some kids are easier than others."

Their drinks arrive. "Two Jameson's kids. Enjoy. It is on the house," said the bartender and left them alone.

"You're in good with the bartender, I take." Rachel sips the stronger drink and listens to Seth. He is good looking, even with the long hair and unshaven look. He appears to be an American drug lord, or rich kid with parents that live in Europe on some vast vineyard she speculates.

"Rachel, I have missed you. I have thought about you and hoped you were doing well. And you are."

"I went to college and had a good time until I had to settle down and study. I forgot about everything and everybody when that time came. Even you."

"And here we are. Watching the sunset high atop the bar in Cortez sipping free drinks," he chuckled and clinked her glass. "Promise me before we leave tonight, we'll get our feet wet in the ocean."

"Promise." She clinked back and smiled.

Meanwhile, at the hospital, the young girl who passed out from some drug at the beach bar earlier in the day, had stabilized and was on the ventilator. She had regained her own heartbeat and breaths, opened her eyes, and recognized her parents. Mary, the part time drug dealer, had come by the hospital, and profusely apologized to the parents and cops. The chief put her on house arrest with an undercover patrol nearby. He wanted to get the friend of a friend, he wanted to find the source. The medical doctor in charge ordered a CT scan for the morning. Tonight, everyone needed rest including the patient. Her parents slept in the waiting room saying they would get rest after her CT scan tomorrow.

The boys, Patrick and Henry, played video games then ate pepperoni pizza. All of it. Patrick did not know this, how could he, but Henry was an adventurer with no apparent boundaries. His own mother did not even know it. He did not break the law, except for driving, he just bent it and did whatever he wanted. He would drive his mom's car at night and go visit his girlfriend. He would take out the small whaler that belonged to his mom's brother out back in the intercoastal waterway. His uncle worked for the Coast Guard, not too far away, and Henry liked to poke around over there, too. He was always learning. Someday he wanted to be the captain of a big boat or work in the Navy or Coast Guard. He was not sure yet. Henry looked at his watch. It was 11:00 pm. Lots of time he thought to himself. He wanted to take his new friend on an adventure. They could be buddies and look out for each other.

"Patrick, what do you say we go on an adventure?" Henry was planning it as he asked.

"Sure, I will ask my aunt. She lets me do lots of things." He replied.

"This one requires only us to know about it. Okay?"

Patrick looked at Henry for a long time. Then in a split second, he decided. He liked his new friend and trusted him already. He played fair and gave Patrick lots of turns and seemed to care about him. For Patrick had seen death and chances at life were not always fair. He would take a small chance. "The adventure must be over by 12:30 am. No exceptions."

"Yes. We will be back by 12:30, even earlier, maybe." Henry smiled. He had a partner now to explore the intercoastal waterway at night.

"What do we need?"

"Flashlights, life jackets and swim trunks. Oh, and a towel. Bring a hoodie as well. It gets cold out there after swimming from the night air."

The boys gathered the items and fled to the small dock. It was pitch black out with calm waters. The wind had died down. Henry got them aboard and released the lines after starting the engine. It was surprisingly quiet. He went slow at first and then sped up. Patrick wondered how far he was going? He guessed he was the first mate and Henry the captain. Patrick was on his first adventure with Captain Henry.

Seth's phone went off with some song she did not recognize. It seemed to be in Spanish. It stopped almost as soon as it began. He looked at her. "Hey, I need to meet someone downstairs for five minutes. I will be right back."

"Okay, sure."

"Stay right here. I will not be long. Let us talk about you and the last 15 years. Think about that," he said as he made haste for the stairs.

Rachel sipped her drink. Things were going well. He was as interesting now as he was back then. Imagine that. Should she tell him about the drama? She should. He might be able to elaborate on some of the things she knew.

She stood up to stretch her legs and walked around the new bar making her way around the east side which faced the intercoastal and then to the south side. She looked down and saw Seth and some dude talking. Instantly, after a second look, she stepped out of view. Who was he talking with? She panicked and covered her mouth. Her eyes grew wide open. The guy looked like a fucking MS-13 gangster she had seen on the television. Covered in tattoos and short cropped hair- he looked like he could knife a guy to death. More panic. Geez. She crawled back to her chair and drank the rest of her drink voraciously. What on earth was he up to? She needed answers. Now. She closed her eyes and tried to listen to the music.

Seth was back in a flash and looked at her sitting in the chair. She turned and stared at him. She looked sad. Confused. He walked over to her. She said, "I'll have another, double shot."

He made the call to the bartender. He took her hands and held them. He wanted to hold her closer and closer. She seemed to be shaking and her hands were cold. The bartender brought the drinks and set them down.

"Who was that?"

"Who? The bartender?"

"No. The dude from the Mexican cartel."

"Oh, you saw him."

"Yes. I wish I had not."

"I will tell you everything but first I want to hear your story. Please, you first."

Rachel seemed to warm up to this idea. If she talked, she would forget about who she just saw with her own eyes. "Where do I start? Let us see. How about my sister? Yes, let us start there."

Rachel stood up and leaned against the balcony facing Seth. She smiled at him. Damn he was gorgeous tonight. "My sister got breast cancer and was cured, then it came back with a vengeance. It was bigger than her. Between diagnoses she wrote books and blogged, conquering the internet, or so she thought. She did not know if someone followed her online but she suspected someone was following her around town. She became very frightened. She did not feel she did anything wrong-so who would want to frighten her? They lured her by showing her pornography, etc. but she was not deterred. She knew who she was. Terrible thing is her husband had an accident and became paralyzed. So, their love life was over. After about a year she read literature through fan fic and steamy novels. This seemed to help with the awful situation presented to them in their young life."

"The internet can be a tough place. Many kinks to be worked out. Guys look at a lot of porn on the internet. I heard it was like 60% or more porn."

"We must protect the young kids and get the bad guys. I get it. Why would they set up women wanting to read steamy novels? Are they crazy?" She asked.

"Why would anybody be following her?"

"Possibly because her husband's brother was a felon. He tried to solve his own case and they took him down. They transferred him around the country from different towns so he couldn't get council. His parents were to meet him in Vegas and what do you know he was gone without notice. They did it on purpose."

"What did he do?"

"He sent an email to a judge. Not nice. Put him away for five years."

"Okay. Okay. Makes sense. They followed the family to trap him more. Or they were just playing with her-the wife."

"This is my sister, the nicest gal you will ever meet. In her most down of times they came after her by following her around town at stores, places she went and then material she read off the internet. Once they showed her violent sex and what she thought appeared possibly an underage girl. She reported it on the social media site. This was after very nice stories she had been reading. Steamy but not illegal. She felt tormented. Seriously. She left the social media sites and began writing her own books. I felt sorry for her."

"Did they ever find out who was doing the tormenting online?"

Rachel looked at him. And waited. She wanted him to guess. This was his line of business, not porn but mayhem, drugs, bad people, etc.

"What? Are you saying it was the big guys?"

She kept quiet.

"The IA agents do all the digging and investigating, then the top IA guys decided to help out some, looking in, and I mean looking in through the TV's, phone lines and bugs causing mayhem with my sister. No one believed her. I did. But I could not tell her why. I know some of the tricks but we swore secrecy."

"Rachel."

"Seth."

"There is a case just prosecuted that speaks to the injustices caused by the defacto, when the good guys become bad guys. The guy who got prosecuted said hundreds of them were doing bad things and he was the scapegoat."

"I guess they clean themselves up. I did not tell you everything. They affected the power grid, too." He grew wide eyed on this one. Lately power grids were in question, was it us or a foreign power?

"I wonder if maybe some other superpower, or country, was involved. Supernovas playing around?"

"Yes. I believe anything."

"Do you think the stress caused her second illness? And what about the brother of the husband. Where is he?"

"They gave a felony to the brother who never touched a soul, no burglary, no rape, no murder, just an honest guy trying to win in federal court. He spent five years in prison, some in solitary when a fellow convict placed a pen in the door. You are not supposed to prop open doors. He is out now and minding his own business. Until he upsets someone again while trying to undo his conviction. As for my sister, she says it felt like a gut punch, repeatedly, would hit her when she thought about it. Yes. It was extremely stressful. Like a door to 1984 and you can only call it a conspiracy theory because these guys are so good. But, the conviction of one, helps."

"Honesty is the best policy. Truth shall overcome evil. Did she know who it was before she died?"

CHAPTER 4

Rachel walked over to Seth. She needed a hug and he wanted to hug her. He held her. He also needed to know if her sister found out who the bad guys were. He was not like that. He told his computer buddies to always act professional. You never know who you are helping or who is watching. He held her for a long time then pulled back and with one hand touched her face on the side. "Please tell me she knew what happened and was at peace."

"Let's go sit on the floor behind the bar."

He led her and they sat facing each other. "Please tell."

"She found out everything and she was not insane, paranoid or telling a lie. One month she started listening to a storyteller online. She always watched the news, too. She pieced together the story and she felt at peace. She got her resolution. She did not want it to happen to anyone else. Think of all the young children who are vulnerable with Tik Tok and other very popular social medias. She wrote all the notes to another book but was not able to publish it as the cancer took her away. To heaven I suppose."

"Can you tell me the peace she received, the story? What

did she say?"

"I know some things are top secret and she will never know it completely. But she said someone came along at just the right time and helped her. Their lives had been devastated, tragically by cancer and an accident. Such good people. Evil. The evil tried to outdo the good but she would not let it. She remembers all the good feelings of love through literature and reading. The evil was from men behind computers altering the AI systems that were being developed to use for sickness and to help society."

"Wow. Rachel. That is incredible. There's likely more we'll never know because some sweep it under the carpet to protect the system."

"Kind of like the evilest thing one could do. Traumatic, really. Makes me want to help the good guys." She was being so honest. Yes. That is how she really felt.

Seth reached over and pulled her close to him. He kissed her. He did not know why. He just did. Very softly. The couple paused for a moment of reflection.

"They bugged her car, too."

"Of course they did. They always bug the car!"

The couple laughed a light laugh of relief after looking at each other with incredibility.

The boys who were skimming across the night on the black water to some tiny islands were oblivious to the goings on. They were intent to swim, have some fun, then return before being caught. If they got caught then Henry's mom would not trust him like she did now. He didn't want that, so even though he was breaking all his momma's laws, he did it anyway knowing he'd return before his partner would be found out. He slowed down so they would not hit land too hard. "Take the line from the bow and put it under a big rock on the land."

Patrick followed orders. Boy he would love to tell his aunt how much fun he was having. He would have to wait though, until he was seventeen or eighteen. He laughed.

"What's so funny?" asked Henry.

"Nothing. This is too much fun. Do you go out every night?"

"Naw, only about once or twice a week."

"Now you have a partner. I will pack some drinks next time, maybe a sandwich or two."

"We could bring a snorkel to see if the bottom lights up."

The boys swam and swam then dried off. They walked a little around the island and thought they heard voices off to the north side. Henry stopped Patrick with his hand on his shoulder, then turned him around and put his hand over his mouth. Patrick looked stunned and frightened. Henry decided they needed to get out of there. So, hastily they did.

The two of them sneakily walked ever so quietly and quickly back to the boat. It was dark by his boat. They boarded and sat down then floated some. They could still hear the voices and rustling. The boys remained quiet. Henry wondered what was going on. Someone else was on his island. He would have to come back and check it out. He told Patrick next time they would investigate the noises. He let the current pull him out some before starting the engine. Once in the clear he let it rip to return to the intercoastal passage to home.

Henry and his mind conjured up adventures. He slowed the boat to tell his new friend an idea he had. It would be dangerous, but not too dangerous, and fun. Patrick just looked at him frightened like. What kind of friend is he? Maybe he should tell his new mom. Mom, he thought about her, the one who died. It had been a while, he missed her at this moment. She would want to know and then guide him on what to do. He would have to sleep on this idea. Just let me get back safely from this adventure before the next one starts. "Okay," he said.

"Okay?" Henry confirmed the answer which was really a question.

The pills found in the purse of the young lady at the bar who was now in Intensive Care on a ventilator, intravenous cardiac drips (gtts), and slightly sedated were found to be Vyvanse and Adderall mixed with a potent Fentanyl. It was liked someone took them and dipped them like a chocolate covered ice cream cone. The police chief quickly put together a team to quietly pursue who and why this occurred. He contacted the local Drug Enforcement Agency and gave him what he knew. He made another call to an undercover agent named Seth. What they suspected would eventually happen just happened.

Seth answered his phone and just listened to the instructions. After a long pause he hung up.

"How about we go eat some food on this date?" He gave her a choice of two places and asked which place sounded better.

"I would love to eat at Coastal Bridges. I heard they have a fabulous grilled cheese with tomato and bacon!"

"Bacon?"

"We could split one, try an appetizer or some hushpuppies,

and order dessert as well."

"I love that idea. Let us go."

"Being under cover can you walk out of here with me?"

"Certainly. I am a man. I can be with a woman."

The date progressed nicely without further interference from strangers. No calls, no meetings, just Seth and Rachel eating dinner near the intercoastal waterway. Live music played and the couple was entertained. It became a real date totally enjoyed equally. They even toasted with a shot of tequila. Why not? Both were off tonight and the night was still young. They inquired about each other's family beyond the dreaded death of her sister and death of her husband a month later. Poor kid lost both parents. It was a sweet thing to do by Rachel to care for Patrick. He admired her strength and love. He told her he looked forward to meeting this kid and added, "but I should probably wait until after the Fourth of July."

"Why should you wait?"

"We need to talk some more. Are you ready?" He contemplated. Seth was having a wonderful evening and he did not want to ruin it. But he had received his call and the plan would be set in motion over the next week or so.

"No. I am not ready. Does it have something to do with your earrings and dread locks like hair?"

"Yup. Most definitely. I got the call tonight and it will be starting up. The thing is I could use more hands-on deck."

"More hands-on deck as in undercover agents with you?"

He eyed her for facial expressions and body language. He could tell she was interested. It was serious business and he needed to be sure. They would test her. He knew that. "Yes."

"How much will I need to know?"

"Nothing. But they will test you and I am sure you'll pass." He relayed.

"What kind of test?"

"You will have to break the law and get away with it."

"Will you be there to help me escape?"

"I will probably be the pick-up guy when you are on the run. That way we will prove we are a couple defying our own laws. That is how we prove we want the business and money. They want us desperate and good at what we do."

"You make it almost sound playful but my skin is on fire. Yes. I am scared thinking about it. But I want the bad guys, I want 'em really bad!"

"I am going to help you get them, because it's not all south of the border bad guys. It is right here in our backyard."

Rachel had no comment. She only shook her head. She was in. She was going to be undercover-for real. Damn.

"Oh, tell me more."

"I will. It is a six-week operation. We will be on a boat, a sailboat, after you prove yourself."

Seth paid the bill and the couple left the restaurant and headed for the beach.

The water was gently lapping the shore and the moon was high overhead. It gave some light on the beach as they strolled along. Nothing beats a moonlight walk on a beautiful beach cooled off now after the sun has set.

Seth stopped her and turned her towards him. He kissed her again. He was becoming overtaken by this gorgeous woman before him. He felt her shoulders, reached around, and held her back. And asked, "May I kiss you again?"

"Yes." She said yes and closed her eyes moving forward to meet his mouth. Nice. Unexpected.

Back up at the parking lot the couple talked before leaving.

"When will you give me all the details?"

"I will come by in a few days to give you the plan. You'll need to take off work for six weeks, say family emergency, and have someone watch Patrick. I am sorry. I hope that will not be too much of an inconvenience. Maybe you want to think about this. By tomorrow morning I will need to know."

"This was much more than a date. I realize it sounds crazy. But we did it once before, we can do it again. What's six weeks? Does it pay?"

"It pays a big payday; you'll like that perk for sure."

"It pays because it is dangerous. You like danger, don't you?" She had to ask it.

"No. No, Rachel. It likes me. I am good at it. Unfortunately, or fortunately." His face contorts and he swallows but continues. "When they threw those little boys off the tops of buildings, I wanted to kill those mutherfuckers. Those bad animals do not deserve life. Sorry. That is how I feel."

"I got you. I am going to help." He slipped in her car to accompany her home. He would walk back he told her.

"We are going to call this **'Operation Lexi'** because the first victim is in the hospital trying to stay alive as we speak."

"Operation Lexi. When will you pick me up?"

"Tuesday morning. I can say hi to Patrick and meet him that morning. We will be working out for two weeks and getting supplies. The boat will be a four-to-five-week venture. You okay with that?"

"I dive and swim. I can boat. At least I think I can for a month."

"Thank you. And goodnight. I had the best time."

"I did too. We waited a lifetime wouldn't you say?"

"We saved the best for last."

The door opens and it is Patrick.

"How was your date Aunt Rachel?"

"Good. Very good."

Patrick turns with eyes almost closed.

"Good night you two."

Seth leans in and gives her one last light kiss on the cheek.

"Night."

"Night." Rachel closes the door and walks in.

"You didn't tell me he was a pirate."

CHAPTER 5

The next morning Rachel drove Patrick and Henry to school in her new truck. The pair was quiet she thought. Everyone in the car was in a quiet mood. She dropped them, told them Henry's mother would pick them up, and that she needed to have a discussion with Patrick tonight.

"Anything important Aunt Rachel?"

"Yes, but it concerns me, not you directly. Everything will be okay. I will explain tonight."

"Sure. See you tonight."

Rachel headed to the hospital. Today was sunny and dry with no clouds to be seen. She did like May in Florida. It was summer without the humidity or rain, which came in June and July like the Gods of Thor. Once at the hospital she headed for the human resources department. She was sure they'd give her a month or two off. She never took all her holiday time nor called in sick. In fact, she thought about asking for a raise but decided to wait until she returned. Maybe they would miss her when she was out and think they really needed someone like her with all her experience.

While there they did a Covid test. It was a random test

the hospital was performing to see where they stood. Rachel had no symptoms but tested positive. Now she had had to tell Seth. Would they be allowed to begin the workout and preparations? She already knew what he would say. So, she went about her day. He had an 11:00 meeting then he was coming over to shore up the next week or two. Driving home she thought about the next six weeks living on a sail boat out to sea, capturing cartels trying to do bad things. She'd be using her skills like swimming and scuba diving, computer hacking and even some cooking for her and Seth. That sounded nice too.

Rachel packed up a few grocery bags to give to Henry's mom. She was delighted to watch Patrick for six weeks. The two would have company starting out the summer. They could even help at the snack and bait shop she had a half mile away. She hoped when she told Patrick tonight that it would be okay. It would be over before anyone knew it. Then things would go forward like birthdays, Thanksgiving and Christmas. Maybe she'd take him up north for the holidays to visit the grandparents.

Seth went to meet his computer guy who worked for the CIA. He was his contact and go between. This meeting was held out in the open. Seth knew certain operatives would be following him around maintaining their eye on the prize. A meeting like this had to be interpreted. If Seth was hiding something they wanted to know before the fact. Two of the surrounding tables had thugs listening to his every word. Seth just wanted to give the thumbs up on his partner and when they would be going out to sea. After today they would not have contact but the plan was laid out in every detail. If something went astray, they would have to meet at the supply store to change any plans. The couple was on their own going forward. If everything went right no one would get hurt, unless the cartel hit someone up, and a couple of top guys were about to expose themselves on both sides.

Seth and his buddy had worked out all the plans' weeks ago. Rachel would be briefed over the next week and a half. In essence, all Seth and Rachel had to do was retrieve the gold and replant it into the cartel's hands. But, oh, do not forget Rachel had to win them over first. Seth was sure Rachel could handle a little action. Most likely it would be a robbery and a getaway. That would likely happen next week right before the gold heist. Seth chuckled to himself thinking about it. He would make sure she was not harmed in any way.

Seth's buddy gave him the keys to a sail boat. He worked at a marina which rented boats. He made sure Seth had the paperwork, keys, and instructions. Seth wrote him a check for 36k which included the rental, insurance, and dockage, if needed. His cartel associate, Valeria, had already given him 40K to cover the costs. The first day sailing came with a captain, after that it was up to him and Rachel. They could do it. Mostly they would be motoring and navigating a few islands and, of course, the treasure if it was even there. He shook his hand and stood up. He could see the others nearby finish their coffee waiting on his next move. He hoped they all cleared out and gave Rachel and him some breathing room. It was showtime.

The doorbell rang. Must be Seth. He was right on time. She opened the door and it was like it was still a few nights ago. He was smiling and staring right into her soul.

"May I come in?"

"Yes, please do."

"What did the hospital say?"

"Oh, that's right." She hesitated for a moment. "I have Covid."

"You sick?"

"No, no symptoms. They were doing random tests. Not sure why."

"I have had Covid. Mild symptoms. No problem. We can work together, I am sure."

"I am telling Patrick tonight. He is staying here with his friend and mother. I have known her for over a year. She is a good woman. Works extremely hard."

"If you don't have any symptoms then we can get started tomorrow with the training and buying supplies. I cannot wait to show you the sailboat. It is a dandy. You are going to love it!"

"You think?"

"How's your sea legs?"

"It has been forever but it must be like riding a bike or water skiing. Right?"

"We'll have a week on it to prepare, practice, go diving, etc."

"Then what happens?"

"We will be collecting the gold." Seth winked at her.

She hoped it was that easy. The way he made it sound was like going to Disneyland.

The parents of Lexi, who was hooked up to a ventilator in the ICU, slept at the hospital and waited for the CT scan to finish before they would leave to go home. It was not good news. In fact, she had become unresponsive immediately prior to the scan. This worried the radiologist and hastened the procedure. As soon as the results returned, he phoned the neurologist and ICU interventionist. She needed a surgeon. Now. She had developed a subdural hematoma causing an occipital whiteout. If it went any lower it may harm the electrical current to her heart which had made a comeback following the fentanyl exposure. Her heart rate and breathing had been immediately affected by the dosage but had returned nicely. The paramedics had saved her life. Now she needed a second saving. Poor girl. This should be swift and easy, though. He went out to talk with the parents.

The parents were shocked. But they understood the bleeding in the brain-it had nowhere to go and must be let out. They signed a consent form and decided to go home, shower and rest and return later. They knew they were helpless and had to trust the surgeon and nurses to get her through another day and evening. The radiologist did his best to give them all the information and said she likely would not wake up until tomorrow or even the next day if they sedate her. The hospital had their number and would call if something happened, positively or negatively.

They held her hand and said goodbye right before they wheeled her bed away. An ICU nurse came and told them who she was and that she would be caring for her when she returned. Lexi would be in good hands. This was a typical procedure. Yes, it had its difficulties but usually produced a good outcome. Also, they must stop the bleeding, so she can return to normal. It was a good thing they caught it so early. The nurse was extremely calm like she did this every day, which she did. The parents knew this hospital had the best reputation.

"Thank you. We will see you tomorrow."

Seth, still looking like a pirate, or hippie, Rachel was not sure, picked her up and they went shopping for six weeks' worth of food and supplies. "I meant to tell you something."

"What did you mean to tell me?"

"Sundays are siesta days. Like a day of rest. It is our day off. We can cook, swim, read or do whatever we want."

"Whatever we want. No bad guys on Sundays." She did not know what to make of that. "Will I be using any nursing skills to save lives, say on a Saturday?"

"Rachel. I do not know. I do not think so. No guarantees."

"Okay." She continued to help Seth load supplies onto their 36' Catalina 2005 rented sailboat. She was determined to not let the danger interfere with the wonderful working time she was going to have. He told her she was well prepared. After all the supplies of food and paper were put away-they loaded the dive equipment and other sports gear needed. Weapons were also installed and would be used if needed. She had packed one suitcase and would live in about three of four outfits. She had several hats, sunblock, and long sleeve shirts. They had batteries, candles, and even bottles of wine and rum for leisurely Sundays.

Tonight, after dinner Seth would review the whole itinerary with Rachel. This would be their last official meal on land. Occasionally, they could dock and eat somewhere nearby. He picked a steak place and the pair chowed down on filet mignon, shrimp, salad and baked potatoes, bread too.

Both went for ice cream and a coffee.

"Captain Seth, tell me the plans. What am I in for?"

"You, mate, are in for life!"

"What?"

"Just kidding! Six weeks of paradise is what has been ordered for you, then you'll get your release."

"But first, a good night's sleep. We both need that."

"Right after I show you the plan which I will then burn up. No plans are allowed on board."

He laid out the plan on paper with a light pencil the whole six weeks and the ending on July fourth. She would do her part. And she would do her part on land before they left. They had almost two weeks of working out, getting on board and off, a couple parties to attend to, before sailing away for four weeks. Tonight, they would sleep. Tomorrow was a party. He assured her she would love it! Did he forget to mention the party with a fashion show and live music? It was at a fancy condo on the water in Sarasota.

Rachel fell asleep rather quickly. She had no thoughts of fighting off other pirates, watching out for sharks, or other watercraft on the high seas. She vaguely remembers him saying, "and we'll take a helicopter over the whole area so you know what's going on. It will help you to get your bearings and keep things lined up or in place."

Seth received a late text. He got up and went to meet Valeria Dave-the dude who looks like MS-13. On the dock Seth received the instruction for his partner. One simple robbery of a popular place. Friday. Ok. No problem. Yeah. Right. Night. He would worry about this tomorrow. He was back asleep in a flash. Things were happening and he needed rest for all of it. He needed to be his best. It was his life and her life. He was sorry he was getting her into danger but he would protect her-that's what he was trained to do, over and over again.

In the morning someone was playing loud music on the dock. That and the bright sun woke them up. Seth made coffee and Rachel scrambled some eggs. There was a little bouquet of flowers in the middle of the table which made her smile.

"How about we start off with a run this fine morning? Get prepped with some energy."

"I would love that. Let's take the boardwalk-it's about four miles."

"Perfect."

CHAPTER 6

It was now down to two weeks before they would depart via the sailboat, go out to sea and dive for treasure. It would be filled with workouts, obtaining supplies, a two-day fashion-music show charity event, a helicopter ride and a robbery. It would not be your typical two weeks in sunny Florida. Seth was ready for this big job-he'd been preparing a long time placing himself in the mix of these drug lords. He sensed Rachel wanted to do this; she had her own reasons. She had a resilience about her, and now, being a mother, she wanted to see the bad guys go to jail. He hoped for exactly that as well.

All in all, it was not going to be the most dangerous job Seth ever did. Maybe that is why he was relaxed about it. They would do their part in getting the treasure, which was drugs, to the bad guys in charge, then the pair would depart and enjoy the fireworks on the Fourth of July. Rachel could even bring her nephew and his friend. That was the ending. Seth always had the goal in sight. Always. When you've done this business, or any business, and you do it well, you develop your own way while you achieve success.

After the run the pair sat down in the shade on a swing overlooking the river. Rachel looked at Seth with his long hair, some braids, dreadlocks, tan skin and bright blue eyes and said, "I'm ready to hear all the plans. Are you ready to inform me?"

"As a matter of fact, I am."

"Good. Fire away."

"We have two weeks to prepare but there's some fun in there, too. We need to run and workout daily and obtain all needed supplies for the boat. We should practice diving as well. There's a two-day fashion-music show which happens to be a charity event. You are going to love that. There will be some big celebs, great singers, and divas with lots of special food, champagne, and dancing. It's all in this high-rise condo on the water in Sarasota. Pretty grand if I say so myself. That charity party, though, is not associated with the bad guys. It's one of our benefactors, she likes to throw a big soiree a couple times a year to fundraise and give back to her helpers. We are her helpers."

"I like this part. Keep going."

"I will probably take us out for a boat ride that night. We will see. Then the next day we have a helicopter ride scheduled with Billy, one of my friends who flies copters."

"It's not dangerous, right?"

"Comparatively speaking, no. Then we finish up the week with the faked robbery."

"I will not get in any trouble, right? You have this all scoped out with the police, etc. Correct?"

"We must make it look real, so we can't tell anybody, but I've got you covered. No worries."

"Seth, man, you are the right person for this kind of business. It is like a big game with you."

He did not answer. He raised his eyebrows and wondered aloud, "I don't know why that is. Maybe you will discover why during our adventure. And if you do, you can tell me. I will accept the answer."

"Okay, I will."

"There are only so many days left to play. Like football my years are numbered, as a player and as a quarterback, leading the team to a win. What do I do when the games end?"

"It happens. Like my sister dying and her husband as well. We move on and take care of others or switch jobs. We fall in love."

"We. Fall. In. Love." He raised his eyebrows again. What a sweet thought. He put his hand on her leg and patted it.

She smiled at him.

"But not before the job is done."

The fourteenth-floor upscale residence was finalizing the décor, flowers, and general preparations for the big event. The grand ballroom held hundreds of patrons, two dancefloors, a musician area and small stage. Condos on the 15th and 16th floors were reserved for special guests and the out-of-town celebrities and sponsors. Basically, it was not basic, it was a fun affair full of laughs, thanks and meet ups!

Sara Callais, aka as Scarlet, was the main sponsor along with a few private wealthy friends. She maintained her stance as an opera diva even though her touring had stopped last year. She played the piano prodigiously and would likely perform both areas of expertise at this event. Another young upstart had been invited and he had swarmed upon the scene in

Nashville delighting the young and the LGTBQ community for he put his sexual preference out there right away. He was very young, black, and held a physique like a workout six pack guy. His stage name was Blossom but he was also known as, Onyx, like the stone. Everyone was raving about him, no one would miss the show when it was his turn. He was singing both nights. What a treat!

From Florida's Gulf Coast, the handsome ex-Navy Seal, and Scarlet's right-hand man, was James Edward Kelly. He and his new wife Megan would be attending. They were the new power couple in this whole operation but nobody knew that. It was so top secret, not even the agencies knew of them and what they were up to. They just made a nice looking, fashionable couple out for a good time. Megan was stunning to look at and probably should be one of the models, maybe she was in fact.

Suzanne was a cancer patient from Georgia and nearly died last year after rounds and rounds of poison put into her through her veins. She did not know how she lasted but she had a goal to find out who was wreaking havoc on these women, these cancer patients who happened to be female. She wanted to get to the bottom of this evil barrel and she vowed she would. She also could not wait to show the crowd how she had changed. Scarlet begged her to come as she knew she did not relish the spotlight. But Scarlet told her it would help her project to show others what can happen. So here she was resting in a condo on the 16th floor with a view of the gorgeous Sarasota Bay. Scarlet wanted her to talk and give a short speech. She had it written down and practiced it from time to time. She also couldn't wait to see James and ask him about his progress.

Scarlet's personal condo was on the 15th floor and it contained a piano for her to warm up on. She liked coming down to Sarasota. It was her second home-she had lots of friends here from all over. Jessie came too to assist her. They appeared to be a couple, maybe they were. One just did not know the intricacies of a long-standing partnership. Her four-bedroom condo was luxurious. She knew she had done very well over the years and didn't mind spending her funds on her two homes, one in Atlanta and the other in Sarasota. Her grandson and granddaughter were coming and occupying two rooms while Jessie stayed in the third and her the fourth. It would be wonderful having all of her family here except her son who was busy with his new wife. That was okay as she wanted him to be making memories and settling down. She looked over her condo and ordered a few supplies for the next few days. Jessie helped her to plan any events occurring inside her place.

Seth and Rachel packed small bags to stay overnight in Sarasota. "You know I don't have anything very fancy for the night you are describing tomorrow night."

"Hey, didn't I tell you? You get to pick out a dress from the rack and wear it all night."

"Wear it all night?"

"Yes. The only thing you must do is model it at the show."

"Model it?"

"Yes, model it. You will be fine. They do your makeup, get you fitted, teach you how to walk and viola, you are a model. It is very fun. That is what the other guys and girls say."

She stared at him. She would just have to trust him. "Do you model?"

"Honey, really? I am undercover, remember?"

An Uber came and took them to Sarasota and dropped them behind the building. Seth took Rachel through a back door and up the service elevators to the 16th floor. He pulled out some keys, found the condo and unlocked their temporary paradise. Rachel looked around. She almost forgot he was always undercover. She did not see anyone around and entered through the door after Seth. Whoa was this ever nice. Like super nice, spectacularly ritzy. Who could afford to even stay here let alone buy a place like this? This was going to be fun. She decided right there to enjoy herself these next 24 hours in a super glam place. Plush carpeting, tall ceilings, big wide windows with silky curtains and the room was large with a huge bed and glorious looking bedding. There was a sitting area with sofa and chairs and a dining room over to the left. She walked around and found a small dance floor. Are you kidding me? Champagne and stemware sat atop a high-top table. The champagne was on ice. She looked at it and then at him.

"That is Sara, she goes over the top. She appreciates her helpers. I am one of her helpers."

"Maybe you should explain to me how you help her?"

"Top secret. But it is all within the law. She is a law-abiding citizen, okay?"

"Okay, if you say so. Thanks for having me. I like the perks already."

"I knew you would like this place. Relax. This will be a fun time, tonight and tomorrow night."

Rachel went to the small kitchen area where she saw an itinerary and picked it up. "Here is the schedule. I will read it out loud."

"Please do. I will pour the champagne."

Rachel took the itinerary, accepted a glass of champagne, and made her way for the modern lime green club chair which faced the beautiful window view of Sarasota Bay. The iconic bridge named the John Ringling Causeway lay before her and she would later see it all lit up as in tonight while cars came and went to the outer islands of Lido Key and Longboat Key, including the infamous St. Armand's Circle. She sipped her champagne and kicked her shoes off.

"Wait, we must toast to our adventure here and the future high seas spectacular project named Operation Lexi." He walked over to her and clinked glasses. They sipped and smiled.

"Okay, here goes. Tonight from 5-7 PM guests may mingle at the bar on the first floor. There will be a table of name cards if you wish to wear a name tag. Please introduce yourself and feel welcome! Enjoy a table of seaside hors d'oeuvres and desserts. Everything is on the house. Tomorrow is pool time after a delicious brunch served poolside at 10 AM. From 2-4 PM is time for the models to prepare with hair and makeup. Feel free to sign up and join in! Five o'clock is showtime!"

"Very formal. That is because she is a real lady. She traveled with all those formalities, all over the world in every city. I believe she speaks some words in every language as well."

"Way above our standard, I suppose."

"That is the truth, however, she will make you feel more

than welcome. And we can handle it, Rachel. We will be fine. More champagne?"

"Yes, please."

She laid the invitation and itinerary on the small table in front of her. It reminded her of a wedding she attended that was formal. I suppose when one is compassionate about something they go all out.

Seth and Rachel,
Sara Callais cordially invites you to a
fabulous soiree filled with fun, fashion, and
frivolities!
Tonight 5-7 PM Cocktails & Hors d'oeuvres
Tomorrow 10 AM Brunch Poolside 2-4 PM
Fashion Prep 5 PM Showtime!
Thank you for attending.
I will see you there,
Sara

CHAPTER 7

Since tonight was informal, Rachel had appropriate clothing. Seth went to a meeting and Rachel took a thirty-minute nap dreaming in anticipation of this middle of the week soiree. She called Patrick and talked with him before laying down. He told her to have an adventure and he wanted to hear all about it when they got back together in a month and a half. Sounds good she replied.

Rachel woke to a knock on the door. Frankly, she did not want to answer it but it persisted. She rose and walked to the door. Looking through the peephole thinking she might see a maid or even the infamous Scarlet, she became concerned when it appeared to be the MS-13 looking gangster. Oh my god-where is my undercover guy when I need him? She looked again, tried to think very fast about what to do, when he turned his head and began speaking to someone in the hall. She recognized the voice. It was Seth.

Quickly, she walked to the bathroom and entered the shower.

The pair walked down to the bar via the staircase. They did this for exercise and to avoid cameras, thought Rachel. She did not ask. She did not want to know everything. She wanted to have a great time tonight and tomorrow. Once on the first floor the couple walked to the bar where the festivities had already begun. A small band played music, tropical delights, and some party goers were already dancing.

"What would you like to drink tonight?" Seth asked Rachel. "By the way you look nice."

"And you do as well. Your conservative casual look fits in nice, especially the leather loafers."

"Thank you. And your drink?"

"I'll have whatever you're having."

Rachel walked over to the name card table and wrote her first name down and placed it on her khaki blouse. First name basis sounded good. She was ready to mingle and chat with folks here for this event. She turned around and ran into a couple with name tags.

"Ginger and Georgie, nice to meet you. I am Rachel."

"Well, hello, Rachel. Very nice to meet you as well. Are you performing tomorrow night?"

"Oh, no. I am just a guest. But I might be wearing one of the dresses for the fashion show."

"Then, you will be coming to see us. We are the fitters and makeup stylists for the fashion fun show." The slender black couple eyed her up and down as if they were sizing her up for a dress.

"Well, ladies, my favorite colors are army green, navy, and light yellow. I think they flatter me best. What do you think?"

Ginger spoke up, "You may be able to pull off chartreuse,

if you wanted to wear something bright and a show stopper. We will scope out the dresses. Come on time and we will fix you up."

"Thank you, Ginger, and Georgie, for the tip. I will. I do want to look fabulous as I am dating this new guy, you know." She muttered out an explanation she had no idea where it came from but it sounded real.

Just then Seth showed up beside her and the makeup stylists gave him the twice over as well. "This must be the new guy," Georgie blurted out.

"Yes, I am the new guy. Seth." He smacked his name card on his chest and smiled.

"We are going to fix her up tomorrow. You will not recognize her," laughter exuded from the couple.

"All that beauty I don't think you will be able to hide it from me." Rachel looked stunned. How did he make her feel like an extraordinary woman with one sentence? She best be careful, as he was sounding more like a keeper than an undercover agent.

"I'm hungry-let's eat," Rachel broke the focused conversation.

Once they sat down, she began to look around and made small talk about the makeup artists. "Were those two males or one of each?"

"I think it is two males transitioned into two women. But I would have to investigate to know for sure."

"You could be right. But I think Georgie is male and only dressed as a woman, whereas Ginger has transitioned to female. Her voice was softer, more feminine and there was no facial hair." Seth stared at her.

"Wow. You are good. I believe you. Good take. Why must we always talk about people who transition?"

"I think it is not that we feel we must talk about it. We are just curious; it sparks our interest to figure things out."

"I wonder if we could go undercover and be the opposite sex?"

"Good question. I doubt it. Our skills are honed from birth to recognize females and males and to know their differences."

"Once again, you know your characters. Lovely people. They will make you look more gorgeous, if that is even possible."

"Thank you. Now, as soon as you are done eating, let us dance."

After a walk around downtown, the couple made their way up to the condo on the 16th floor. Such a pretty sight at night with all the lights everywhere. The bridge shown bright in red, white, and blue, maybe in preparation for Memorial Day. It was stunning from this view. The couple was still dressed when another knock came on the door. This time Seth answered it. It was Scarlet, or Sara Callais.

"Please come in. I do want to introduce you to my friend."

Rachel came over and introduced herself shaking her hand, "I am Rachel. I have heard so much about you and I'm thrilled to meet you and be here for your event."

"Oh, Rachel, how kind. I have heard a little about you as well and couldn't wait until tomorrow to meet you."

"Please come in and let's sit at the dining table." Seth stated.

"I won't keep you long, but I do have important

information to relay, and I wanted to meet Rachel." They all sat down and waited for Scarlet to continue.

"Do you want the good news or bad news first?"

Rachel and Seth pondered for a moment, waiting on each other to give up a clue.

"Rachel, I know you are here to help Seth perform a dangerous mission for our cause. He selected you. Did you know that?"

"Um, I saw his photo on Instagram and followed him. So, in essence I was the one who followed."

"Sweetie, not really. We put his photo in front of you to see if he'd catch your eye. He did and then followed back."

"You wanted me."

"Yes. I did. You are perfect. There is no other person that could do the job you can do."

"I suppose, you could have asked me, outright." She thought out loud.

"Rachel, it worked. You wanted to see him as well. Now, I have both of you here to help me. I thank you from the bottom of my heart."

"Scarlet, I do want to be here. You are very kind. I see why Seth likes to work for you."

"What's the bad news?" Straight up, that's Rachel. She asked about the worst first.

"Project Lexi is very important. The young girl in the hospital has just died. Her name was Lexi and she was 22 years old about to graduate from college. Fentanyl is what killed her. It has reached Florida and a few other states. That is the bad news. I am sorry. Truly sorry." Scarlet paused. "The good news is that Project Lexi has just been given a five-star status. The funds have been doubled, as well as the backup personnel, and it remains at a high alert. It must succeed and y'all must win. I know you will."

"Rachel, what this means is that there are twice as many people looking out for us and will assist us to make the bust. We will not fail. I feel terrible about the young girl. We must save others before it hits the streets."

Rachel reached out to Scarlet and picked up her hand and held it with both of hers. "Thank you for entrusting us. We will succeed."

"Good. Be careful when you are diving down to the bottom of the ocean."

"Sure thing."

"Seth, I wondered if you could take one of my guests out for a boat ride tomorrow?"

"Tomorrow night, you mean?"

"Yes, that would work after he sings and the fashion show is over around 9:30 or 10:00 PM. His name is Blossom but he goes by Onyx."

"Do you want to come as well?" Seth asked.

"Oh, no. I will let y'all have the fun!"

"I'd love to take a nighttime cruise aboard Susan."

"Your boats name is Susan?"

"As in black-eyed Susan, my favorite flower."

"You have a favorite flower?" She asked the question but she did not know why it mattered. He did not answer. Scarlet stood up and walked to the door. He opened it for her and let her out but not before asking if she needed an escort to her room. She replied it was down one floor and she was fine. Thanks. Goodnight, she spoke. She waved to Rachel and said how nice it was to meet her. Likewise, from Rachel.

The next morning Suzanne appeared at the brunch and seemed to be the hostess greeting everyone poolside. Megan and Rachel were there minus their significant others. Megan and James were married partners and Rachel and Seth were business partners. Suzanne chatted up Megan and Rachel.

Where were the guys? But, of course, their business was private. Top secret was more like it. Their communications were making all of this project go forward. Scarlet was not at the pool either. So, Rachel figured out the three of them were having a special gathering of intelligence minds. Cool. She could handle that. Seth would do his part and she would do hers. She was highly trained in diving, computers and medical care, such as life support and resuscitation. Seth was a sailor, undercover agent, and weapons expert. He also had the ability to sway others pretending he was someone else. That would be his natural ability to blend in. Maybe he was just a good actor-she did not know. Now they were a team. Six weeks.

Rachel relaxed on a chaise lounge next to Megan. The two exchanged histories and found a likeness in each other. This was the beginning of a friendship it seemed, when exchanges occur naturally. They enjoyed themselves and had a few mimosas after the bountiful brunch. Megan explained to Rachel that they were friends of Sara's from Georgia where she had a ranch. She has been building it for a while and calls it her plantation. "Suzanne's been there recuperating from an illness and a few of the people here actually live there, temporarily that is," explained Megan.

"Where do you live?"

"I live in Destin. It is magical. My family and I live there and go fishing. My kids go to school and my husband works remotely. He will be at the function tonight."

"Yes. I would like to meet him. My partner will be here tonight as well. We just started dating, it is rather fresh right now. We will see how it goes."

"Well, I wish you luck. I know I got lucky. He is super. Everyday I kiss myself hoping it lasts forever. See, I had my boys before I met James. Then we adopted a little girl we call Amelia. Life is precious."

"Let's share photos tonight."

"Sounds good. Maybe we will be at the same table," Megan said.

The ladies went for a swim, mingled some and then turned over to tan the other side. About 1:30 PM Rachel bid goodbye and told her new friend she must go as the soiree was providing her a dress tonight and she needed to be on time.

CHAPTER 8

"See you at 3:45 after my dress fitting and makeup." Rachel called back to Seth as she left the 16th floor condo overlooking Sarasota Bay. She was told to go to the 14th floor where all things soiree would occur. Apparently, the fashion show itself would be in the grand ballroom downstairs along with the musical entertainers. The makeup and fitting rooms were across the hall. She found the door-it had a sign on it and walked in. There she found Georgie and Ginger assisting a few women.

"Darling, come here. Oh, I am so glad you came early, too. Come. Look. I have selected about ten dresses I think would look absolutely and extremely gorgeous on your body." She pointed at the dresses on hangers and all in her size. From the looks of it they seemed like ball gowns, or pageant wear.

"Wow. Dressy. Glamorous!" Rachel exclaimed with her voice and big eyes.

"I know, right?!" Ginger nodded in approval. "There is a dressing room right that way. Go try them on, pick one, and put it on. Then, we will do your makeup."

Rachel did as instructed and found hooks in the dressing

room with many mirrors. First, she selected a few by color, then style. In the end she could have picked out three but settled on the chartreuse swanky gown. The taffeta material was a bit much but she did not care. She called out to Ginger, Ginger totally agreed. Next thing she knew she was getting her hair curled and styled and makeup applied. How fun. Georgie did an elegant updo on Rachel's highlighted medium length hair. He, rather she, put a few jewels in areas atop her head. They were at the ends of bobby pins. Georgie did have a magical touch. She seemed to love what she was doing!

Rachel thanked them and offered a tip. The pair stated that they were paid very well for their services. They assured her she would see them tonight. "And Rachel, get up and dance tonight so everyone can see your fabulous dress, makeup and hair. Mwah!"

"I will most definitely."

Rachel couldn't help looking at herself in the mirror, every chance she got, on the way back to her condo. When the elevator opened, though, there he was. The man who spooked her, gave her an unwanted look, and if she could ever kill anyone, it would be him. Was she misjudging him by looks alone? She had not even talked with him. She closed her eyes, turned sideways, and shot off the elevator. Why did she keep running into him? Hurriedly, she almost ran to her room. She found her key and opened the door quickly and shut it even faster.

Seth just stared at her. "Oh my god," was all he said.

She took three or four steps and plunged against him and into his arms that were not fully opened yet. She wrapped her arms around his shoulders, laid her head on one of them and let out a gasp.

Seth was bewildered. What just happened? "Um, are you okay?"

"I am now. It was just a stranger, just a stranger. I wig out every time I see him. It's like my brain has been electrocuted and my hair is standing on end. My nerves get all tingly and I know my blood pressure must be 200/80."

"Okay. We must get this under control. You are my right-hand accomplice and I need you on board. Period."

"I know."

"It is likely just nerves. You are not in imminent danger and we even have more people on board. Most of the cartel is in Mexico-the big guys, anyway. If someone comes here, the US patrol might kill them. Or a rival gang member will combust his ass and take over."

"Wow. You seem to know what you are into. I believe you. It is just that one guy you deal with. I have seen him like two more times."

"Valeria Dave. Oh, he is a higher up. He is not here to hurt you. He looks damn tough, though, I know. He will be telling us what your job is to prove yourself."

"Is that why he is hanging around here? To frighten me and scare me to get out?"

"That is too many questions. When he gives me your job he will be leaving. I think that is tonight."

"Maybe once I know what that is I'll settle down around him-knowing I can kick ass, that is." She laughed now. Some courage arrived and she used it to calm herself and get ready for the party.

"You are beautiful Rachel. Stunning. We are going to have

a great time tonight. I have got my boat lined up at the docks and it's stocked with supplies for an evening run or cruise, whatever you're into. Onyx is coming with us. He is one of Scarlet's proteges. He has been working at her farm and living there for about a year. He has got fantastical music talents as in singing. You are in for a treat."

"Thank you."

"Thank me for what?"

"Thanks for inviting me here to this event. And thanks for assuring me I can do the jobs and be your side kick."

"I believe both of us like a little danger. You are the nurse; you tell me why that is when you figure it out. And you are welcome. Now let us go have some fun before the danger sets in."

Rachel and Seth arrived fifteen minutes late. That is considered fashionably late as the first thirty minutes is all about finding one's table-getting a drink, then locating your seating. Eight attendees to a table which were lined in white tablecloths, set with a Bird of Paradise flower arrangement and a formal place setting. Name cards instructed you where to sit and waiters came to pour wine, take a drink order and set champagne to chill nearby. One could see the head table was oblong, near the dance floor and stage. Rachel counted the seating there and it was fourteen with Sara Callais, aka Scarlet, in the center accompanied by her butler, or partner Jesse. While Jesse wore a white tuxedo, his companion tonight wore a magenta-colored taffeta long evening gown. She looked so pretty thought Rachel, especially for her older age. She had taken care of herself she just knew it. She had protected herself from the damages of daily living and had aged well thought the nurse. Maybe she had a secret ingredient, secret food that singers eat or even a special drink.

After thirty minutes and with the crowd seated and enjoying their table talk, an emcee emerged and began announcing the evening's details. He introduced the head table and waited for the applause, then told everyone to have a great time before continuing.

"Before dinner we will watch the fashion show. Some models are professionals and others are you who came and needed an evening dress with makeup and hair. Thank you for allowing us to present you this evening. All of those that participated please come out to the hallway at this time. After the fashion show we will have a musical number by a wonderful new performer named Onyx and then a short speech from our lady Sara about her causes, fundraisers and benefactors! Dinner will be served at 6:30 and dancing begins at 8:00 until 10:00. Let the party begin."

Seth learned that donors could bid money on a dress worn by the models, professional and party goers, followed by boutique owners who could wish for a certain dress they liked to sell in their shop. Once a certain dress was spoken for by a wealthy donor it was placed on a mannequin in the hallway for shop owners to wish. They could put their name on three dresses and the results were picked by someone from the head table, notably a person selected by Scarlet. Megan was chosen to be the selector. The fashion show lasted about an hour with numerous gowns in all colors, sizes, and lengths. Thirty gowns in all were shown, each costing more than seventeen hundred dollars. The bids all started at three thousand dollars, many reached ten thousand dollars and ten made it to fifty thousand. One surpassed all with a seventy-five thousand dollar bid! The event would fold in more than seven hundred and eighty-five thousand dollars in dresses alone minus the cost of each which Scarlet funded herself. The dinner and dancing were another way of amping up the funds and it did with plate costs of eight hundred dollars and there were a thousand people attending. A million five hundred and eighty-five thousand dollars for a soiree that was super successful was a win. And even though Scarlet did not measure the money, she did this for the people that worked for her, she relished what she could do to further promote her causes.

The appetizers were delicious, both agreed. Megan was in the hallway when Rachel was headed to the bathroom. She was selecting the wish list for the boutiques. "What a fun job you have!" Rachel exclaimed.

"It was a surprise for me." She reached in and selected a winner for Rachel's dress. Obviously, there was a duplicate. "Your dress won you know."

"Won what?"

"It was the highest bidder settling on seventy-five thousand dollars."

"Lordy, that is way above me. Good for the cause. Man."

"Fun to have a night like this and see how the few who made it big can spend their dough." She smiled.

"I know. It has been extremely fun! A couple of dances and we are going for a boat ride. Will I see you tomorrow?" Rachel asked.

"Yes. We are staying another few days. We made it a vacation, even though we live in Florida."

"See you tomorrow but first on the dance floor!"

Rachel walked the length of the hallway and turned the corner. She followed it and went to the farthest away bathroom so it would not be as crowded. She walked past a sitting area and saw her man. Here he was again. He stood up and walked right over to her.

"Rachel?"

She stared at him disengaging herself from the typical fear which usually set in. "Affirmative."

"Huh. You are funny."

"What do you want and what's your name?"

Both stared each other down. Valeria Dave was the first to break eye contact. Yes. She said to herself. She could break this guy.

"You know who I am." He paused. She remained silent. "I want you to rob a place. Here is the date and time. You wanna play, you gotta say … yes."

He handed her a note and left. She read it. She had her orders. Her test would be a simple robbery. Seth would say no problem. Do not worry.

Rachel met Seth back at their chairs at the white linen clothed table. Champagne was poured, the lights were dimmed and a new musical guest appeared on the stage in front of the head table near the dance floor. The candle lights from each table flickered in the grand ballroom. The emcee introduced the singer as Blossom with a nickname of Onyx. He would sing three numbers with the first being a Dolly Parton tune named "Jolene."

He held the crowd with this number. It was super quiet, joyful because of the event, but troublesome and somber due to the nature of the tune. It made Rachel feel cold. This sad song made her feel lonely, more alone than normal, yet reached within her to feel the ignition of someone else's loneliness. Tragic. Like her patients who coded, there was a tragedy about to occur. The singer was good and so young. One could tell he worked out as he was all fit and trim. The very next song he took his shirt off, which was orange blossom in color, and showed his six-pack abs. He had a small tight pink vest on with buttons. Yup, he worked out all right. He strolled through the tables and sang two more tunes. The people loved him and clapped generously at the end of each.

CHAPTER 9

Onyx made his way to Scarlet's table and gave her a hug. Then he walked right over to Seth and Rachel's table and sat down at his spot. Rachel did not realize that spot was for him. They all made introductions while more champagne was poured and drank. Rachel almost forgot about her instructions. She put the paper in her purse and would discuss this later with Seth, maybe on the boat ride. For now, she remained calm, even talkative. And hungry.

"Blossom, or do you prefer Onyx?" Rachel raised her glass to toast this fresh young singer.

"Onyx is my name. Blossom is my stage name. But we will see which one catches on more."

"To Onyx and your beautiful music!" Rachel toasted.

"To Onyx and that wonderful performance!" A toast was raised by Seth to the young performer sitting at his table.

Suzanne took the mic and made her way to the stage. She had been feeling exorbitantly fantastic. Her enthusiasm showed but she had to be relative. Her experience was not what others lived. Only her. She would tell HER story without infusing or injecting herself into others. To each his own and seize the day. That was her mantra.

"Welcome to everyone here tonight. Sara thanks you for your generosity and I'm sure she'll tell you that later. I am grateful for her. My name is Suzanne and around four years ago I got the big bad cancer. Not researching or getting a second opinion I became filled with chemotherapeutic chemicals. I was a walking hot mess. It destroyed my appetite and I was living on the verge. On the verge of death that is. A couple of my nursing friends flat out told me. Dear-you know that stuff can kill you. Watch out for yourself. Sometimes healthcare gets too busy to care about the person inside. I never read the fine print-lo and behold there are so many side effects, you are literally a petri dish waiting to burn up. Too bad I could not turn on a switch from the inside to put a stop to the tumor. I did have the tumor removed and the chemical installation via the vein was a protective measure. For what, to make sure I hit close to death on the way to survival? You get the point."

Suzanne presented a picture of her in the good old days, she pointed to it up on a screen behind her, then a picture of her last year and the crowd was aghast. She was telling the truth. Deathly skinny, pale and with sunken eyes she did look like the typical patient who was on their way out. Like in a few days she would be laid to rest.

"For sure, I should have gotten a second opinion, maybe even a third. I do realize this is the best care we have but is it really? They sent me home to hospice care where I laid in the bed for five days. The morning of the sixth day I had a dream and woke up abruptly. In my dream I saw a big house with a garden that I was walking up to. On my nightstand there was a card. I picked it up and it said *I Can Help* and I have no idea who put it there. But I left the house that day, after I called the number and had my driver take me to her place. What tiny energy remained I put into her. Her beautiful soul received me and told me she could help. My will and her soul fixed me, I know it. No more tests. I do not want to know. I was dying on hospice and here I am. At least for a while. You never know if you are in good hands. Here is a picture of the day I presented to the farm-Scarlet's plantation home in southern Georgia. And these next few are me recuperating with her as she and her team took excellent care of me. I was in good hands. Finally. Thank you, Scarlet, for your loving ways and a new take on cancer care." Suzanne blew a kiss with her hand. One could see her happiness and the courage it took to get up, and out, and trust another. With the help of a beautiful soul who kept her going, she was here tonight.

"I'm here to show you and support Sara Callais, aka Scarlet, in her efforts to shake things up in the medical world, transforming our health towards a more natural transformation post cancer. I had given up after my chemo and did not see a way out of it. I felt like I needed a miracle. I prayed. My prayers were answered. Someone helped in my plight. Maybe it will come back, but me not worrying right now is better than anything. It is worth the life I have. She gave me that. The audience clapped in appreciation towards a new hope for the hopeless and dying.

As soon as Suzanne was seated the waiters brought the plates to the patrons. It was a busy sight to see. Things were going well. Rachel looked around she certainly did not see Valeria Dave anywhere in sight. What kind of name was that anyway? Why was she bothered by him? He spoke nicer than he looked. That she knew. Maybe he was not as evil either.

The waiters asked, "Steak, lobster, chicken, or pasta? We have surf and turf as well."

After dinner and a small talk given by Scarlet the dancing began and Seth and Rachel joined many others. Later, the couple with Onyx said their goodbyes and made their way to go for a boat ride. Seth had made a cooler and brought some blankets to his boat earlier in preparation as it could get chilly with the night air. They crossed the downtown street and made the way to the dock where his boat was tied up. He helped them aboard and untied the lines after starting up Susan. They all found a seat and were excited in anticipation of going out on the bay and intercoastal waterway.

"Does anyone have any time constraints?" Seth asked his guests.

"No. Tomorrow night I play again but the day is mine, and this night too," replied the young singer.

"I am with you, Seth. Let me know how I can help. I am yours," she blustered out.

"Well, okay, then. We are off on a nighttime adventure."

Seth sped away. There was no traffic on the water tonight. Immediately, he had an idea to take them to his small house he had over north of Holmes Beach on Anna Maria Island. It would be a trek but, hey, they had all night and half of the day tomorrow. Tomorrow was meetings and a helicopter ride over the islands to give a visual of the next six weeks. This was their last time to themselves. It would take over an hour but sounded good right now. He turned up the music and found his vibe. The water was smooth, no wind or waves, and most of the light was behind him. The bridge was portside and it sure was pretty all lit up in the American colors. He supposed that was significant for him and Rachel in what they were about to do. He smiled at that thought.

About forty-five minutes into the voyage, he heard the cigarette boat before he saw it. He veered to the right to give him more room, just in case he did not see his boat. Seth had his lights on. Then he saw another scarab cross before him. He came out of nowhere. What the heck-there was more activity out here than he planned on. He slowed down while figuring out his next move. Then he saw a third boat, a large cabin cruiser hitting the speed pretty hard. That's when he saw someone with a gun, or so he thought, and it was pointed at the cruiser. Why he put his arm up skyward he did not know. What was he thinking? He would stop a bullet?

"Fuck, man," he shouted. He pulled his arm back down. He felt the burn but he needed to get his passengers out of this mess. "Rachel, grab me a towel. I got to move faster."

She was not sure why he wanted a towel until she reached for one and handed it to him. He slowed the boat for a few seconds. She saw the blood. "Here, oh God, you've been hit."

She wrapped it around his hand quickly. "Good. We got to hit speed and get out of here."

Onyx was in the back of the boat and really did not see what was happening. Then Seth took off and went left to a small island out in the middle of the intercoastal. He was at top speed clearing more distance between the other three boats. He had to make sure they would not come after them. He cut his lights momentarily and went to a secret dock on this little island. No one really knew it was there. He slowed as he approached the small inlet and curved around cutting into it. They were hidden now. His lights were still off but going slow he could see the dock ahead. He looked at his passengers. Rachel looked at him then out and did not see any followers. She told him so. He told her to get a line and tie up both ends and he would see to his wound.

"Everyone please remain quiet. I think we dodged them but we will wait a while here." Seth instructed.

Onyx saw his hand and the blood. "What happened?" he whispered.

"I do not know, man. But I would say we got caught in a crossfire."

"Like a shootout?"

"Yes, unbelievably, out here. I must call it in. I just want to check my wound first."

"Let me look, Seth." Rachel, the nurse, examined the wound. "It is topical, fleshy, but did not penetrate. I do not think. Can you move your fingers?'

"Yes, I can move but man, I didn't want to wait for more exchanges. What the hell?"

"Seth, you got a gun, right?" Onyx was checking.

"Sure. But that is not the mission tonight."

They all sat way down in the boat and waited. For what they did not know. Seth was sure his boat and they were hidden. He figured they must not be from around here and were trying to get to someone. He called it in very quietly giving descriptions of all the boats. The Coast Guard would be right on it. The Coast Guard told him to give them an hour before departing from their secure location. Seth told his boat mates he could go out to the ocean under a nearby bridge but then they'd have to anchor off the beach and get wet. The nurse and the singer decided they would wait the hour because no one really wanted to go in the ocean tonight. Seth opened the cooler and they waited until they could make an escape. He laughed quietly to himself. Gunshots on the bay. What is next? A lot more excitement in about two weeks or so. The bleeding was not severe and Seth was able to move his fingers. He placed a bandage over it and listened for the Coast Guard. The danger seemed to be headed towards the mainland as they were lots of inlets with natural areas for trails.

When Seth turned the boat back on, he kept the lights off until he felt sure he was in the clear. He traveled slower, better that than some derelict tracking him. If he was picked up, he would explain and the officers would give him the benefit of the doubt, especially once he gave him his ID. After the second bridge he turned his lights back on and headed for the marina and his dock over at the island. He saw maybe three other boats out tonight. Not much traffic except for the racing boats earlier. Once he was docked, he would call back in to the Coast Guard and check on an update. They slowed and went through narrow passages past other docked boats on the way to his dock. Finally, they made it. He told them they were almost to the beach on the other side.

"A quick walk on land and we'll be there!"

CHAPTER 10

"Thanks for the information." Seth stood outside on his front porch talking with the Coast Guard official taking in what he just said.

"No. Thanks to you. All is well. Enjoy your evening."

He walked into his cottage on the beach and found his guests in the kitchen.

"What happened? Did they say?" Onyx was relieved but interested in the outcome. He removed his shirt and laid it on the counter.

"Yes. They did." Seth looked at Onyx and his six pack abs or were they an eight pack? "But first, man, you are built, dude."

Onyx smiled and blushed a bit. He touched his abs and said, "My workouts are working out, I suppose."

"I agree. But your singing is truly amazing. Let me pour us a drink and maybe you'll sing us another song. Maybe?" Rachel gushed a bit.

"I agree. But first a tour. I'll show you your rooms."

Rachel poured them a drink and Seth procured the tour while both listened to Seth's report of the mishap on the water.

He turned on the lights as he walked around leading them here and there. He had bought the place last year after someone had updated the bungalow. Cedar floors and ceilings outlined the place while white painted the walls and bed spreads, sinks, too. The kitchen had cedar cabinets and a green stone covering the counter tops. Seth turned on the outside lights which showed a large truncated tree spanning out to each edge of the property. Outside was a portable hammock on green grass with an ocean beyond tall sea grass. His guests were truly surprised.

"Seth, thank you for keeping us safe tonight and bringing us to your beautiful home. And on the beach."

"Cheers." Seth clinked glasses with Rachel and their new friend Onyx. "I do keep extra swimsuits out here, or you can go in your undies if you prefer. Who is up for a night swim?"

He gathered towels, chairs, and a small cooler for the beach. He had to admit it was nice to finally have a couple guests here with him. Comforting. Rachel went and changed out of her prom or pageant style dress to a one-piece swim suit and Onyx stripped down to his undies. Seth did likewise. While they had not thought about swimming earlier, they changed their minds when they saw the night ocean.

"Here's some flashlights as the beach can be rather dark before the moon shines bright."

The sand was cool and the ocean a midnight blue. It was after midnight now and no one was down here. They were alone, laughing, drinking and ready for a calmer adventure than earlier. Seth had placed a large Band-Aid over his wound. He forgot about it. He set the three chairs down by the water's edge and Onyx placed the small cooler in front.

Rachel carried the towels and put one over the back of each chair. Time for a little private party she thought. She knew the rough stuff was coming, it just was not here yet. Small talk prevailed in getting to know their guest.

"How do you two know each other?" He asked the inevitable question. Rachel let Seth take control. She was not sure what to divulge with someone from the event. She was not even sure Onyx knew what Seth was up to. He probably did not know a thing. That is what she presumed.

Rachel poured them another drink, rum, and coke, and added a cut lime to each. She sat down and waited for Seth to speak. They all stared out into the blue depths of this oceanic solitude.

"Onyx, we met when we were in high school, became friends, then went our separate ways. Recently, we decided to date again, to give it a try as in last week."

"Oh, very recent. Do you work together?"

"Well, not exactly. Rachel's a nurse. And you know I work for Scarlet, part time that is."

"Scarlet, she is a gem. I met her last year; she loved my music right from the start. I was just getting going and she put me on the fast track. She has tons of connections. I've been to her ranch, or plantation, as she likes to call it."

"Many people at the event have been there. Sounds impressive." Rachel commented.

"Oh, you should go if you can. She is inspiring. She wants me to inspire some of her young kids there."

"That is a plan. What else are you up to?"

"Well, I am going to do that and put on shows. Kind of like the fashion event but even more theatrical with song and dance. Hard to believe. I guess I am on my way."

"Let's toast to Onyx, or Blossom, and his theatrical singing tour!"

"To success wherever you go!"

A long silence ensued.

"You asked if we work together. We are working together for the next six weeks." Seth added.

"Is it a secret or something?"

"Rachel, go ahead, you can tell him what we are going to do."

"Are you sure?"

"Now, I am intrigued. Please tell. You must."

"With his permission," she points to Seth, "we are doing a little sting, an undercover thing."

"Shit no, really?"

"Really. I want to be honest with you as you are very special to Scarlet. So, mums the word, except to her."

"No problem. You are going to get the bad guys then. I love it. Know, that when I am singing, I'll be smiling bringing you good luck when you put yourself in danger."

"What a sweet thing to say." Rachel said.

"I'd like to invite you back down here for after The 4th of July party on the fifth to celebrate the completion of our job. I am sure you can stay at Scarlet's or even here. Yes, stay here."

"My tour is on break for the first two weeks of July. So that may work."

"Perfect."

"Perfect. But no boats with guns going off … just fireworks."

"Fireworks, lots of fireworks!" Rachel joined in. It was a plan.

The beach goers went for a midnight swim followed by more chatter, laughter, nonsense, and another round until Rachel suggested a late-night mini concert. Onyx was more than happy to oblige. The three of them headed back to the cottage and placed their chairs outside. The party ended on the grass under the large tree behind the cottage. Seth made a late-night snack for all of them.

"Would anyone like a night cap?" Seth asked.

"I am going in. I am feeling perfect and I do perform again tomorrow. I will be doing more of my theatrical show, so I need to get my beauty sleep." He winked at Rachel and said his goodnight to Seth.

"Sure. The boat leaves tomorrow for the mainland at noon after breakfast. So, sleep away."

"I'll be on that boat."

Seth and Rachel had a nightcap inside in the living room. Rachel began the conversation. "Are you going to tell me about your boat name?"

"I thought I did. My mom's favorite flower is the Black-Eyed Susan. That is the name."

"Did she grow them or plant them?"

"She did."

"Seth, is she still alive?"

"No."

"Tell me the story of your mother. I do remember meeting her once, I believe."

Seth looked at Rachel and thought to himself he might as well get this story out there. Better before Operation Lexi takes hold of them.

"My mom went back to college after her kids were grown. I was out of the house overseas. She studied and studied and obtained her degree in like two years. Then she went to law school, became a lawyer and finally a judge. When she made the judgeship, she went out and cut all her Black-Eyed Susan's out around the house and garden. She brought them in and put them in vases. Dad threw her a small party and everyone came. I was there. I was very proud of her. Six months later a drug lord got the wrong address and came and robbed our house looking for his dealer. He shot my mom in the dark. She later died. It was a sad time for all. At her funeral her former law firm she worked for sent four vases of Black-Eyed Susan's with a card."

"We are so sorry."

Seth began crying letting a few tears slide down his cheek but he had to finish the story. He choked but continued. "The Black-Eyed Susan apparently has meaning; it means and represents justice. They sent four vases for her family of four, and of course, they knew how much she loved those flowers."

Rachel came and sat next to her friend and put her arm around his shoulder. "That is the most tragic, yet sweetest story I've ever heard. Oh, Seth." She cried with him and held him.

"Now you know more than you likely cared to know. I am over it but when I tell someone from my past it gets to me. Killed in her own home by a lowlife. It beats me up for sure."

"You are going to get these guys. And I am helping."

"I wish we could stop them from becoming them in the

first place."

"When we are sailing, we will come up with ways to prevent their existence. Maybe the sea will help us claim that ability. I think it might. We will try."

Seth kissed Rachel on the cheek, then stood and said goodnight.

"Goodnight."

"Miss Rachel, you are overdressed for breakfast." Onyx exclaimed.

"I know, but it's all I have." Rachel twirled about and bowed. "Sir, may I have this dance?"

"Sure." Onyx played along while Seth cooked breakfast.

"A cottage breakfast coming up for all," Seth said. Seth was glad he had shopped and loaded up the cottage with food. Usually, he only went there on the weekends by himself.

On the way out in the boat Seth had to go slow via the canals before he could put speed into their journey. Rachel was looking towards shore as they began to speed up. She looked and took a second look and saw Patrick and Henry in another boat. She asked Seth to slow and waved to her nephew who was now in her care, albeit temporarily in her friend's care. The small boat came over to theirs and she talked with Patrick. He assured her it was okay that they had permission and all. He told them he was going to dinner at her Mexican restaurant where she worked and maybe she could meet them the day after next. She looked at Seth and he said that would be fine. She would come alone. Patrick waved at the pirate and Henry pulled away and off they went for a ride. Rachel looked at her dress. She was totally unprepared for that.

Seth looked at Rachel. "Small world, my dear."

Back to Sarasota went the boating party. There was much to be done today, meetings and a helicopter ride with his buddy Billy from the Air Force. Onyx had another show and the fun was just about over for now. He turned up the music and ran Susan as fast as he could through the intercoastal waterway. It was a beautiful day with boats everywhere going every which way seeking fun via beaches, bars, and music. He docked the boat and they retreated to their rooms to shower and change for the day.

Rachel had left her purse in their room. She suddenly realized she forgot to mention the piece of paper Valeria Dave had given her. She must get it and tell Seth. He was in the shower. She reread the note. Rues Place on the river this Friday. That is all it said. She had to rob a nightclub. What?

"What's the matter?" he asked.

She held up the note. He took it. Read it. "We have your test."

"Can I, do it?"

"Piece of cake, yes, you can."

"Okay, so we'll have to rehearse this, right?"

"Sure, I have a plan."

"Good, because I've never robbed a place."

"I know, but you're going to be awesome."

"Awesome?"

"You'll prove them you are the one to be afraid of, that's all."

"What am I doing?" She laughed.

"I am going to teach you. Tomorrow. How can I be so good at getting the bad guys if I don't know how to be bad, or know how they do things?" He looked intensely at her.

"Oh, I forgot. Okay. Okay, teacher. I am ready. Tomorrow."

CHAPTER 11

The helicopter tour was set for 2:00 in the afternoon. The sun would be westerly overhead and visuals would be perfect to scan the islands. Seth and Rachel walked a few blocks to a high-rise that had a rooftop landing. The helicopters are held at the airport but the pilot friend would pick them up here downtown Sarasota. Exciting is all Rachel could think about as they took an elevator to the top floor, and walked up steps to the floor above the top. They climbed more stairs and stood in a waiting area looking out towards the pad. A couple of guys stood outside waiting as well. Rachel checked her phone and it was 2:05. That is when she heard a loud noise and saw the wind hit the guy's hair and blow it around. The helicopter landed and waited for them to come aboard. Seth took Rachel's hand and opened the door. Both of them walked briskly slightly bent over to the open door of the helicopter. The two guys helped them to board, get settled, and apply a seat belt and head phones in which to hear the pilot. The pilot had a co pilot today and both greeted the pair. The co pilot handed Seth and Rachel a map of the area. They could take notes of what they were seeing if they chose.

Off they went in a quick swirl motion after ascending off the building. The pilot headed for Longboat Key across the bay. Water was everywhere thought Rachel and soon she would be diving in that vast ocean, very soon. But for now, she felt exhilarated seeing this beauty from the sky. Blue, blue oceans and islands, or keys laid out before her giving a path for the pilot to follow. She took out a pen from her purse and marked her map as Seth or the pilot pointed out. When they went sailing this would give her a good idea how it all fell together. To know her little nephew was down there and she was responsible for him made this mission seem more important. Then there was the girl who recently died named for the mission. How awful for her family. She did not stand a chance with a fentanyl coated pill. Wouldn't the word on the street get out about these pills, that bad people were making a killer? Much more needed to be done but she and Seth would start with this operation, knocking a big bump in their avenues for distribution. She smiled at that. And all done undercover. On a sailboat. In the Sea.

The pilot maneuvered the helicopter and flew smoothly over the length of Longboat Key. The beaches were glorious with gentle waves lapping the edges over and over. Boats were everywhere moving slowly leaving a white wake behind. He pointed out a few bars and restaurants that might be of interest in case they came ashore for dinner. Rachel wrote these down, she saw docks that could take large boats, or watercraft, while one went to dinner. Two bridges lay ahead and the pilot named those. Seth pointed to Cortez, where they had their date, reminding Rachel with a smile. She smiled in return. Then she saw her restaurant where she worked and pointed to it.

"Amazing," is what she said aloud, not that anyone could hear her. Seth held her hand in confirmation. She looked at Seth and saw he had not shaved. Probably he was going back incognito after the big charity event. He was. She just knew it. Maybe she should get her hair braided or a few braids put in it. She would look more the part. Except once she proved herself it did not quite matter. The brainless blood hungry idiots wanted to kill our children. Damn them.

The helicopter reached Anna Maria Island and all the little roads and places scrambled about until they reached the point. Bean Point was like a miraculous miracle of beauty. She could not take her eyes off the beach and waves surrounding the most precious sight in all the world. How is nature so awesome? Seth pointed out his cottage by the sea. "We'll go back there after we're done." He said out loud and she looked forward to that.

The helicopter tour went around Egmont Key after passing Passage Key and noted the depths out there. The pilot showed them the area where the big cargo ships go through and on into the Tampa Bay to load or unload. Fascinating. And above were airplanes headed to Sarasota and likewise ones that were landing in Tampa. Such a busy place thought Rachel. The pilot kept going out and out towards the oil rigs. They looked at two of them and he said the last one was beyond these two pointing in that direction.

Onyx slept and later rehearsed for his performance. He was showcasing the big event. He would perform for two hours to a sold-out crowd in this ballroom. It was a mixture of attendees. Scarlet invited those who could not make the first night as well as guests who favored new artists. Tonight, there was no dinner or fashion show but an opening musical act by some unknown, followed by Blossom and ending with a few numbers by Scarlet herself. She would play piano and sing a couple of her favorites. Afterall, she had an immense fan base, especially of the elder and more sophisticated crowd, the more well-traveled folks one might say. She knew many people did not appreciate opera as they never listened or had not been given the opportunity. That is why she went last. But she would keep it short, maybe she would find new enthusiasts.

Blossom was the main show and he would play for two hours, the opening act would play for a half hour and Scarlet a half hour for a total of three hours plus a thirty-minute intermission. Drinks and appetizers were available as well as the tables for seating. It was going to be a magical night setting this newcomer off in a great direction. Blossom would change three times beginning with a tuxedo and ending with a wild orange shirt with frills and pink bellbottoms below which flared out above high heeled boots. Scarlet was sure Blossom would get a standing ovation tonight. She was sure of it. That is how much she fell for his musical performance.

When they returned from the helicopter ride Rachel went to the pool to meet Megan, and Seth reported to Scarlet for a meeting with James.

Scarlet sat at her dining room table as Jesse poured her a second cup of coffee. She had just finished lunch and was waiting for her guests, her top performers in the business of top secret, high level, undercover government business. She had been appointed by the highest department in the land to forge this underground, yet, open minded, very sophisticated cyber security firm involving men and women who regaled America, as their mother, a duty to protect, see all sides and be within the law. She thought it was going pretty well; she had her own security detail to protect her business. A philosophy of one does not always know about the other served her well. And she kept the most important level down to a few as in three. Her top three were James, Seth, and Jesse. No one knew about Jesse; he looked like an older man who enjoyed treating his boss very well. But behind closed doors he was her mentor, her friend, and her lover. He had ways of getting facts and info just like the very young hacks and beyond. Seth was her hands on man, he was willing to fly to the moon if she asked him. She loved working with a chameleon, a perfect specimen of greatness with minimal fear. And James was so comforting. He had been with her from the start, right after she began a couple years ago. His background covered all the bases and he had access to anything she desired in the way of assistance. His new wife Megan had begun to assist him in the cybercrime division.

First, she started with the house hospital for special cases, then she made a network of citizens who wanted to help, founded the plantation to help troubled youth and cancer patients, created the charity fashion show event (to make money added to her own), and the sting operation assisting the ever-busy law authorities in charge of drugs, vice and cyber-crimes. No one suspected this grand dame of anything except her singing and helping some young men and women with cancer. Possibly, she might recruit this new girl that

Seth brought on. She would watch her performance of this big mission in drug curtailing and see where she could help. There was a knock on the door, Jesse answered it promptly and in walked Seth and James. She was delighted. This would be a good meeting.

The gentlemen shook her hand and gave her a kiss on the cheek. Both sat down immediately and she got right to it after Jesse offered them coffee.

"Thank you both for being such fine gentleman and making me very proud of our mission and very soon numerous accomplishments. First up, let us discuss the fishing tale from the gulf. James, tell us what you know."

"Scarlet, thank you for giving me this chance to work on this ultra-important mission. We closed out by taking our own fishing trip out of Destin. We caught many fish that day but took a picture of three king mackerel and a mahi mahi." James pulled a picture from his phone and showed it to her. "My wife is the one that pointed out the significance."

"I am intrigued. Do go on with this fish tale."

"She watched the mahi-mahi caught, brought up, and all its beauty, all gloriously green and blue, and glowing, with a yellow belly. Then later it paled out and became grey. She said it reminded her of the whistleblower who thought himself doing the honorable thing, only to be targeted and chased out of the country. Why wouldn't others want to know what he found out?"

"Megan is wise. You found yourself a real treasure, James."

"Three King Mackerels are all above him as in the IA, investigative agencies, yet he, is on the run and found out.

The whistleblower is the Mahi-Mahi fish turning grey as his life becomes endangered from trying. Real people can decide for themselves. Knowledge and truth, though, win the game, but the final goal determines how we proceed."

"When does the final goal occur?"

"Soon. Much of this is done under cover but shall surface likely in the next few months. You, Scarlet, are why this is happening. I absolutely love what you have done. I am in for life. Ha ha."

"If we perform, then we proceed again. Once we prove our worth, we will get paid." She acknowledged both. "You saw Suzanne at the event. What did you think? You interviewed her, undercover. And you saw how terrible she looked."

CHAPTER 12

"I cannot believe the change in her. Of course, chemo helps many people, but in her case, it was killing her. She talked about psychological waterboarding, and I knew it happened to her because we learned those very techniques to clobber the bad guys, or guilty ones. Ordinary persons in the public do not know those things! It was an act of terrorism performed on her. She told me to not look at her, because the eye contains the exact movie of what you have seen. If she told that to another person, they would think her out of her mind. That is what they wanted her to think. He paused to reflect and looked at Seth. "Her house was bugged, every smoke detector in every room, tv's, phone cameras turned on at times, and then putting her name on a car next to hers at a resort further annihilated her sanity. It was the car from her first novel."

"Who did this?" asked Seth.

"Who do you think? And she is not the only one."

"Bad dudes who know too much. But who directed them to act that way? Who toyed with her, over and over?"

"Yes, those are great questions. We have got the evidence,

characters, witnesses, and security details, along with the progress they were making to put her sanity out the window. Terrorism. A further question is how many others were given this treatment? These women were targeted in an awful way. They either had family with select cases before the government, or service members in the family, one even with ties to a movie company. Some were writers and property was stolen."

"Good work, James. Oh, this brings me so much happiness. My husband would be very proud of you all." Scarlet smiled.

"We have them laughing on tape about their escapades. We cannot let things like this go on. We have daughters, mothers, sisters, aunts, hell, the whole other half of our population!" James sighed and his eyes watered. He was human, too, and he showed it. "I feel sorry that this elderly lady had to endure an illness, then surveillance, followed by a cyber terror group of assholes, and left her with a punched in the gut feeling. She was right. She told me I needed to make sure this did not happen to others." Seth stood. He put his hand on James's shoulder reaffirming his support and the jobs they promised to Sara Callais. Scarlet sipped the last of her coffee. Jesse walked in to see if anyone needed anything.

"Seth, you are up. What is up?

"While James is helping those women and the cyber security areas, I'll be undercover presenting to the drug lords as an ex American soldier in need of cash. I will be there to assist them in getting it here, inside our towns, inside America. They are moving and trying anything right now because of the open border that will soon be closed. Other avenues will be opened to get their drugs here."

"Eventually, I'm guessing they will be moving it through these other avenues, if they haven't already." James sat acknowledging Seth's plight.

Seth paced around the dining room looking outside at the gorgeous view. "Many things go away on their own. But if a single pill can kill you and it is sold like candy molded in different colors a child or teen might experiment. They will not experiment if the supply goes away. My partner and I are going to make the biggest display of wrongdoing go wrong."

"Sounds awesome, Seth." James was interested.

"That it is. I will be smiling July 4th, that is as much as I can say. I will not be in the headlines but the bad guys will," smirked Seth and winked at Scarlet.

"Now you know James why Seth is the undercover guy. You got to have an explosive dose of confidence to pull off this sting with the cartels."

Seth smiled. Not a cocky smile but an all knowing, I am doing this for you gratitude smile.

Jesse cleared off the table. Scarlet made future appointments with both guys for the ninth of July to assess business. She joked maybe it would be a fishing trip, or maybe a boat ride to Key West.

Rachel and Megan enjoyed the afternoon poolside. Mango margaritas with salt were going down smoothly, partnered with quite a few laughs, and released any stress either were holding onto.

Seth and James emerged and joined them. The four of them would go to a rooftop bar and later celebrate a dinner by themselves toasting success with their business partner.

All was good in paradise.

The funeral for Lexi was held on Thursday five days after her death from surgery post fall succumbing to an accidental fentanyl overdose on her part. Her parents were stricken with unbelievable grief and could barely hold up during the ceremony at the local cemetery. The minister spoke while the attendees sat in chairs placed for family and friends of this young individual. Her mother placed a bouquet on top of the coffin and returned to her seat. They sat while time moved forward, and, in their oblivion, neither spoke a word. On a black top road off to the side a black SUV pulled up, out of view of the mourners, and rolled down the window. Inside sitting in the back seat was Valeria Dave looking out at the gathering. He contemplated what the family was experiencing at this moment. Certainly, heart ache for their loss. He tapped the front seat. Time to go. He sent a text to his boss.

After the funeral a small celebration for Lexi's life was held at her parents' home. Her mother and father had it catered and asked that any attendees bring photos or stories about Lexi and share them into the evening. A large board contained a few pictures while others brought prayers and letters to her parents about Lexi and pinned them accordingly. The police chief and his partner came, not dressed in uniform, and offered their sympathies and further support with any information to solve this tragedy. The parents were not worried tonight about outcomes, only that Lexi's life be told from loving hearts ringing with sadness interspersed among merriment and joy.

The only person not invited tonight was Mary Peters. She sat home alone weeping for her mistake in the incident. She felt like the driver who lives after a fatal car accident in which the driver was at fault. She would likely forever be full of guilt. She meant no harm but now she was the guilty murderer. She gave her the stinking little pill and if she had not the girl would be alive. Alive. That is all she could whisper and think about. Maybe she should end her life. Maybe. Sunday she would go to church and ask forgiveness because she was not giving it to herself. How could she have participated? Time heals all wounds. How long does it take to get over this? She got up and poured herself a glass of white wine and took a sip then cried. She cried. And cried some more. Then she prayed and cried some more. She told herself that she was a piece of trash. She got up and walked to her front window. She looked out at the street. The streetlights were on as it was just passed dusk. She saw the car down the street with a person sitting inside. She was a criminal. She wore an ankle bracelet. They were just waiting to arrest her. It would be soon. But not soon enough. They had to find the source. She waited at home while they investigated.

Seth and Rachel finished dinner with James and Megan in a private room at a downtown restaurant then left separately. They had a fun time getting to know each other and said they looked forward to the next time when not incognito and both had another success to share.

Rachel and Seth headed to the sailboat. He discussed what they needed to do tomorrow. "First up, we will go for a morning run and hit the gym. It will be a light workout as I do not want you hurt or strained.

"Okay."

When they get to the boat Valeria Dave is standing on

the dock. Seth tells Rachel to get on board while he deals with the guy. Rachel cannot figure out what he wants but she overhears him say, "It is twofold, just a light addition. You and I will be her driver."

"You mean the get away car? Sure, which car?"

"I will bring it. I'll pick you up from the dock after the rue and we'll drop her at a house, she'll go out back and follow the dry bed and go through the highway ditch. We will pick her up from the other side. Got it?"

"No problem. As long as there's no gators in that creek or dry bed as it is night time."

"Tell her to bring a gun or a knife, whatever she knows better." He smiles.

"Who is she stealing from?"

"Tekani Rez."

"Carlos's competition? Are you crazy?"

"Yes. No."

"Do me a favor. Make sure he is not home."

"I can do that. He is going to a wedding tomorrow night."

"I never said my partner was a fighter. I said she can scuba and retrieve."

"The house will be empty. The safe is upstairs. Good luck to her," Valeria said then investigated the sailboat looking towards Rachel.

Seth looked at him. This seemed strange like he was asking too much. He was going a little overboard to prove her worth.

Rachel saw him leave. A chill ran through her. Seth stared after him just a little too long before he came aboard.

"Hey dear, let's get to it."

"I am putting my pajamas on. I am ready for bed. Maybe you should tell me in the morning when I am fresh and ready."

"Sounds good."

Meanwhile two older men met at the Sunshine Skyway Bridge just off Terra Ceia. One is in a black pickup truck and the other is in a big black SUV. They are pulled over at a rest stop for fishermen and parked in the dark. The guy in the pick up is Carlos Mendez and he oversees cartel work in the south. He is meeting a businessman named Izan interested in working with him. He wants to help him unload his large shipment. He owns storage units across Tampa, Sarasota, and Naples, basically the west coast. He has some empty units and Mendez needs a place the first week in July. Why so secretive? Because its business. And Mendez does not want to fill out paperwork. That's what he tells his fellow Mexican. So, Mendez is willing to pay more than usual. Izan tells him he doesn't want to know what he's storing as long as it's not lethal or explosives. No guns, alcohol, or explosives he says. No problem he returns. "I'll be loading after hours," he says, "is that okay?"

"Yes. Anytime. The remote opens the gate and the key opens the unit."

He hands him the keys and numbers to the units nearby and Mendez hands him an envelope of cash. Deal done. Izan returns to his car and both drive away unseen by anyone except the night cameras newly installed by the city. When Izan gets home, he counts the money, he has been paid four times the amount owed. He thinks to himself could it be illegal? Should he care? He has built up such a fine business. Carlos had been referred to him by a young guy with a double name.

Rachel and Seth go for a run on the beach near her restaurant. They stop to get a coffee and Seth relays the plans about the job. "Here's what is going to happen …"

Patrick and Henry have been getting along great. They both help Henry's mom at her store, it is his uncle's store but Henry's mom manages it every day. It is nearby. It has been busy lately with all the fishermen coming in for licenses, bait, and lunch to go. She lets them take one of the boats out during the day. She does not know about their nighttime excursions. Henrys planned another one and he tells Patrick. Patrick is getting used to Henrys adventures. They do not seem so bad. He is sure his aunt, or new mom, would not mind. That is what he tells himself. Maybe one or two final adventures before she returns. She promised them they would all be together on the Fourth of July. Perfect. Fireworks. Friends. Fun.

CHAPTER 13

Henry is having a great summer. Occasionally the boys help Henry's mother at the bait shop. He, and Patrick, who is two years younger, love video games, pizza, and snacks, and going out on adventures on the boat or mostly swimming in the ocean. But occasionally, Henry, who looks older than fourteen has slipped out unnoticed in his mother's car. He drives over to his girlfriend's house and visits with her for an hour. He guesses he taught himself how to drive. Henry has long dark hair which touches his shoulders. His mother told him he could wear it long through the summer but would need to get a haircut before school started this fall. Sometimes he pulls it back in a pony tail. He is rail thin as he forgets to eat at times. His grades are average. He is average, but hey, that is a good place to be right now. He's approaching eighth grade and his mom told him he'd have to start studying and planning for his future. Especially since he told her he wanted to go into the Coast Guard. His mom told him she would look into it and they'd make a plan and work on it together. He did not play a sport or engage in hobbies at school. He told his mom when she asked, he guessed it was swimming, boating, fishing, or anything on the water.

Patrick, on the other hand was very smart. He had always studied and achieved good grades, with or without studying. He had no idea what he wanted to be someday. Maybe an astronaut he told his mother before she died. Patrick had sandy blonde hair and wore it crew cut or as the stylist like to say high and tight, the public called it blended. It was getting a little longer-maybe he wouldn't cut his until school started like Henry was doing. He had a buddy this summer and everything was great. He was swimming, learning to operate the boat, dock it, and even fish. He could bait a line, drop it, wait for it, and even pull a fish up into the boat. They hung out together from sun up until sun down. They had been twice to the island at night. The first time had people on it. The second time no one was around at all. Henry was planning another adventure when his mother was going to stay with a friend overnight. That night was tonight. The next day after that Patrick was meeting his mother for dinner. This time Henry planned a picnic, swimming and they would bring his mother's spare phone. He did not have one yet. His mom said, "Xmas of eighth grade I'll get you a phone, not until then."

"Henry," yelled his mother from the kitchen.

"Yes, mom."

"Come here. I have some instructions to give you."

Henry followed orders and sat at the kitchen table waiting. His mother was hurrying and bustling around cooking as she readied to leave for her overnight. She turned off the stove top and put the lid on dinner. She came over to the table and looked at her son's steely blue eyes. She brushed away the long hair from one side. "You having a good summer?"

"The best. Really, I mean it."

"Dinner is ready. You and Patrick can both eat the pasta. There's a salad in the fridge and I made brownies for dessert."

"Thanks. What time you leaving?"

"Like in a few minutes."

"Hey, do you mind if I borrow your other phone?" he asked.

"Here it is. Call me or text if you need anything. I am only a few miles away. I will be home before noon."

"What's the celebration?"

"Just a girls night in. How about that?"

"You really go for it, mom."

"Now you are teasing. When you can drive, have a phone and maybe a job I will go out more."

"Then, that is next year. Not too long." Henry smiled, took the phone, and stood up. He gave her a kiss and left the room. The news had come back on and he saw clips about the fentanyl crisis, cartels and a huge immigration problem. He wondered what police were doing about it. He thought about the Coast Guard, they must be on it locating drugs and cartels. If he were old enough, he could be helping.

Patrick had gone to his place to get more clothes. His new mom had given him a key in case he needed it. Patrick was going to be in sixth grade this year and he was super excited. He would be in middle school and halfway to being done in the school system. Science fascinated him and he thought robotics was the bomb. He wanted to be on the team this year and hoped his new school had one. He went to his closet and grabbed a hooded sweatshirt, more swim shorts and clean underwear. Then he saw the water shoes his aunt had bought him. He put those in the bag as well. He would wear those on the boat when they zoomed to the island tonight. He locked the door and went to Henrys. This was convenient living so close. His mother had left already. Henry was watching the news when he walked in.

"Henry, what time are we leaving tonight?"

"How about we eat and then set out. We'll go earlier, take my mom's phone, snacks and drinks and explore the island while it's light. We can come back in the dark," Henry explained.

"Sounds good to me. Maybe we will run into other explorers tonight going for a swim. Do they fish at night?"

"Not so much at night but early morning, yes."

The boys ate dinner that Henry's mom had prepared. It was rigatoni with meat sauce, meatballs, and garlic bread. They forgot about the salad in the fridge and packed up the brownies to go with them. Henry made a couple of meatball subs and put them in plastic containers, grabbed a couple of cokes and placed it all in his backpack. Patrick helped and was excited about tonight. It might be one of the last times they went exploring at night because his new mom, Aunt Rachel, might not let him do this when she returned. He turned off the TV after watching the news finish. He could see why Henry wanted to join the Coast Guard someday, it seemed rather exciting and Henry, well, he liked excitement. Patrick sure was glad he had someone to show him the ropes around the water.

The sun would be setting in about a half hour to hour as the boys pulled away from the dock. The trip would take about forty-five minutes or so but they had all night. Henry was the captain and, on occasion, he let Patrick steer the boat. He taught him how to start and stop the engine, reverse, tie up, anchor and some general safety rules while aboard. Henry noticed the Coast Guard boat tied up over at the opposite shore. That was unusual. That post had not been used in quite a while. Maybe he should show Patrick the boat up close. He only had to cross the inner coastal or channel and they could get a better view. The water was calm tonight. It would be a perfect trip. He maneuvered his motor boat and went slowly past the 47-foot life boat. He knew it was 47 feet from the numbers on it.

"Cool. It is big, Henry." Patrick looked and studied it intently.

They drove past the boat and then Henry saw a small dock ahead of it, out of the way around the mangroves and hidden out of view. Maybe, he thought.

He pulled up to this unused small dock and saw a path leading up and over to the big docks which held the Coast Guard boat. He did not see any *no trespassing* signs. He looked at Patrick.

"I say we take a closer look."

Patrick knew what that meant. They were going to be adventurous.

The boys tied up their boat securely and exited onto the abandoned dock. They walked behind the shrubbery and found the path. Tall bushes on each side hid them from anyone seeing them. It looked like maybe an abandoned condo or old house lay inland. No one was around. They were extremely quiet as if wondering should they keep going or not? They kept going. Patrick's heart was pounding but he wanted to see it as well. The path led to a small old building and a big dock. At the end was the 47-footer. Before walking on the big dock Henry looked around in every direction. His heart began pounding as well. He did not let on to Patrick. He turned around and gave him the pointed finger to the lips. Patrick knew. He complied. Once Henry knew there was a clear path the two walked the wooden planks out to the end. No one seemed to be on board. He found the entrance and signaled to his friend. The boys quietly, and seemingly, all knowing, boarded the vessel and quickly walked up the steps onto the large craft. They looked around and decided to check out the interior. Investigating this large ship was thrilling. Up to the front they saw a place where a person who could perform gunnery action. Henry pointed to the area and their eyes grew big. They envisioned a big artillery gun like in the movies. Big action called for big bad action on the high seas.

"Just like in the movies, man," whispered Henry. Henry spied some storage spaces and opened a door. One could hide in here he thought. He heard something. He peeked out a window. Someone was walking on the dock. He heard steps. Patrick heard it too. "Quick, let's hide in here until they leave, then we'll get off." They stepped in and found numerous compartments. Hiding behind life vests, lines and other equipment, the boys remained out of view.

It was quick and unexpected. Once on board someone started the motor and another must have lifted the lines as the large craft began leaving the dock. Slowly, then urgently, it sped away. But to where? They were getting a ride but where were they going? Henry made sure Patrick was okay. He whispered in his ear, "What goes out must come back. We will be fine."

Patrick shook his head up and down like he understood. No way was he going to say a thing.

It did not cross the young boys' minds that it wasn't the Coast Guard going out for a ride, until the vessel, after what seemed an eternity, slowed down and almost completely stopped. Then Henry heard some shouting from one of the guys aboard. They would just have to wait out this trip until it was finished, then deboard and find their small boat before escaping this.

Henry heard the men talking. They were looking for something on an island when the boat came to a complete stop and made Henry and Patrick fall into each other.

"There, there it is. Quick, let us get off and pick it up. We have no time to waste." One of the men in charge yelled to the other. Henry was thinking. He wanted to see what they were after and get a look at them.

He did not hear an anchor go down, this trip was not permanent or going to be for a long time. He had to get a quick look. He whispered again to Patrick. Patrick said, "All right, but I'll be watching through some of these windows while you look. Then we must return to this safe space."

The two men walked across the sand and entered a light forest of growth and woods. Henry opened the storage door and went up to the main deck to see the men walking into the woods. There was a piece of material on a tree near where they entered. Just then Henry heard a light footstep from down below. He turned. Shocked. A small boy around six or seven years old appeared. Henry immediately put his finger to his lips again.

"You, okay?"

The boy shook his head from side to side.

Henry kept one eye on the shore and took the little boy's hands. "Is anybody else here with you?"

The little boy said, "No."

"What's your name?"

"Jose."

"Hi Jose. I am Henry. Were you sleeping down there?"

"Yes. My dad watches the building and I went for a walk. On the boat."

"Here is the plan. We are going to go back down there and be quiet. These guys do not know we all got on the boat. Can you do that?"

"Sure."

"Then when we get back to shore, you can be with your dad again. Okay?"

"Yes. That is what I want."

"Walk back down there and my friend will help you to hide."

"I hid under the bed, then fell asleep."

"Patrick, put him in the storage with us. His name is Jose and his dad watches the building at the old station."

Patrick brought him back down the steps and into the storage area.

"We're like passengers on a ship and those guys are the pirates," Patrick did his best to explain the situation.

CHAPTER 14

Henry kept a look out and saw the two guys emerge from the woods carrying two large rectangular looking black boxes. It looked like two trunks of some kind. The men were not Coast Guard employees. There were no shirt emblems or uniforms. They wore black shirts and black jeans. He saw multiple tattoos on one of them. Both had dark hair and appeared to be outdoorsmen as in they were very tan, like they worked on boats or roads. He took a good look at them through a small window up top, then retreated below and prepared for the journey, hopefully, back to where they came from. The way back was far less treacherous than the first hour not knowing anything. Soon it would be dark as the sun was setting. He saw it on the horizon. What was up thought Henry? It sure did not seem right. Were they in peril? He just figured to remain quiet was the best way forward. At least the guys had placed the packages on the main deck and were not hiding it below. Because then they might be found out and if it was nefarious, he did not know the outcome.

The ride back went faster and once Henry determined they were docked and the load was lifted off they could breathe easier. The guys were just about off the dock and headed to the parking lot next to the building. He decided they needed to move fast. He needed to check on Jose's dad or else the kid would have to come with them. Once on the dock the little boy went running towards the building, the older boys made haste and ran the dock as well. Only they went off in another direction. Henry went up to the windows and peeked inside. He saw the father and son reunite. The father was shaking his head and looking at the coffee cup in front of him. He checked his watch and acted like they were late to be somewhere. Henry and Patrick made haste to their little boat, boarded, and started the engine. They exited and never looked back. The plan was just delayed not disbanded.

Henry and Patrick did not talk until they were on the island. And safe. The thrill made them feel exhilarated, only because they were safe now. And they would talk about it all night long.

Henry purposely slipped the boat on the other side near where he thought the boat had gone two hours ago. He was near enough to peek and with his mother's camera he would snap a couple photos. Suddenly, he felt like a policeman or an FBI agent. That made him wonder about what was in the black boxes.

"Patrick, the two guys brought containers off this island and onto the Coast Guard boat. What do you think was in them?"

"I hate to think about it. Honestly, it does not make sense. Any of it."

"But give it your best shot."

"Drugs and drugs. Because guns would be too heavy."

He stated matter-of-factly.

"Then that is what it is. Nobody keeps fish over here and I haven't heard of any divers discovering any sunken ships lately. And I always watch the news, every night."

"Henry, you saved us, all three of us. We were not supposed to be there, neither was the kid. They must have drugged his father. My, oh my, it could have been worse. Thanks man. Maybe you are a hero."

"Patrick, I am no hero. Because we were not supposed to board a Coast Guard boat without approval. I wonder if this will prevent me from joining up."

"I do not think so. My mom said they expunge your record when you turn eighteen."

"But something like this could hurt me. I do not want to be untruthful but I must think this over."

"We did not do anything wrong except explore. I can tell my mom and she will know what to do. Do you want me to ask her?"

"Yes. Because I cannot tell mine, then she will know. I would rather she still believed in me. I will take some pictures and you can show miss Rachel."

"We did help that little kid," Patrick reflected. So, they settled it after a real-life pirate situation, they would tell someone but did not want any hero status or notoriety.

It was dark so they used flashlights to explore. Once they found the tree with a piece of material on it, they walked in. Nothing really existed just a narrow opening and footsteps in the softened dirt floor. Henry took a few photos with the flash on, then he noticed something discarded between the trees hanging on a branch. It seemed to be a shirt like someone hung it to dry. Inside the pocket, because of course Henry pursued the inevitable, he found a shipping label. He slipped it in his pocket but left the shirt. "Let's get out of here."

The pair went back to their boat, swam, explored, ate, drank, and talked about Henry's girlfriend. Patrick listened intently. Maybe someday he would have a girlfriend. What an exciting, thrilling and beyond adventurous day he had had.

"Maybe tomorrow you should come to dinner with my mom and I," said Patrick.

"I like that idea. Then I can see if she thinks it is important or not and I can still go for the Coast Guard after high school."

Patrick and Henry laid on their towels and looked to the stars while laying on the cool sand. It was a quiet and very still night with the full-scale excitement at their heels. Now they talked about the future, dates with girls and their moms. Both did not want to disappoint their moms. Driving and cars were in their future as well. And more boats. His uncle was getting a couple of new boats and would rent them out. Certainly, he would let Henry use them. With content in their hearts and future highlights to explore the boys left the island around two in the morning. They would be in their beds by three and tomorrow would reveal any ill fate.

Meanwhile earlier in the day Patrick's mom was preparing for her assignment. Seth was prepping her with locks, guns, and thieving. He would be right there every step of the way, except the actual heist, because then he would be with Valeria Dave waiting to celebrate her success.

"When I get my phone this Christmas, I am going to get

an app that let's me study the stars. Then when we come out here, we can point out the constellations!" Patrick got excited at this prospect. He wanted to know what was up there!

"Oh yeah, man, I know a few. Let me tell you what I know." Henry studied the stars a couple years ago with his uncle. "There is an archer named Orion, and the Seven Sisters. Let us find those."

"My mom did tell me how to find the North Star but I can't remember."

"Okay here's what you do … find the Big Dipper and go off the end of the cup straight up to the North Star."

"Henry, you are amazing. The Coast Guard will be lucky to have you on board."

"Find it now. Look around."

Patrick searched the whole sky before he found a formation looking like a cup, but he found it and traced the ladle and then over to the cup and straight out not too far found the North Star. It was in the northern sky according to where he thought north was located.

"There it is. But it is not too bright."

"Now for the Archer, which happens to be my birth sign. I am a November kid. That is where all this adventure comes from."

"Find it. Find it."

"Okay. Hold on. It is usually in the southern sky, sometimes towards the east. There it is. Do you see? It is bright." Henry drew an archer with his hand showing him the outline beginning with the three bright stars close together which formed the belt.

"Cool. I see it."

"The seven sisters are nearby ... but I forget right now. We better get moving. Do you think?"

"Sure. I am ready. Thanks for this day. I will never forget it, Henry."

The boys traveled the calm waters after a treacherous start. Seemingly an innocuous situation which presented itself became a thrill neither boy wanted to tell anyone about. For some reason Patrick thought Rachel would know what to do. She was a nurse, someone trustworthy and helpful. He would tell her tomorrow night when they ate dinner together before she went off on some job with her pirate.

The boys slept great and did not wake until 11:30 am when Henry's mother walked in.

"Morning guys. How was your evening?"

"Oh, pretty boring." Henry stated.

"Your food was great. Thank you very much." Patrick recalled.

"Okay, all right. That is it?" She asked.

"Yeah, nothing much happened."

"How was your stay inside date with the girls?" Patrick quickly remembered.

"Thanks for asking. Let me tell you all about it." Henry's mom said and then went on and on about women, wine, and movies and then a comedy show followed by a few card games all amidst a pajama party. Mom, Henry thought, is getting younger while he was growing up.

Henry and Patrick went with Henry's mother to the bait shop to get some bait for fishing. She went and talked with Henry's uncle while the boys walked around the store looking at this and that. That is when they saw a man and a little boy walk in to the store. Henry took a good look; it was the kid from yesterday. What now? Henry had to think fast. He nudged Patrick and the two of them thought best to stay out of sight. They went to the storage room and hid.

The man went to the counter to get some squid for bait as he had a fishing trip in the morning. The two men talked about fishing and the customer's other job besides fishing. He told him he did security work and sometimes guarded old buildings and docks, even the old Coast Guard building across the way. Henry's uncle asked him if he ever caught bait on his way out into the big water. He replied he did do that from time to time when going way out. But he was taking his grandson out to just drop a line and bottom fish tomorrow. Someday he would take him out on a real big trip and catch *Ballyhoo* for bait when he got a little older.

"Ballet-who (Ballyhoo)," said Jose. Jose pulled out some cash out of his pocket. "Dad said you could buy me a fishing pole." He laid forty dollars on the counter.

"He did, did he?"

"Yup."

Henry's uncle pointed to the fishing poles which were located over near the storage door. Jose walked over and checked out the poles. The boys were looking out through the crack of the door and watched as Jose selected a pole. They slid away and out of sight, breathing heavier, still not knowing what to do. Another time thought Henry. He needed more time to think this plot through.

"I'll take this one."

CHAPTER 15

Rachel had practiced for two days on how to pick a lock when Seth told her they were going to steal the cash when the safe was already open.

"Why did you make me go through all that training?" She looked at Seth in puzzlement. "Why?"

"It's good knowledge to have." He waited for another question.

"Really?"

"Now you know how to pick a lock in case you are ever in that situation again."

She laughed out loud. "Should I teach you how to scuba dive, just in case you ever have to do that?"

"You should. Don't you have to have a buddy with you?"

"I thought you had that covered. You do, don't you?"

"I think you will have to teach me something when we get way out there."

"How deep am I going? I will tell you if I need a buddy."

Seth opened his computer. "Let me check the depths out in the Gulf. It will be on a shelf, so not as deep as the deep blue sea." He smiled.

"Tell me the depths."

"Can you go down twenty-three or twenty-six feet by yourself?"

"Sure, I will just stay on the line from the boat. I do not have to go all the way down to see the bottom. I can go say 15 feet and rise if needed rather quickly."

"We're also going to check out an abandoned oil rig platform."

"Oh, exciting."

"Yeah, I thought you might like that."

"Are we going fishing as well?"

"I suppose we could catch our dinner a night or two," Seth said and smiled at her. Once this heist was done tonight, the rest was smooth sailing. That is what he always told himself. After all, why did it have to be any other way?

Rachel dressed in jeans and a tee shirt, pulled her hair back and placed a cap on her head. "I am ready. In and out, drive away, lay low and then onto the next gig."

"You are ready. The first place is Four Oaks Pub, a quiet little bar that has been here forever. It will be in between shifts, employees out eating, smoking and no one paying attention. That is when the safe will be open. I will distract by ordering a beer and then step outside and sit at a table. It is in the back room right before the kitchen across from the lady's room. Likely four thousand cash. Be quick."

"You got me covered right? Like no one is going to arrest me?"

"Rachel, we are undercover honey. If you get caught, you will get arrested, you just will not be charged. It will be fake."

"Ok."

"Just like we are returning the money later on after the big sting."

"Let's go before I think it over any longer."

Outside Rachel asked where his car was. He pointed to a slate blue metallic muscle car.

"This is yours?"

"Hop in." Upfront it was a two-seater black leather with a full back seat.

"Wow, Seth. You like cars?"

"This is a 1966 GTO fully restored. I just bought it. I am glad you like it. It is going to get us there and out of there before anyone knows what hit them."

He revved the engine just a little and the pair took off. The night was young and the sun had not even set yet. Rachel was going to follow her instructions and be very quick.

He parked the car and the two exited at the same time. There was a party going on outside with a local band and picnic tables scattered here and there. The song playing was an oldie. "The night they drove ole dixie down …" The couple walked inside and Rachel went to the lady's room but did not close the door. Once she heard Seth asking for a beer, she peeked out and opened the door across the hall. Sure enough, the safe was in there and open. She immediately reached in and pulled out the cash, two tall stacks. She stuffed it in her shirt which was tucked in her jeans. Stealing. She never stole anything in her life. Quick. Do not think. Get out of here. That is when she heard Seth order another beer. He must be getting someone's attention. She peeked out and went to the bathroom again. She flushed the toilet and exited. She took a big swig of the beer-drinking half a bottle and said, "Let's go outside."

Seth drank his beer and both walked outside. The band had moved on to another old song. "Sweet Home Alabama, Lord, … I'm coming Home …"

Quietly and quickly the couple slid into his new car and muscled off the property. He turned the radio on to Allman Brothers singing "Midnight Rider…" They did not look at each other or talk until fully out of site down the road two lights and a turn towards the river.

Once safe, Seth stopped, turned, and asked, "You, okay?"

Her heart which had been excited was not racing. That was the easier of the two gigs tonight. She could not wait until this was over. A car pulled up beside them. It was Valeria Dave. He came over to the passenger side and put his hand out. Rachel reached inside her shirt and pulled out four thousand dollars though she had not counted it yet. She slapped it in his hand. "You are making some money tonight. Do I get any?"

"You will get your payday at the end, July 4th. But I did get you guys a bigger sailboat. Adios."

"This life of crime pays well. Man, I see why people get involved, there are no taxes or loans. It is all cash." Rachel went on and on shaking her head sideways.

"No. Crime does not pay and drugs kill. Remember the plan. We get the bad guys in the end, at the end of the sting."

"You're cute, you know."

"I am, even with all this scruff?"

"I do wish we were just going out on a date right now."

"Me too. Where would we go?"

"Well, we could watch the sunset, go for a walk or maybe

get a late-night bite."

"We can still do that tonight after our next gig," Seth replied. He winked at her. He made a game of this treacherous business. She guessed that is how he survived all this time. "Let's watch the sunset, then go to the next place which has a much higher net."

"How much higher?"

"Way higher."

"As in …"

"Three hundred thousand."

"Then there's cameras or an alarm, I suppose."

"I have scoped it. Valeria says that is why he picked it- there is no alarm. The guy trusts his granddaughter and does not think anyone knows he has that much cash."

"A big surprise is coming."

"Here is the deal. I drop you down the road-you walk in. Go through the garage. The daughter smokes cigarettes in the garage with the lights out. Then she goes back inside. She usually orders a pizza when he goes out, not sure of the time. The loot is upstairs in a spare bedroom. You take a garbage bag and bag it all up. Throw it out a window and retrieve it when you leave. Do not let her see you."

"Then I pick it up off the grass and run where?"

"You run to the back of the house and follow a dry bed all the way to the highway. There is a tunnel-go through it to the other side of the highway where we will be waiting in my car. Valeria Dave will be with me. Then your test is over and the cartel has your back with the job ahead."

"I am checking your attitude and copying it. No worries here. Solid plan until she finds me in her house. Does she have a gun?"

"There are guns in the house but no one is home except her."

"Okay."

"Here is a knife you can strap to your arm or leg and here's a gun. Put it in your side pocket or keep it in your hand."

The couple watched the setting sun and enjoyed this quiet time in the car together. The date would be continued after the gig. Seth started the car and drove to the next job for Rachel. Rachel's heart started to pound. She had a knife, for the dry bed, which might contain snakes or alligators and a gun for the house and the stealing of six figures from one cartel for the other cartel. This was a game of cartels. Rachel. Think serious, not board games. She would not kill the girl, no matter what. She would use the gun as a diversion if needed. Rachel wondered what was sold to reach three hundred thousand dollars. Damn. That was a ton of cash!

She did not even want to know right now. She would find out later. Rachel had a lot of confidence in Seth. He knew what he was doing and people respected and paid for his knowledge. He and his team were on the forefront in this adventure after doing a couple smaller details and gaining their trust. Seth drove out and away from the city into the country and entered a small neighborhood. He pointed to where he would be waiting on the highway. He was giving her forty-five minutes. He pulled up to an empty lot after driving past the house showing her. Sure enough, the garage door was up.

"Here is the garbage bag. I do not want you rummaging

through her kitchen cabinets and drawers." Seth handed her a black bag rolled up. He gave her the thumbs up. "See you in forty-five minutes."

"Forty-five." She left the car, quietly closing the door and began walking back to the house in the gig. She made her way to the back of the houses two houses before the one in question. She stayed close to the sides of the houses and then there she was in her back yard. She looked and saw her playing on the phone while sitting on a sofa in front of the TV and opposite to the kitchen. Perfect time to get inside. Quickly, she set about entering the garage keeping an eye out for any people strolling outside. Rachel made her way into the left side of the garage when suddenly the door opened. Out walked the teen with a cigarette and lighter in her hand. Rachel squatted down on the other side of a vehicle out of sight. Okay. She hoped it was a one cigarette moment. Rachel thought why isn't she vaping? She thought all the kids did that now. Until she smelled it. Oh no, it was not a cigarette, it was a joint. Was she going to smoke the whole joint by herself? It is a good thing the lights were off. It seemed like forever. She waited. And waited. Then the girl went inside. Time for Rachel to get near the door, maybe check out the front window to see where she was located inside. The staircase was in the back near the kitchen, that much she knew. Suddenly, a car was pulling into the driveway. Rachel slithered to the front of the car out of sight. It was her pizza guy! He got out of the car and took a pizza with him. He made his way to the front door. When Rachel heard the doorbell ring that was her biggest cue to make haste. And she did.

She tried the door handle and it was locked. Rachel pulled

out a credit card and slid it up and down. It worked. Man, the things you learn when on the opposite side of the law. Who would have thought a credit card might come in so handy? It is good housewives across America do not know this trick. Inside she stepped and could hear the girl talking with the pizza delivery guy. She told him to wait one minute while she got a tip. Rachel quickly closed the door, locked it, and hid in the pantry. The girl came back into the kitchen and retrieved some cash from her purse on the counter. Once the girl went to the front door again Rachel took off for the stairs a few feet away. Up, up, and out of the way. She hoped she had a little time while the girl ate some pizza and played with her phone.

CHAPTER 16

Rachel searched all the rooms upstairs, three in total. The final room seemed to be a spare bedroom, like no one slept there. She checked the closets, the dresser, the bed and finally an extra table next to a sitting chair by the window. Funny, she thought, why would there be three empty pizza boxes up here? Maybe the girl saved her used pizza boxes. For what? Maybe she recycled and stored them up here. Wait. She opened the top one. Bingo. The cash was in plain view filled to the brim with hundred dollar bills all neat and tidy. She checked them all and quickly emptied the cash into her garbage bag, one by one until all three spilled the cartel cash, then emptied a large air pocket and went to open the window. It was on the side of the house. No lights were on the house next door. Good sign for her. Rachel dropped the bag to the bushes below and closed the window. She restacked the boxes and left things as they were. Good. Just in case the girl came up here and brought another box to stack she might not see anything amiss. Now she had to escape and not be seen. She crept down the stairs and peeked around the corner when she neared the bottom. The girl was eating her pizza and watching TV. Suddenly, she stood. She paused the show she was watching and walked towards the front of the house through a hallway. It was bathroom time. Perfect for Rachel. Or so she thought. After scampering across the kitchen floor, she opened the garage door and found a car pulling up onto the driveway. Oh no. Slowly it came right up into the garage. Without a moment to spare Rachel closed the garage door and made her way through the hallway to the front of the house and then hid in a dining room out of sight. She had to either wait for the girl to exit the bathroom, or make a run out the front door while the person in the car either came into the house or went outside for mail. She heard the garage door go down. One way out. Get out now she told herself. Like a cat in the night, she pounced without a sound, opened the front door, left sideways squeezed through a narrow opening and closed it behind her. Her eyes needed a second to adjust and then she took off running taking a quick right to the side yard, looked up to the window and back down again to find her loot. She gave a quick look in all directions. Seems whomever came home turned the lights on out back. Rachel went to the front of the house next door and sped across their drive and yard before hitting the way to the back of the houses. Better to be safe than have someone see her come through so close to the gig house. Running as fast as she could she felt like a bank robber except no one was after her. Seems these crooks need some security. She guessed because of the wedding there was none tonight. Fifteen minutes to get in the house, fifteen minutes to scour for the cash in the house, she figured she had ten to fifteen minutes left through a dry bed just up ahead. Also, the dry bed was in a lush tropical forest. No way.

She was not entering that bitch. No knife was going to slay a gator or a python. What the actual fuck? Did Seth know she had her limits of frustration. Certainly, he must know. He was so keen on everything. She traveled close to the monster, the forest, so as not to be seen. She had gone maybe ten houses when she spied the highway. Nearby was the tunnel. She had another idea. Her gaze lingered on that circular dark beast with cement towers on each side. Barely five seconds later she knew she was better at scaling, reaching, climbing, and existing in the open than walled off for two hundred feet on her elbows and knees face down.

She ran towards the cement blocks and jumped up high before reaching it, throwing up her bag of loot and grabbing hold, then she threw a leg up and struggled, relentlessly. She was strong for sure and that saved her as well as her light frame. She made it. Why did she just not climb up the grass off to the side, well, because of a damn fence much taller than her. She crept low. She looked for their car across the highway. Not there yet. Traffic out here on I-75 went in spurts. She wanted to make it in one giant quest across the whole thing. She studied to see if that was possible. Since they were not there yet she made a fast and furious decision. Be there before them, then they would think she came out of the tunnel like directed. She would fool them both and be cleaner in the doing. She scoped it and at the perfect time, she rolled over the berm and took off. She could see lights way down the road on both sides but to her amazement, the south bound lanes were barely in use. Running on the highway she was pretty sure she had just broken another law. What the hell, Mr. Seth, were you getting her into? He was getting her into the cartel and Valeria Dave would be her new boss. For now. Once on the other side Rachel hid down the embankment near the opening of the tunnel but not over the cement blocks. She waited. She had three minutes left.

Sixty seconds left according to her wristband. That is when she encountered a snake slithering through the grass. Thirty seconds left. She looked down the highway and a car slowed. It pulled over and eased up just in front of her. She climbed up a few feet and checked to make sure it was a 66 GTO. Valeria Dave was the passenger. That she could see. She went to the back door, opened it, and threw herself inside and laid out flat on the black leather seat. No sooner than that, Seth took off. She was dizzy and panted a few breaths. Waiting. He pulled off the highway and took a few turns and pulled into a vacant parking lot near a building. She waited. There was Valeria Dave's car under a tree but clearly out of sight.

"Any complications?" Seth questioned her.

"Not really," she replied.

"Valeria, I got a present for you." She pushed the bag towards the front on his side. And waited.

He took the bag, peeked in, smiled at Seth, and said, "Rachel, what was the hardest part?"

"Definitely traveling through the tunnel to the other side. That took most of the time."

"You didn't take the tunnel."

"You are right. I have my limits of torture."

"See, you passed. Because if you had taken the tunnel-we would still be waiting for you, or worse yet."

"What's the worst yet?"

"One never knows what lies in those awful places, sweetie."

"Good. Glad I passed. Now I want that date you promised me Seth."

Valeria Dave left the car. Seth pulled away while Rachel laid in the back going back over her gigs. No gun used. No knife used. Not that she would not have pulled out either. Three hundred and four thousand dollars in theft, she surmised she was a pro now. Big time. Time to celebrate. Time to escape. She was on the other side all in the name of the law. Seth's law.

"Honey, you did good. You will get paid well when this finishes, I promise."

"I believe you. I am going to pass out-let me know when we get to our date."

Seth drove towards Tampa by way of the Skyway Bridge. All lit up it was beautiful. Job done. Time to celebrate over near the beach at an out of the way little place. Dancing, drinking and a late-night bite is just what Rachel ordered up. He aimed to please. He pulled up at his place, a small one-bedroom condo two blocks from the beach. Rachel woke and looked around. She heard the trunk close and there was Seth with a package in his hand. He opened the door and led her out.

"We're here."

"Where?"

"A place to have a little date. Just us."

They walked to the condo door and he opened it. He handed her the package which contained a dress and sandals. "Take a shower and get dressed. We will go get a bite, maybe dance some."

"Yes, sir."

Rachel was already forgetting the events of the night leading up to this and a shower helped immensely. She dressed and fingered her hair in place. Seth was waiting with two glasses of red wine. "Oh perfect."

Seth wore his hair back tonight, gelled back into a pony tail. He wore a Tommy Bahama Florida shirt mostly teal in color with sailboats and islands and khaki shorts. Handsome is what Rachel thought. "Looking good," she said and sipped her wine.

"Likewise, my dear," he replied. Rachel looked exquisite in the light green, yellow and fuchsia flowered halter styled sundress. He also bought her dark brown open back heeled sandals, perfect for dancing. Her light blonde hair fell everywhere, especially around her face.

"Thank you for the dress. So nice."

"You're welcome. Tell me where the money was at the gig?"

"I thought you'd never ask." She laughed in relief. "It was in three empty pizza boxes upstairs in a spare bedroom. The teen girl must be helping her father."

"Hmm. I will need to look into that."

She emptied her wine glass and said, "Shall we go dancing?"

"Let us go. It is close."

The couple walked two blocks towards the ocean and turned the corner. Music could be heard and they followed the sound finding a small little place with a courtyard and inside tables that were placed upstairs overlooking a balcony with an ocean view. They ate upstairs first. Seth ordered oysters on the half shell, Rachel ordered fried green tomatoes and both ordered a cheeseburger to follow. The tables had hurricane lamps with candles and the setting seemed romantic with dim lights and white table cloths. All while the ocean across the street made continuous white falls landing on the sandy shore dissipating its thunder.

Rachel devoured her cheeseburger and fried green tomatoes.

"Dessert?" asked the waiter.

"We'll take two to go whatever she wants."

Seth paid the bill and the couple departed to the main floor where the band played. A small group of dancers were swaying on the floor. They set their desserts and phones on the bar back in the corner and joined the others. The set finished with a slow number and Seth invited her to finish much closer. Relaxing the pair swiveled around and settled in close. One would think they had known each other for awhile or longer. They did in fact but it was fresh, exciting, and intimate. Like when two people begin dating and they are falling in love … ever so revealing.

Back at the bar Seth conversed with the bartender, who he knew, and Rachel talked with the couple next to her. The guy was a jokester telling one joke after another. They were much older and totally enjoying themselves. He ordered them a round of tequila shots and proposed a toast. And then a second round. Tequila was firing them up while laughter began releasing any inhibitions.

The couple said no to the third round and bid them goodnight.

Inside the condo Rachel undressed and Seth took off his shirt. He pulled the covers down and laid his beautiful Rachel on the bed. She was his flower waiting for him to make love to her.

He did.

CHAPTER 17

Driving over the Skyway Bridge the next morning, Rachel felt alive, as though this was the very first time she had ever seen so much water. But it was not the first time. She smiled riding in the slate blue 66 GTO, wearing sunglasses. Onto the next adventure. For sure.

Seth dropped Rachel at her place and she went to Henry's to see Patrick. They were not home. She texted Henry's mother, she said they would be back pretty soon as they were at the bait shop down the road. She went and waited for him at her place. They would have a late lunch together, talk and then she would be out sailing and gone for weeks.

Patrick walked in and was happy to see her. It had only been about two weeks with four more to go. He seemed happy and his hair was longer. "How's the pirate?"

"He is good. You know his name is Seth. You can call him Seth."

"Okay, next time I see him. When will that be?"

"The Fourth of July you will see him. We will watch fireworks, listen to music and have a picnic. Sound good?"

"Yes. Can Henry come too?"

"Sure. I believe so. Maybe his mother will want to join us?"

"If she's not doing something with her girlfriends."

"Good. Patrick, what do you say we go to a late lunch? I would like to take a quick nap first."

"Sure. I am going to take a shower."

Rachel was a bit surprised he wanted to clean up for a lunch. She looked at him.

"We went swimming last night and looked at the stars while lying on the beach. I need a good wash to get the salt out of my hair. Look at it."

"It does seem to have a mind of its own, all wild and standing up."

He left for the shower. So, this is what it is like to have a boy. They kind of surprise you. First, they are all wanting to be independent and dirty as in no shower, then they turn and are all human and desiring to be clean. Go figure. Someone told her they will guide you-being a parent is a natural endeavor. The child is the guide. That is a relief. Still, though, she would read some books or ask other moms like Henry's to make sure she kept him in line and safe.

About an hour later, Rachel and Patrick walked to the Mexican restaurant and were seated at a table in the back. Patrick told her that Henry was going to join them and that he had given him his order to place. Was that, okay? She assured him it was. He would be coming in about an hour and that gave them plenty of time to catch up. She would not be telling him too much of what she was doing but couldn't wait to hear how his days have been with Henry and his mom. He cleaned up well and his hair was now back to normal and covering his ears some.

"Aunt Rachel, can I ask you something personal?" He asked after they sat down and the hostess placed menus down on the table.

Rachel had no idea what he was about to ask. "You can ask me anything and I'll decide if I can answer the question."

"Well, because I'm with you now, and I guess that's forever, um, can I call you mom?"

She smiled. What a nice question, a big one too. "You would like to do that?"

"Yes. I have been thinking about it and I know it's only been a few weeks. But we should just move forward. That is something my mom always did. Each day she woke up and just pressed forward, even after a bad day before. She would want me to do that, because that is what you are now. I know it."

"Patrick, it is your decision. However, I would totally like that. But do know if I think someone, or someone, like you, are out of line then I must act like a parent. I will tell you no or correct you if something is wrong. Fair?"

"Yes. That is fair. Now Henry and I have moms but no dads."

"Which could change if ever that happens, you know," Rachel replied and added, "though it seems neither of us has a partner right now."

"You mean you and Seth are just friends."

"We are friends but also coworkers. I will fill you in after I finish helping him. I will be scuba diving in the ocean off of his boat in search of endangered fish."

"Sounds like an adventure. Is it hard to scuba dive?"

"It can be. But I am not going very deep so nothing bad should happen."

The waitress came and took their order and dropped off a couple waters. Both ordered tacos and cokes. While they waited Rachel asked Patrick how the boating and fishing was coming along. He looked at her and readied himself. He was about to spill the beans. Would she be mad or disappointed? He told himself it was okay. Do not be nervous. Tell her everything except that Henry drives to his girlfriends. He could not tell that. It was not for him to fink on something he was not involved in, or was it? He was not sure but right now he would not.

"I have learned to drive the boat, put an anchor down and retrieve it. I know how to tie a line around the wooden post on the dock and we have fished a little. I can hook some squid on the line and use a lure. I am still learning what to do though as I do not know all the fish."

"And there's quite a lot of fish out there in that big ocean."

"I love it down here. Thank you for having me."

Their food arrived and so did Henry. He did not tell her yet about all the stuff. Maybe they should eat first, then tell her. Yeah. That is what he would do. Everyone was hungry. Few words were offered for the next twenty minutes. Even the waitress came by when all the plates were empty and asked about dessert. Both boys said yes to brownies and ice cream. Rachel ordered a coffee. Rarely did she have an afternoon coffee but this seemed like a good time after Patrick's declaration of what he would call her.

"Did Patrick tell you?" Henry started in.

"About what?"

"I wanted you to eat first."

"Please, go ahead."

"Mom, please don't be mad but something happened yesterday and we aren't sure what to do about it."

"Yes?"

"Let me tell the whole story first before you say anything. Okay?"

She looked at both boys as they returned the gaze. Neither of them was hurt-so that was good. Here goes her first challenge as a mom. Oh brother. She could hear the single guitar player singing *wasting away again*. Maybe she should have ordered a margarita she thought. Then Patrick started in.

"One night when we were out in the boat on an island, we saw some guys at the end of the island going into the woods. We decided to go back there and see what they were doing and check it out. That was yesterday. But before we made it over there, we stopped by to see the big Coast Guard boat docked over across the way. It usually is not there. Henry took us near it and we saw a place to hook up and peek. And then we walked the dock out to the boat. It was super cool." He paused. She said nothing and waited. "No one was there. It was all by itself. So, we boarded it, very carefully. And looked around. Except, suddenly, a couple men walked the dock and we went below to hide. We did not plan that, I'm serious. It all happened so fast and we thought we were in big trouble. We hid down below. But the guys were fast and the boat started up and took off in like three minutes."

"We were safe Miss Rachel. I promise."

"We could tell we were going fast. That boat is not slow. Later it stopped and the two men got off. We looked and we were on that island near the woods. We peeked and Henry took a few pictures. Then, oh my gosh, a little kid came up from below. He said he was sleeping. We told him that we needed to be quiet and that pirates had gotten the boat but if we stayed quiet and out of sight, we would be all right. He did what we told him. Henry really saved us all. He was quick to think and we hope we did the right thing after doing the wrong thing. The guys were bringing two big boxes aboard, so we hid back down below and waited for them to return. They did. Then when we were back at the dock they unloaded and left. Once in the clear the little guy, Jose, took off on the dock and went in the office building. His dad was in there. We looked in the window and he seemed to be telling his little son he drank his coffee but did not know what time it was. We took off seeing that Jose was okay. Quickly we got on our boat and headed out to the island. We did not look back. He must have been a guard watching the boat and fell asleep. We made it to the island and looked around. We found the hiding spot but it was empty except for a shirt and this was in the pocket. It is a shipping label. We left the shirt. Henry has some pictures. Did I leave anything out?" Patrick handed the label to Rachel.

"Yes. We stayed on the island and looked at stars identifying constellations."

"So, it was a field day for school? A science project that lasted into the night."

"Mom, are we in trouble?"

Her face was not so happy now and her eyebrows were raised. She had no idea what to do.

"I forgot, there's more."

"Please Patrick, no more."

"Earlier this morning when we were at the bait shop the guy, a guard, I think, came in with the little boy, Jose. We hid out of sight. He bought his grandson a fishing pole and Henry's uncle started talking about little fish and big fish and then he says, "You'll both have to go out and catch the Ballyhoo bait someday when he's older.""

She sat there stunned. Really, did it have to be this big of deal with the first item to have a talk over? Rachel wanted that margarita more than ever.

The boys looked at her. "Miss Rachel, we had to tell you because I cannot tell my mom until I have all the facts. I want to go to the Coast Guard Academy or work with them after high school."

"I see. Here is what we are going to do." She paused, contemplated, then continued. "I am going to find out more information. I am new at this mom thing. But you both are fine and the boy and his dad are good. All safe. That is the most important thing. Next, I will find out about boarding a vessel not guarded. Third, those men might be very bad guys and I do not want them to know about you both. Do not tell anyone until I get back with both of you. Promise me."

"Promise."

"Promise."

"I am serious. This could be bigger than all of us, even the Coast Guard. I would imagine there are cameras and such. I have a person I can contact. Eventually, we will tell your mother. Know that, Henry."

"I'm sorry to put you through this." Henry stated.

"Henry, give her the pictures."

CHAPTER 18

Seth picked up Rachel after she had transferred the pictures to her phone. Tonight, she would run this situation past Seth. He of all people would know how to handle this. Thankful is how she felt. She liked his new ride and enjoyed the view as he drove her to a new marina off the end of an island after they had crossed several bridges. A bigger boat was waiting for them. They arrived at sunset. Tomorrow would be shopping and getting it ready. The next day would be the beginning of four weeks out to sea.

"I bought us a couple of sub sandwiches for dinner." He placed them on a table in the sailboat. Then they walked around putting their things away. Seth opened a bottle of wine and poured them both a glass.

"I know we have business out there but this is super nice. You sure about being the captain of this bigger vessel?" She asked.

"Yes. For as far as we are going. Now, if you asked me about sailing the big seas or across the Atlantic, then no. I am afraid I would not be up for crossing the Atlantic or Pacific."

"I do not want to do that either. I had an aunt who did

that several times but she had a captain who knew all about big seas."

"Rachel, we will be close to the shore but it will not be visible. Are you okay with that?"

"Someone, or a rescue boat could reach us if needed. Right?"

"Yup. For sure."

They started in on the sandwiches and Rachel began to disclose her earlier conversation with the boys. "I have something to ask you about protocol for something I know nothing about."

"What is it?"

"Patrick and Henry have been doing their own little investigation and I believe it might be far bigger. Here are some pictures they took. And here is a label they found on a small island out past the river, probably one we will be going by."

"Two big tan guys carrying a shipment container out of the woods?"

"Here's the whole story," she started. She told him everything. "And Henry wants to join the Coast Guard later after high school or maybe even try to go to the academy."

Seth took in this situation. He realized the kid is still a kid. But he wondered if this was part of a bigger picture and connected to what they were doing. "Could be criminal."

"I wondered too. What do we do? This is my son and his new best friend. We must report it, I know."

"Yes. But let me check with my authorities and alert them. It might be another way the drugs are coming in and we do not want to scare anyone off before we bite them."

"Thank you. I feel relieved already."

"The kid thought quick on his feet. He did what an ordinary person thought they should do given the situation without harming anyone. That stands for something."

"I know, in this business things are not always black and white and deserve consideration of the whole story. Especially since you are working for the good guys." She smiled at him and drank her wine.

"The little kid had a nap while likely they drugged his dad. The boys acted in good faith. What if the thugs left him on that island? Could have been dreadful."

"Okay. He wants to call me mom."

"Patrick?"

"Yes. Isn't that sweet?"

"Can't wait to get to know Patrick under normal circumstances."

They finished eating, cleaned up and drank more wine. They had separate quarters and retreated for the night. It would be an early morning and then departure was set for ten in the morning. Seth left the boat and made two phone calls. One to the top boss of Operation Lexi and another to Valeria Dave. Rachel fell fast asleep and dreamed of quiet seas and sunsets mixed in with some scuba diving looking at fish.

The trip to the grocery store presented the couple with an opportunity to explore what it feels like to be a family buying suppers and staples necessary for a long excursion. Selecting steaks, chicken, pork, vegetables, and fruit, as well as coffee, wine, beer, and rum. Only a couple salads were selected as one week out and items like that would not last. Seth liked oatmeal and sausage while Rachel preferred eggs, bacon, and waffles. He picked up a few candles and cleaning supplies while she made sure they had toiletries and paper towels. She told him she would catch fish and cook them after he told her what kind was good to eat. He agreed but said in case they did not he had plenty of meat to cook on a grill or inside if it was raining.

"I had not thought about the rain. Do we have rain gear?"

"It comes with the boat. That and blankets and fresh water. But I bought more if we need it."

Four weeks of supplies came to $875. They used the trunk and back seats to load up. Driving back to the dock was the last of land for a while. They were ready. She was ready to be a first mate. She had sailed before and assisted, just not with Seth nor by themselves.

"Ready?"

"Ready, Captain Seth. Tell me what to do. I am yours."

He liked that. He wondered for a moment *how did this happen?* He had not planned on Rachel helping him at all. One day out of the blue she followed him on Instagram, and now, here she was on this adventure. Must be karma. Even though Scarlet says she planned it. He did not see it that way. One of those "supposed to be" things he had heard about.

"You will release the lines up front and I'll be in charge of the stern lines."

"What's the front called again?"

"The bow."

They released from the dock and motored out to the river taking it slow and maneuvering through the harbor. "Teach me those words again for the front, back and sides."

"The front is the bow. That will be your job. The back,

which is mine and yours, is called the stern."

"Okay, bow and stern, or bs. Continue."

He laughed. "The sides are port side to the left, and starboard to the right."

"Okay, wine to the left and stars to my right."

"Sure. I will test you until you have got them."

She pointed to the front, said bow, then to the back, said stern, to the left and said port side, and finally, to the right and said starboard. Bow. Stern. Portside. Starboard. "Why can't it be front, back, left, and right? Instead of bs, wine, stars."

"I think you should google that, or there may be a manual down below."

"I should read the manual. I will do that." Rachel looked around. Today was smooth out on the river and not too many boats were out at this time she thought. Maybe they were already out there fishing or pleasuring.

Seth turned the music on and cruised the river out to the small islands off shore and beyond. He passed the barrier island which was a touristic paradise dream. He made note of the small island in question. Nothing happening he noted. His two phone calls would handle that. He had told Rachel that this morning when they had coffee. He guessed it was her first worry being a mom. Something like that he told himself. She seemed very relieved.

She saw some wave runners, or jet skis, coming right at them. Didn't they see their big sail boat? At the last minute they turned and pulled in front of them. They bobbed slightly, nothing really. The dudes need to pick on someone their own size if it is a thrill they are giving out. They had just passed a tiny island which contained only beaches and birds. The other small island coming up had trees and was much larger. Maybe that was the island the boys visited. She saw Seth fully staring hard at this place. Must be. It looked like a place you might want to visit and walk around if one wasn't working. Rachel gazed across the quiet but strengthening waters. While they were cruising extremely slow, she saw a current carrying a small log. Just then she imagined a big shark looking for dinner. Girl, leave that alone. Do not bother. Do not think about sharks, not now. Lifting her head up and away from the salt water she looked to shore and watched sandpipers perusing the shore with each lapping wave. Seagulls were flying above and everywhere. This was their territory!

"Rachel, after we pass this island, we will put up the sails. Prepare." She did as she was told. Once they were way out the seas were almost empty of other boats. Sails up and with the light wind the journey would be smooth and take about three hours or less. One could not see the old abandoned oil platform, built before restrictions were set in place. Three of them were out on the west side of Florida. Not in use. Not that the industry did not want to use them-its just too much red tape. For now, they existed out on the Florida shelf. Seth had gotten a tip about nefarious industries trying to use these places. Undercover, he and Rachel, are out looking for endangered fish and they like to accumulate near these platforms where smaller fish thrive. If they were lucky, they might catch red fish, mackerel and maybe even an amberjack.

The sailboat cruised about 4-5 knots or around 5 mph. Three hours of sailing would put them out 12-15 miles and somewhere around the 83 degrees longitude and 27 degrees latitude. He would have to plot the other platform after investigating this one. Four thousand abandoned oil rig platforms existed in the Gulf of Mexico. Did anybody know that? He never heard anyone talk about that. He knew it because he was going to go into one and find out who has been there or might be using it. At least they were not seen from shore-then everyone would know about these things. From shore one could see about three miles out. They did not even mess with the sunsets. Most of the abandoned rigs were outside Louisiana near New Orleans. But a few existed here before restraints prohibited the use. He relaxed once the sails were set and it was easy cruising. Two more hours and they would tie up or anchor, he had not decided yet. He would choose the safer route by eyesight.

Seth had Rachel steer the boat for a while as he studied the weather forecast. Winds from the west, as they generally were, with currents and depths he calculated for most of the week they could tie off or anchor right near by on the east side of the platform. Looks like it would be calm until later in the week. No thunderstorms. Nice beginning. Another hour to go and he would drop sails. The sea calmed him for sure. He gave it a thought as in what else would he do? He did not know. He did like being around Rachel, quite a lot.

Rachel looked around. Well, this was easy, just steer the boat in this direction. Gentle lapping waves were not a problem. She tried to look as far as she could see. It was endless. An endless sea. She thought about going for a swim when they anchored. That sounded refreshing. Apparently bad guys hid out here. How is that possible? Then again, she did not know what a bad guy looked like. She thought they looked like Valeria Dave. He looked bad, but was he? She contemplated the strange relationship Seth held with him. Was he a player or the main honcho? Why did she have so many questions? Go with your instincts Rachel.

"Land ho!" Exclaimed Seth. He pointed ahead of him just out of the hull.

Abandoned.

CHAPTER 19

Valeria Dave met with Carlos Mendez for coffee at a small riverside café. They ordered cinnamon rolls, freshly baked, and sat at a table discussing business. Valeria Dave tried a caramel iced latte for the first time. Hell, there was a first time for everything. Carlos seemed perturbed and lost.

"Carlos, how are you this morning?"

"Davo, not good!"

Both sat down hidden out of view from street goers and passersby. Carlos was already sweating and had not even started on his hot coffee with two creams.

"Why so shaken?"

"I do not know what happened but my loot was stolen or misplaced. I am sure it is misplaced. My granddaughter is looking into it. That is all."

"Your loot?"

"My personal affairs."

"You still got the keys to your storage unit. Those were not taken, right?"

"Right here. I am ready for what is coming. Should be a two-million-dollar sale with two hundred extra big ones for me." With seven hundred his take and two hundred as a bonus he would be set for life. He acknowledged that and made a short brief smile under his hat which hid half his face, including his eyes.

"Good. I am glad. Did you make the arrangements for travel before and after?"

"It is all set. He is using his private jet-we've cleared a small runway just north of here. Then my other guy brings the Americans in and we take them to a private marina where the goods are. They load up, drive to storage, payment is made and we all leave. My third guy comes to the storage and loads up the next morning. Off he goes. All done. Everybody happy. With my loot I make minus the three I lost; I am out of here to some island-never to be seen again as they say. I do not know how I got into this. Except I do."

"I know how you did. They killed your family. All you have left is her. The granddaughter. What is her name?"

"Margarite."

"We need to look out for each other. I got your back, man. Margarite needs you; she is still young and not ready to be out there. It is dangerous. She deserves a good life after losing her parents and grandmother. I will see you through. In four weeks, this will be over and you will go wherever you want. I promise."

"I am not sure how you can promise that? But I trust you Davo. You have been nice to me. Maybe I will leave you my landscaping business. It is all legit. Do you want it?"

"Well, of course, I will think about that. I need a real job. I love working outside. Maybe I will have orchards of fruit trees, and crops of tomatoes or strawberries. I will become a farmer."

"You are a funny dude. What if they kill you?"

"Carlos, I have to kill them first."

"Good luck with that."

Valera Dave winked at him and got up to leave. He walked away confident and assured. A plan was set and it was in play. He turned around and gave four fingers to Carlos, as in four weeks, then he made a splice to his own throat, as in over and dead. Done.

He had another errand with someone he had not ever met. It was secret, maybe somebody from the top, and new to the area. He hoped it didn't mess with his arrangements.

Carlos went home and gave his granddaughter a big hug. He'd been hard on her after the money went missing but it wasn't her fault. It was his own. This lousy business was wreaking havoc. But he remembered the words from his meeting with Davo today. He had his back. He wondered what that meant. He trusted the guy but did not really know all his contacts. For now, he really had no other choice but to follow his orders. Hopefully, this was the right choice.

"Grandpa, I made some schedule changes for you today with the landscaping."

"That is great. You handled it with phone calls?"

"One of the guys stopped by and told me he added three more homesites with full coverage every month."

"Great. Business is good."

"I put them on the schedule and called the guys who need to do the jobs."

"I am so glad you are taking an interest in my company. That is great news I could sure use."

"Also, I am going to cook for us this week. I want to try some new recipes I found on Pinterest."

"Pinterest?"

"Social media. It has everything."

"Maybe I should be on social media. Can you hook me up?"

"Sure, I can. You should start and maybe advertise on a couple sites. I can do that."

"This is great news!"

"Tomorrow, we will sign you up. It is so easy. All you need is an email to begin."

Seth dropped the sails as they approached the abandoned oil rig platform. He then motored up closer to it observing the metal structure. He checked the depth which fluctuated between 27 and 32 feet. Rachel would be able to scuba here maybe with his help to make it safer. He would anchor for tonight, go over the plans with her, eat dinner and rise early to get started in the morning.

Seth fired up a small outdoor grill back near the stern while Rachel prepared a salad, vegetables and a couple baked potatoes. She poured two glasses of wine from the bottle already opened and brought everything up top to the outside table covered from the sun during the day but now the setting six o'clock sun filtered in through the platform. She looked around and did not see any other boats out here. She guessed fishermen were in for the day and barges had reached their port such as Tampa Bay. She had found dishes down below in the kitchen, wiped them off and set the table. Seth finished up the steaks, cooked some chicken for tomorrow before letting the charcoal expire. He brought them to the table and sat down.

"Here you go. This one is medium and that one is medium rare. Take your pick."

"Medium is fine." She toasted her wine glass to his.

"After dinner we will discuss the plan. Sound good?"

Seth and Rachel only had each other now to depend on and consort with. This would be close quarters like an extended vacation with some work intertwined. Once the dinner was finished Seth started in first with the safety features aboard, followed by first aid kits, protection from fire, how to use the radio system for help and weather, and other systems aboard keeping the refrigeration and cooking intact as well as the heads and showers.

"Kind of like getting a cabin in the mountains with no services connected to the outside world for a whole month."

"Like a long journey. Preservation is key but we are not far from land to get back. It would only take a day."

"Unless the weather acted up, then how long?"

"Looking for the worst are we?"

"No. I just want to be prepared."

"A storm could last three to five days I suppose. But we should get warning of that and we will depart if that occurs."

"Seems to me storms, wind, and rain, are very likely in Florida come the month of June. I have experienced them before. Lots of rain, hurricanes, too."

"This is why I am so glad you are with me Rachel. You are keen about that kind of thing. Whereas I get lost in my job and lose focus. I only think about the mission and forget Mother Nature might stop me."

A bigger wave knocked the boat more than the gentle waves had previously. Still, it was quiet tonight. Seth turned on some music to play as he discussed the safety plan and the real plan. Into the Mystic by Van Morrison played and the two enjoyed the beginning sunset. She poured the rest of the wine in both glasses while Seth cleared the table. Then he joined her again.

"Here is the deal. We are lovers doing a summer class from the local college to study endangered fish in the Gulf of Mexico."

"Are there any endangered fish?"

"Good question. We need to look that up."

"Seriously, you don't even know?"

"We are studying them; we will make it up and sound official. There are books in the dining room down below."

"Okay, I'll do some reading tonight."

"There are some test tubes and what not, official looking items below, as well as notebooks. You have your scuba equipment and I have a camera for photos. We are not experts just students getting a PhD or something."

"No. No way, not a PhD. That is too much. We are taking a class so we can open a scuba shop and run a business. You are taking the business class and I am studying the fish."

"Perfect."

The clink of glasses is heard as the sun sets and shines some light for a while making a pink painting over most of the sky.

"Tell me the real scoop. What is the low-down dirty work we are to do?" Rachel stared at him intently waiting for the official assignment.

"We have four guns which are easy to use. Just aim and fire. There are ten flares for extreme conditions alerting the

Coast Guard, but before that we can radio for support to my guy with a cigarette boat."

"How far away is he?"

"Thirty or forty-five minutes."

"Except in a storm or hurricane."

"Right. We have got rope to tie someone up if need be and handcuffs. I have got pepper spray and a taser gun. That will disarm most anyone. We also have smoke bombs."

"Oh Lord. You have smoke bombs?"

"You'd be surprised at how that disarms a crowd, instantly."

"Really? I had no idea."

"Yes. No one gets hurt either. So, it is very temporary."

"Do you foresee using any of these tactics?"

"Yes and no."

She looked at him quizzically.

"Our lives are the most important thing here. We will protect each other first. Then if a foe interrupts or makes attempts at our lives, we have the authority to defend ourselves. That is how it works. Pure and simple."

"And just who is going to get us out here where nobody is?"

"Cartels move in mysterious ways. And I do not always know who is on my side. I am undercover and you are, too. But some rogue idiot who wants to be the big guy might make some moves."

"Like Valeria Dave?"

"Valeria Dave is mysterious but I have worked with him now almost two years. He supervises but does not randomly kill. I have never seen it from him."

"All right. If you trust him, then I will too."

"Tomorrow, we climb up to the top of the rig platform and break into as many places possible. We will spend four days here searching for clues and products while two of the days you go in search of fish."

"And then?"

"We go sailing to another rig. We do the same. The third one is much farther away so it will take longer, maybe five days there, five or six days back depending on currents."

"Here's to fishing and exploring!"

"Cheers! And wear a hat and sunscreen out here as much as possible until you get tan."

Rachel went below to research fish. She retrieved the notebooks and started a make-believe journey of studying. She made notes, drew pictures of fish, noted their colors and depths, and made a small corner for her findings. Seth made a back pack of supplies for the morning when they traveled from sailboat via dingy to the rig platform. They would also wear a life vest-he got those out and put them next to the supplies in the back pack. Rachel packed a lunch for tomorrow including drinks. Her mind was always working. What could go wrong? Plan. She put a few tools in her back pack like a knife, a hammer (for breaking windows), first aid kit, camera, two-way radio, screwdriver, and a portable ladder. She was not sure how rusty these rigs got out here. The Florida sun burnt everything up over time. Bedtime came and went and both were up at the crack of dawn excited to begin.

They ate protein bars for breakfast, drank coffee, loaded the back packs aboard then lowered the dingy, boarded, started the motor, and away they went about fifty yards to the abandoned adventure.

CHAPTER 20

Finally, the pair saw the business in front of them. Everything mattered going forward. There were no do-overs. They would send a record of the daily activities to an agent in town and then delete the info. Rachel wore a bathing suit with shirt and shorts over, a hat and sunglasses up top and some cool water shoes that held a tread for climbing steel ladders and such. Seth and his dreadlocks were long now and he had a deep dark tan, He wore a visor, sunglasses that reflected a blue tone with opaque white frames and the same apparel as Rachel only swim shorts. Once at the ladder to the rig he tied up the line times two. Better safe than sorry because they were quite aways to swim back to the boat. Not impossible at all just not what they needed to be doing. Plus, he did not want to lose the dingy. He figured Rachel might fear sharks as well.

The oil rig platform was massive. He wondered out loud how long these things lasted.

"I don't know but I did see a picture of one tossed sideways."

"Hey, you're scaring me."

"You going up first?" she asked.

"Sure. Be careful. See you up top."

Observing some rust each step was evaluated first before placing weight. The steps were about two stories off the ocean surface. She peeked behind her and down. Do not do that she told herself. Up, up, and up following her partner she went. At the top was a beautiful view of the ocean and more ocean. She steadied herself from a moment of dizziness and looked to see if Seth had the same experience.

"Dizzy?" He asked.

"Slightly."

"Let us get to work. There are about three floors here. Just scope it all out looking for an oddity."

"We stay within voice distance and always on the same floor."

Each one looked around from top to bottom, opening doors if present and peering into storage areas. This fixed oil rig had one and a half stories. The platform where the guys worked and possibly an upper quarter where they lived. After about an hour they regrouped coming up empty. They found the stairs to the upper level and looked around up there, opening lockers and storage areas as well as a small kitchen and toilet area. What looked like a bed area to sleep had been removed and only table and chairs remained. The view out a window and balcony area gave way to a feeling of being on a giant ship and determining which way you were going to proceed.

"Let's eat at this table." Rachel pulled up a chair and retrieved their lunch.

"Sounds good."

Just then a loud noise caught their attention.

"What in the devil was that?"

"Sounded like movement from a barge or tanker, very steel driven I might add."

"Must be something loose or moving down below."

"Think we're, okay?"

"Yes. That is the first time we heard the sound. I did not hear it last night or this morning, or since we boarded this old devil."

"Same. Hey, we should give these rigs names as we go on each one."

"What's the first one called?"

"Well, you just named it, devil. So, Steel Evil or Devil Works, which one?"

"Steel Devil."

"Yeah, that is it. You mighty Steel Devil."

"I believe number one is done. In case the two others are bigger and more floors we might break for number two earlier."

"Sounds like an adjustment to the plan. I am in."

"Let's see if on the way out we can figure the metal sound we heard."

"Okay, name change, too. Metal Devil or Devil Metal?"

"The games survivors must play to keep sane. "

They decided on Devil Metal when they heard the sound and saw a large piece swaying when the wind hit it just right. Last night being peaceful there was no rig music. Day one done. They sent the report and then deleted it. Rachel drew the rig in her notebook and placed the name over it. Tomorrow was scuba diving and fishing, next day onto oil rig platform number two and then three. Calm seas and no drugs made them let their guard down some. From time-to-time Seth would engage Rachel in safety such as gun use, smoke bombs, taser use and other useful tricks of the espionage world. It was his game and he knew it well. He just did not let on too much. He was enjoying this trip or work travel with Rachel. He liked her quite a lot and wondered if she felt the same. But he would not enter that gray area until the Fourth of July.

The next morning, they sailed away from *Devil Metal* under clear skies and minimal wind. Seth raised both sails and put the motor on as well. The other platform was nearby. Rachel made them a hearty breakfast using the cooking stove top for eggs and bacon. She decided to make her favorite omelet, something that would last them until dinner much later tonight. Quickly she made biscuits as well and served this with honey and strawberry jam. She cleaned the strawberries and sliced them, then added them to the plate with a dusting of powdered sugar. This morning felt like vacation aboard a vessel. Maybe it was. She brought the breakfast up to the outdoor table and went below to retrieve the coffee. When she arrived up top Seth greeted her with a big morning hello followed by a hug. She returned the hug. It felt good. They dove into the breakfast while slowly sailing to the next destination.

At one point there was nothing in front of them and nothing behind them. Nor on either side. The horizon was completely blank. The feeling made them aware of each other even more. Incredible. To be only two creatures on earth moving across Gods greatest creation besides humans, the all-mighty ocean. A grandeur that did not go unsaid by either one of them. After breakfast and before drinking their coffee, this sightseeing pleasure was followed by a long kiss. Neither one of them expected this to happen. The pair was in sync and smiled while drinking their coffee staring at one another. Respite was all Seth could think of. He had not planned on any feelings and tried to push them off until the Fourth of July. Was it the boat, the ocean, the mission, the aloneness, or was it each other drawing them closer?

Rachel cleaned up breakfast as Seth sailed the boat to their next destination. After three hours of sailing, he spied the next rig. Good their course was steady. Rachel had been below writing in her journal and reading about fish and colleges over in Bradenton. She researched which bait the fish liked, etc. When she finished making pictures and notes she thought about lunch. What should she make for lunch? It had to be very simple as breakfast and dinner were the big meals for today. She decided peanut butter and jelly sandwiches would be appropriate. Not exactly healthy but totally workable, easy and no cleanup!

She prepared for her afternoon of scuba diving as well. She had heard Seth give a shout when he spied land a few moments ago. Well, not land as in land ho but land as in another oil rig. They had kissed this morning at breakfast and it felt great. They both wanted it to happen. A bit of magic she told herself. She let her mind wonder over the idea of Seth, of dating Seth with his crazy business. It seemed important, dangerous, good paying and he liked it. She was able to assist in a small way as well. She smiled when she thought about the bigger purpose. They were saving the world, at least lives, from harmful substances. And life was all that was important. It was her Hippocratic oath to do no harm and save lives when able and to care for the sick and those unable with respect and dignity. Maybe it was nursing 3.0. Maybe. Her mind ran to Patrick, her boy now, back home who she would take care of forever. A dad would be a good thing for him. She smiled again.

"Penny for your thoughts." Seth walked partway down into the cabin. "I just need a water." He helped himself and returned to his station.

"I'm happy."

"Me too."

Later with sandwiches prepared she went up top. Seth had the vessel anchored, sails down and was ready for lunch as well.

"What will you do while I'm scuba diving below?" Rachel inquired.

"I am not sure. Maybe I will go snorkeling and watch you from above. I should do that as you are supposed to have a partner, correct?"

"Correct. Okay, just do not scare the fish. As they do like the comfort of a boat to hide the rays."

"Do you think I would scare them off? We could put that in our thesis, our summer thesis."

"I'll watch them and report on that."

"I do have a book I could read, some spy novel about Mexican cartels doing business in America."

"You are funny. Make sure the guns are loaded. I do not have time to load up as my shot is a bit shaky, or will be when my nerves get me."

"Laugh now. Because there is nothing funny about a cartel who wants his four million dollars yesterday." Seth became serious. He wanted to show her that this was business, serious business. "But my beautiful lady, I feel we have time. Showtime will likely be the last rig, the furthest away."

Seth did know his business. They had a few days here to play the part of college course studies for the summer learning the fish and scuba business. Seth helped her with the tank and applying it to her back. She checked all her equipment and headed to the back, applied her fins, and prepared to jump in. Seth tied a line with an extra buoy and wished her well. He would join her and watch her while he snorkeled up top. This time the boat was closer to the rig. Seth thought the abandoned rig might give way to more fish.

Rachel went down and down and down. She plotted her course, eyeing their boat, the rig and all the other directions. It was a sandy bottom, about 17 feet in depth, and she noted schools of fish right away. Seth had given her the camera and she fired away. She could see him up top and gave him a thumbs up. She was also going to catch a few fish if she could, one to eat and two to dissect or save. She cut some plants as well. It was peaceful down below and she fell into a rhythm propelling herself towards the areas planned out.

Seth maneuvered himself around so he could be as close as possible. Both were swimming in the ocean blue. He thought she might see the most living things-where the water was cooler near the rig and the schools swam together hiding from the big fish.

When he hovered over the surface area under the rig, he saw Rachel and her fins moving about. He waved at her and she saw him. He saw a few large fish but was not quite sure what they were. He wondered what kind of fish she planned on catching. She would probably surprise him. She took a couple bites of squid bait in a baggy with her. They would have plenty to talk about tonight over dinner. He speculated about Rachel while snorkeling. He thought he was falling in love with her. In fact, he was sure of it. Maybe he could not wait until the Fourth of July. He thought maybe she was falling for him as well.

He swam back to the boat when he saw her heading in that direction. The he heard her emerge.

"I got one. Let us get out before a shark comes sniffling around."

CHAPTER 21

The pair quickly emptied the contents from the ocean unto the vessel as if almost in a race. Then laughing in delight. "You caught a cobia, a large cobia!"

"I was not sure but I let the harpoon gun go and bullseye. I got it right off the back of the boat."

"It will make a fantastic dinner. I have wanted to try it for some time."

Seth put the fish on ice. Cleaned up the harpoon hook and set the gun away. Rachel went below to shower and put fresh clothes on. She set her camera on the table to show him pictures later at dinner and then retrieved a cookbook and wrote down a recipe on how to grill cobia. She placed her plants on the table as well, not sure what to do with them. Rachel showered and put a dress on for tonight. She braided her hair and pulled it up and back to one side. She also put some jewelry on around her neck and gold hooped diamond studded earrings. She found a couple rings and placed them on. A small amount of makeup toned her freshly sunned face. Lipstick added color. Then she found her seaweed with a couple small buds and put it in her hair. Too bad she did not have a real flower.

Seth cleaned up too. He wore a very white light linen short sleeved shirt, so modern, and paired it with crisp linen knee length shorts supplanted by a brown leather belt with a silver buckle. Dashing he thought. He hoped she thought so. He retrieved a couple beers and a bottle of tequila. Rachel turned on the music. The sun was almost set when the two of them popped up through the cabin stairs and started the party.

"Cheers."

"Cheers."

"Down the way … where the nights are gay …" began playing to the crowd of two.

"What a great day, Seth!"

He smiled.

"I had a fantastic time today. It even beats stealing cartel money and robbing juke joints."

"Ha ha."

"I'm serious." She stated loudly.

"I have something for you. Let me get it." He jaunted down the steps, fumbled around, and returned quickly. "Here." He showed her a flower then attempted to put it in her hair. "Nice."

"Thank you. I will take a selfie. Maybe I can send it to Patrick."

"Sure. Why not?"

They sipped their drinks as the sun set while the alcohol cooled their lips but warmed their souls.

"So, this is what they call a working vacation?" she asked.

"Idk, I've never been on one."

"Maybe we should have a fire drill to be better prepared."

"Let us worry about that tomorrow. Okay honey?"

"Sure, honey. Let us cook before we are pure jelly and the fish want to eat us."

They went below and made a dinner, including dessert, and decided to eat below for the first time. After dinner they went upstairs for an after-dinner drink to reflect on the cobia and their future.

"The cobia was a perfect fish."

"Yes, I loved it too. They call it a lemon fish or black bonito. This time of year, they travel up to the north gulf area from here or to Massachusetts from the Caribbean."

"That will be our study fish. You know so much about it."

"And now we know what it tastes like. It is very plentiful because the other fish are over fished some."

"What else is it good for?" Seth is intrigued.

"I am so glad you asked. It has selenium, magnesium, B vitamins, omega 3 fatty acids and is a good fish for your cardiovascular system."

"So, they say. Even with that buttery taste?" Seth asked.

"Yes, and it did not fall apart. I put mine on a very light bun to make a sandwich as I was starved and it made a perfect grouper replacement, which is my favorite fish sandwich next to lake perch."

"The lemon mayo mixture gave it a tart flavor. Loved it. You are a great cook!"

"Thank you."

"You're welcome. You made breakfast and lunch and dinner, so I made you dessert. Are you ready?" He asked.

"Not yet. Let us dance up here for a while," she says.

Everything feels right for Seth at this moment. "You are so beautiful. I really mean it. Thanks for coming on this venture with me. I am so glad."

"I hope I help you. It is exciting. So far so good."

The couple sways to the music, the moon is out now while they transverse from side to side making the boat rock some. They begin to kiss and now nothing matters but them, not music, not the moon, not their dancing. He takes her hand and they descend below to the berth. Seth has put out some battery candles which light the way forward. They find the sailboat bed and undress each other while kissing and kissing, skin to lips, lips to skin. Falling onto the bed he puts himself on top and begins to explore more. Rachel closes her eyes and relaxes even more. She does not even realize she's on a sailboat out in the ocean with a moon overhead and a sea of stars above her head.

He turns her on her side and she pushes him over to topple his body. Now she sees him fully laying there vulnerable to her stare and fingers caressing his being. Nothing else matters but going forward. He turns her over again and the time is nigh. There are no expectations left only energy to complete this act of love. Breathlessness and heaving sighs give way to reckless moans aboard this vessel. The stars shine and the moon moans a soft cry. It is the night and this night is full of love and darkness.

"Bless you my sweet Rachel."

"Almost heaven, Seth."

In the morning Seth received a message that good news had arrived. She could not wait to tell him when he returned.

Also, she warned him of a possible storm in their vicinity. "Be careful."

He deleted it. The pair dressed and made haste to explore rig number two which was very close. The sun was up and they departed in the dingy headed to explore its contents that should not be there. Now they were more natural having done this job already on number one. This one was about the same size only newer, so there was not anything creeping or making metal noises like "Devil Metal."

"What should we call this one?" asked Rachel as she climbed up the ladder.

"Well, let's wait until we are atop."

Rachel noticed that once she was walking around the platform the wind picked up. Seth noticed as well. The previous gloss on the ocean was gone now and slight waves were kicking up. Good for sailing he thought. But he better look on his navigation and reports as he had been warned. They looked in the enclosures and closets and found nothing. One more staircase on the platform took them to the second floor. Rachel tried to imagine what it would be like working on one of these large platforms. It must get rough out here with the wind whipping and storms must make it treacherous walking around when it rained. Maybe it was slippery even scary, possibly lonely if you were out here for a long time. It is all metal, no greenery, only steel and a silver or blue ocean to color your view. It could be peaceful though if you were escaping an annoying life.

More looking around-opening and closing metal doors. They noticed a faded shirt hanging from a hook. Strange thought Seth. He walked towards what appeared to be overhead storage in the kitchen area. He looked around some more and found a step ladder in one of the closets.

He looked at Rachel. Maybe this was something. He climbed up the step ladder and opened cabinets above him. He stared. And stared. He opened all three.

"Bingo," he shouted.

She looked up and saw large bags in all three. Her eyes got big. He pulled one down and handed it to her. It was the size of a large suitcase with clear plastic and duct tape used to seal each end. Inside was thousands of pills.

"I'm presuming its fentanyl or some other narcotic."

"This is what you're looking for, right?"

"Yes. It is a motherlode for sure."

"Why way out here?"

"The cartel is planning as the border may get closed soon with the coming election. They must find other ways to transport their drugs."

"Hasn't the word gotten out that they kill folks? It is not a buzz drug."

"The word is just getting out, plus drug dealers are liars."

"I guess they just want to make America sick and kill them while doing it."

"People want to go right up to the edge of the cliff, and not look at the wonderful view and be euphoric, prompting them instead to be stupid and jump off and hit the rocks below."

"Seth, we got to get this out of here. We do not want any boats snooping around or get caught, right?"

"You got it. Let us go."

Quickly they package up the clear plastic bags in dark

trash bags and take them to the first floor and then to the ladder. Seth ties them with a rope and then he goes down first. He has Rachel swing it over and down to him placing it in the dingy. He covers it with a piece of canvas like a camouflage. She sends all three bags down to him and retreats herself. The couple motors back to the sailboat. They take the drug treasure below and put it on the bed until Seth can store it properly out of sight. He prepares the sails after checking the weather reports.

"What should we call oil rig number two?" Rachel inquires.

"Bingo."

"Motherlode."

"I like Bingo."

"Bingo it is. One more to go. It will take a few days to get there but with this wind picking up we should have no trouble arriving on time."

"Seth, we have a time schedule?"

"Only to get to all three rigs, return and watch fireworks on the Fourth of July."

"Oh, okay. Yes. I like that timeline. Is our personal vacation time finished for now?"

"Regrettably. Yes."

She went to him and gave him a big hug. "Then this will do until the fireworks."

He hugged her back. "I think we are in business, I mean Operation Lexi is going forward full tilt. Prepare for full sail for three days."

She looked around and saw a big boat in the distance. She watched it for awhile and saw that it was coming for them.

"Seth, look out over the stern."

He watched it for a short while. "It is the Coast Guard. Should be no problem." But it kept coming as he was preparing to leave.

Five minutes later they were next to them asking questions.

He gave out his name and city and asked them their business out here near the rig. Seth reported to him about their summer school class and looking at fish. He asked Rachel to go below and get the notebook and specimens. Meanwhile, one of the guards boarded their boat at the stern. Coming on he asked him for his ID and where they were headed. Seth complied and Rachel rose from below with the evidence of students studying the ocean and its inhabitants.

"Who's the owner of the boat?" As the guard asked more and more questions Rachel became nervous and felt awkward. Seth replied about the boat being rented and from which marina. The guard looked at Rachel's sketches in the notebook. She showed him her plant exhibits.

"What fish are you studying?" Seth and Rachel looked at each other in shock but replied.

"We are studying cobia, which have mostly gone up north to Destin, etc., and how they are loner fish."

He looked them over and contemplated the story. It was a story but sounded real, just something he had never heard after boarding a boat. "Sounds good. There is a storm coming this way, not a hurricane, but you never know because it is season. Just watch out for water spouts and tornadoes hitting the land."

"Thank you, sir, for the warning. We appreciate it." Seth replied.

CHAPTER 22

They waved goodbye to the Coast Guard in their massive boat. It was fast, too. Within minutes they were gone and almost out of sight. Rachel wanted answers out of Seth and began to ask the questions. "I know we are undercover, but, the Coast Guard?"

"Here is the deal. You tell one guy and then another guy finds out. You must be in all the way. That is the best way. He might brag at the bar about meeting a couple out here studying fish off oil rig number two or "Bingo" and someone else hears, passes it on. Then we are compromised. I know I told Blossom but he is on tour and far away, plus he is in with Scarlet."

"We are covered for lying?"

"We did not lie honey. See, you have been studying cobia. We even ate it."

"Let us get this notebook below and hide our loot down there. It is a good thing he did not ask to go below. I think the notebook saved us."

She smiled. It probably did.

Seth hid the large bags in a storage area that looked

decorative. He could not figure out why there was money with the drugs. Nobody leaves money unless they are coming back or someone else owed is distributing. He shook his head. He was puzzled.

Seth reviewed the events of the day before beginning sailing. He wanted everything placed in order so he could move on. That is when he remembered there was some good news within the business. Maybe it meant Scarlet had solved the Georgia case. Pretty soon both cases would be over. What was next he thought? He looked at Rachel.

Rachel got comfortable sitting off to one side and had a book in her hand. That is perfect. She would be relaxed and they were almost halfway done with the trip. It was pretty on the water. He would see fish jump and occasionally a couple dolphins rode his tiny wake out back. Today though, he knew the wake was going to get bigger. After checking the weather, he found that winds would pick up immensely much later today, tonight, and all day tomorrow and not be quiet until the following morning. That meant two full days of rocking and riding out here on the ocean. He loved it. He hoped Rachel would weather this storm. He would help her.

The clouds began to form and the wind picked up. It was directly from the west. One imagined the whole United States above and their little boat in the gulf taking the weather, from Mother Nature, and riding it out hoping to survive. She read her book not knowing what lay ahead of them for two days. Seth made a list in his mind of what to do when he took the next break. He would retrieve two life jackets and make them be worn. Lock up any food or loose items, recheck his navigation, lights, and radio.

Rachel relaxed on the bench seating as it had a plush cushion. She read her book for a while and closed it when she became sleepy. She laid down used a small pillow for her head. She put the book on her stomach and drifted off to sleep. She even started to dream. The water had gentle waves and a slight wind from the west. Seth was the captain of this boat and doing a fine job of navigating the waters offshore from the pink palace which was on St. Pete's beach. She could not see it but knew that as the last thing she saw when leaving a few days ago. It had been exciting to walk around the oil rigs, knowing they used to be collecting oil for our energy and power us to where we wanted to go in life. The Coast Guard was the only boat they ran into thus far. Why was that? Maybe because a storm was coming and everyone else got the cautionary words-go home!

Her thoughts blended in with her new son. She would focus on him after this Operation Lexi. She would go out and buy a book on pre-teens and teenagers, parenting and the future. She had an idea that Patrick and her needed to have a similar hobby, whatever that may be. Because she worked, she wanted to spend some fun time with him, when the watch dog of a parent was lessened and both could relax. Maybe that was fire building, or fishing, it could even be a sport. Then whatever time she had leftover she would cook a couple times a week. How about dating she pondered? Was Seth the one? He sure was attentive and kind, always adventurous, and seemed to be courting her some. Her mind told her to wait until they returned to his cottage and catch the everyday life. Then she would know. Would he know? She wanted to observe him around Patrick and vice versa. That sounded like a great plan. She kind of missed him and wondered if he would like sailing. Was he the sailor type?

He watched her sleep. She seemed very peaceful, at ease. He thought she likes this sailing thing and was not too bad at it either. However, today, tonight, and tomorrow might be a kill joy, complete buzz out here on the ocean. He hoped she did not mind the boat knocking around, slippery floors and salt in your face. He chuckled. The war of the ocean was about to erupt. He could not wait. Soon though, he should get their lunch, raingear, and life jackets out and prepare for the sky to shower them with winds and the likes of a stormy day.

Rachel woke when her book fell off her stomach and hit the boat floor. She leaned over and picked it up, smiled at Seth and wondered what time it was. It did not really matter. She looked out to the sea and saw that it was gray with large gentle waves rolling around. Seth seemed happy at the helm and content. So, all was well.

"I'm going to let the sail out and slow our speed so we can go below and get lunch."

"Perfect."

"Okay, let's go." Seth headed down below and made sandwiches for both. He told her to get the rain gear out and put it on. He retrieved the orange life jackets and threw them up top over the stairs.

"What shall we drink for lunch today?"

"I think we should have juice or water and save any caffeine drinks for later."

"Because we are going to be up all night?"

"Something like that."

"My go to wake up meal is chocolate and coffee, works every time."

"I do not really have one. I guess I am always up."

"I agree on that. Maybe you need to eat more, get some meat on those bones."

"Are you calling me skinny?" He teased her.

"You need a milkshake!"

"Okay, let's go right at the corner and slide through the McDonalds drive through. In fact, get a meal for midnight," He joked.

She put the food in a bag and up they went without a milkshake.

"Here is your life jacket. We must wear them all the time from now on."

"Safety. I get it. Is it likely one of us goes overboard?" She asked calmly.

"No. It is only for preparedness. Like in case the boat tips over."

"No way. We are not spilling. I demand a new captain. No spilling. I will not make it."

"We will slow when the wind gets gusty and surging as we are in no hurry. Let us have fun and weather it out."

"Weather it out. Okay." They both had rain gear on and bright orange life preservers.

"Let's eat."

"Tuna. Yum."

They ate. They laughed. He kept his eye on the ocean and wind. She enjoyed herself all bundled up. She felt safe, for now. They were sailing in the Gulf of Mexico in a tropical storm. Nothing to worry about here she thought. She had even speared a fish and cooked it yesterday. She had a notebook, drug loot and cash with a cute guy sitting nearby having lunch with on the sea. What could be finer? She smiled big.

"What are you thinking? You look so happy."

"This. All of this. Lunch on a sail boat with you makes me happy." There she said it. She named her feelings. Good girl.

"Tell me how you feel in a few days."

Valeria Dave was on his speed boat at the dock when he saw a man and his daughter approach. He looked like one of the cartels from Mexico and had not seen him around doing business. Immediately his antennas rose and he tried to figure out what was up. Did this guy know something he did not? Always something arising man, he thought. Maybe he should take over Carlos's landscaping business. No time. Here we go.

"Valeria, Valeria Dave, I mean." A young Latin looking man with a blonde streak of hair falling forward approached him in curiosity.

"Who is looking for him? I will tell him."

The little girl walked right up to him and said, "Hi."

"Hello there, what's your name?"

"Xochiquetzal."

"What a beautiful name." Valeria climbed out of the boat and stood on the dock. "And who are you?"

"Xochi's dad."

"I gathered. What is your name? I have got a busy schedule today, every day."

"My name is Coyoti."

"I know what you do. I need your name so I can inform my boss."

"I am your boss. The name's Coyoti."

Dave stood there. Unfazed but whirling inside. Big guns.

Dave pointed to the picnic table in the shade and walked to it then sat down. He chose that as he needed time to formulate a plan or have a defense in line. He was not about to be manipulated at the last hour. The father-daughter duo walked slowly and sat down waiting to have a meeting with the trusted source in America on the Suncoast.

"I have a small detail to affix, correct, and then I'll be gone."

"What is that?"

"A new operative has stored a few bags for me and the payments with it. I need to pick it up and pass it forward. It is really a favor for my wife's brother. He just moved here but had to go back for his own wife's funeral."

Dave did not even want to ask for more details.

"I am told it is out on an oil rig, not far at all. Easy. Go out, go up, clean house, return. A one-day operation. Out to eat that night."

"No problem. I must clear my boat, check its schedule, let you know."

"Your boat has a schedule?"

"I told you lots of business here. Step in line, that is how it works."

"Check the schedule. I want to know before I leave."

"Tell you what. You get a hotdog at the stand and I will be right back."

Valeria Dave walked back out to the end of the dock and made a phone call. Then deleted it. He returned walking slow thinking things through.

"There is a storm in the gulf. We will go the first day it clears. That is three days from now. No sooner. I do not capsize my four-million-dollar boat."

"It will be a pleasant and fast ride. There will be five of us going for the ride. Thank you."

"How many adults and how many kids? I need to make sure I have got life vests for everyone."

"Cautious. Bien. Dos ninos pequenos, tres adulta."

Coyoti and Xochiquetzal walked away. Not holding hands and the little girl running to keep up. She just lost her mother. Maybe he better investigate it tonight. And who was he bringing?

CHAPTER 23

"Shall I go make us some coffee?"

"Yes. That sounds good. Then we can have our second cup when it is time for our individual duty, or watch."

"So, we take turns tonight?"

"We can do it together but at least once we should each take a three or four-hour sleep."

"Black?"

"You guessed it."

Rachel stood and grabbed onto the back of the bench seating. The boat was gently rocking over each medium size wave. Now was just the beginning of white caps. It was not considered rough yet. Or so she thought. She walked a few steps towards the cabin and hit a puddle on the floor. She did not know the ocean had splashed a couple waves of water onto the boat. She had been asleep. She tried to catch herself and put forth her right arm to seize the door suspended back allowing passengers to walk down but she missed and plunged forward when Seth hit a wave and the boat suddenly rocked hard to the left. She came down head first onto a steel plate with sharp edges. Wham!

"Ah!" She shouted but Seth barely heard her as he was checking his position after that large wave. That is when he saw her fall to the floor and roll over. He saw blood everywhere. He set the boat on auto and hurriedly went to Rachel. She came to and then blood dripped in her left eye and on down her cheek. Dripping from her chin all over her.

"Let us get you down to the cabin. Can you walk?"

"I think. Am I hurt bad?"

"You are bleeding like crazy but your bones are in place, I believe. Easy. Let us go down and I will clean it up."

"Who's running the boat?" After she spoke this, she fainted and he carried her down the rest of the way. It was only a few moments. He laid her on the bunk down stairs and quickly found sterile gauze and a clean towel. He got right to work.

"Who is running the boat?" she asked again.

"Darling, it is on auto pilot. We can do that for a short while."

"Is it bad?"

"I forgot; you are the nurse. It is open and bleeding."

"Any bleeding under the forehead making a bigger bump?"

He looked around. "No."

"Probably, it is a clean slice and dice. How many inches is the wound?"

"Looks like three to four inches."

"We are not sewing it up out here in these conditions. Clean it, dab it with peroxide, dry it and before you put steri-strips over securing it in a nice line you must put slight even pressure over the wound for five minutes. Then, if the bleeding has stopped, which it will in a matter of four to five minutes, apply the steri-strips."

"How do you know this?"

"Because most people have bleeding times of five minutes or less."

He held pressure on the long wound after clearing the excess blood, cleaned it, then dabbed it with peroxide, dried the wound gently and opened the steri-strips. He applied them pushing the skin together making a seam.

"Done."

"Now we will bandage the head holding down four by fours of gauze, in case of future bleed or a wrecking ball fall into something, with that long roll. Go over my forehead and around the back of my head securing it in place but tape down the front for extra protection."

He did as she instructed. Hey, she might have made a good army nurse he thought. Him too. But he was the killer in the service.

"Thank you. I need a cap like a skiing hat, not too tight."

"I have exactly that."

"Seth, just in case you have to monitor me for any neuro signs faltering, I must tell you what to look for."

"Like what? Keep you awake?"

"Just monitor me for alertness, dizziness, pain, etc. I can sleep, you just must wake me up every two or three hours, okay?"

"Yes, got it. And if something untoward happens, then what?"

"Damn it pirate!"

He was stunned. "I think your neuro signs are affected."

"You radio for help. You get a god damn helicopter out here and save my ass."

"Yes, ma'am, sailor!"

He kissed her and she kissed back. The boat rocked.

"I will make the coffee. You sit here and get your balance. We will walk up together."

He had it made in two minutes and poured it into safe drinking mugs. He put them in his rain gear pants pockets and up they went. Rachel secretly hoped that she had gotten her fall from grace out of the way.

They sailed and sailed, quietly, allowing the rising storm to have all the attention.

Much later after the couple had drunk their coffee they began to feel in sync. This storm was rising in power and magnitude. Seth signaled to her the white caps over the starboard side. She looked and saw them splitting after a wave rose too high. She supposed they were mini waterfalls. She told herself get over the poetry of the sea because all your senses are needed right now. She noted the white foamy crest and that the ocean appeared darker out here. The sky was grey with strands of blue and purples appearing and the rain had not come yet but likely it would. She licked her lips, and though, she had not been swimming they tasted salty like a potato chip. The sea emits the salt on those that sail its waters. There was no way getting around or escaping its natural emissions.

Seth told her the plan for the next twenty-four hours of how he would manage the storm. It was a tropical storm but could turn into a small hurricane at any time because of being out on the ocean. She wanted to say are you kidding me? But she knew the answer. She also did not think he would sail in a category one hurricane, or would he? Well, she would survive she told herself. This ship will not go down and they were far but not too far from shore. They could be saved. They did not need all the sails out as he was not in a race and it would put their boat at a disadvantage turning on its side. With any large swell and speed their vessel could capsize. She understood that principal. He informed her that certain winds produced certain wave sizes. Their wave size seemed to be four to five footers and his boat could handle that. He reassured himself, and her, that by tomorrow night this storm would be on its way further east. It would clear up as fast as it started.

After a while the wind began picking up and the ocean swells were increasing in size. Rain had begun to come down in a sideways fashion. The only sail still up part way was now the mocha colored sail retaining the water pelted on it. They were still able to sail and maintain balance.

Seth went to make some dinner. He was not sure where they would eat or if even they should. Maybe a sausage biscuit was in order. He warmed up four of those and came back up. They ate them and drank some water from water bottles. This might be it for twenty-four hours.

The food was good, simple but pleasing. Seth checked his navigation and turned the radio on for any information. Rachel had no idea about these items. She reminded herself to check out the shark navigation and names app when the weather cleared in two days. Patrick had told her about it. It sounded fun to know where they were swimming, what size and name was below the surface.

The sprays from the ocean were hitting more frequently

now. One must be careful of the floor and remember not to slip. The drops hit like mini pellets waking you up. Rachel got a second wind and was wide awake. Bring it on, she felt strong. I am going to give it right back at ya Mother Nature. I know you are the better of us so you win, but I am going to give this battle my best shot.

"I will go make our second cup of joe." He gave her the wheel and told her where to keep it headed for direction. She was the maiden up top steering them onward to a new adventure. He went below to make coffee but laid on the berth and closed his eyes. He fell asleep. He did not mean to abandon her and leave her all alone up top.

After about forty-five minutes Rachel realized her partner had not come back up. She pondered that he probably fell asleep, or was he hurt? He was not hurt. No, he fell asleep. She kept steering and sailing and smiling and navigating the storm. It had not reached its pinnacle yet. She would give him another hour or two before she went to retrieve him. She was not ready for sleep as she was indeed challenged by the ride. It was rough, large swells came and went, and made for more ocean to cover. There was no tropical blue water, only darkness and no stars because of the clouds. The rain picked up some but it was not torrential. She felt akin to a sailor, to sailors and why they love sailing. Day times and sunsets were wonderful displays of nature near the ocean but darkness mixed with swells became madness you could not escape. You had to conquer them. You had to drive right out of it, or sail out of it. You had to be the conqueror of a world you could not control. And this was power, very powerful indeed. Over correct or put up too many sails to go too fast and your fucking sunk as in flipped and drowned. She carried on in the darkness knowing eventually the lights would turn back on. Maybe she was made for this. She was a good nurse, caring for and making patients better with her insight and skills. She had life skills. This pleased her. For what else is there if not life and the big beautiful ocean monster to overcome?

Tonight, she was partnering with the ocean monster and it was a good ride. If one could have seen this sight: a delicate woman with a head bandage over a recent wound in rain gear steering a big sailboat by herself in a storm at night. Her strengths though were overcoming this situation blended with a wound that should hurt but did not. Yes, tomorrow was another day but Scarlet, you should see me now. Her new business partner would be proud of her, she would sing it loud and proud clearly in dramatic theatre.

Just then a large bolt of lightning shook the setting like dynamite. She counted the seconds. Six. Six miles away it was. She wondered if that girl scout measurement performed the same when on the water. She looked around for rubber. Her shoes had rubber and certainly her rain gear held a little rubber, the life jacket she did not know. About five existed between her and a lightning festival. She would have to go below and retrieve her partner. He would know about lightning and if it could harm a sailboat. She hoped he knew anyway. In thirty minutes, she would go below as her speed would take about an hour to reach that part of the storm.

Rachel thanked God for her life. It seemed like the perfect time to honor the being for which all this beauty, even the dark extreme beauty, existed. She said a little prayer and thanked him for her new son and meeting back up with Seth.

She included her land job as a nurse and the waitress thing she did for fun with Mexican food, margaritas included. She did not know what the future held. Maybe God was preparing her for the future out in this storm-testing her to see if she could do it or even like it. Yes. Yes, she told herself, she could. She already missed Patrick and wanted to be there for him. Her old friend and new love was below sleeping, testing her to see if she could do what a man does. She did not want to be a man but she did want to try out the fun parts, exciting parts.

CHAPTER 24

Hours and hours went by so it seemed. She heard her name called. Rachel looked over and Seth appeared coming up the stairs to the deck. He smiled. He looked around. He pointed to her and made a head gesture for sleep. She said yes and shook her head up and down. Yes. She needed a break.

She stood and he gave her a big hug and checked her bandage. It was dry. He kissed her lips and held her head. Then she retreated downstairs to the bed berth. She removed her rain gear but kept everything else on even her water shoes. Just in case she had to quickly rise or if in an emergency she wanted to be ready. The swells had been immense and there was the lightning coming. She forgot to say something. Seth would figure it out and act accordingly. He would keep them safe. She fell asleep immediately, noticing only a couple of dips with the swells before slumber took her away. She would not fall out of bed because it was a v shape. She might roll over against some pillows. Rachel prayed morning would come soon and they could see the weather pattern on the ocean better.

Seth studied his gauges and their vessel's approximate location. Rachel had sailed just fine through hours of the storm. He wondered if she had been scared. She did not act it. His turn. The fact that his vessel was headed northwest and the storm was headed to the east, possibly they were in the worst right now. He saw the lightning ahead. Water and electricity were evil. His mind was hoovering over the possibilities of what he should do when he saw the lightning strike ahead of him. One second later he heard the thunder. One mile. He opted to steer for another fifteen minutes then bring down the sail, disconnect his instruments, and then retreat to the cabin hoping for the best. The storm would pass that was a known fact. The rain kept coming, soaking him and the swells seemed to enlarge before his eyes. He wiped them. This storm was an unexpected surprise and must have just formed a couple days back. He saw another lightning strike and the thunder coexisted. Time to exit the deck. Finish disconnecting.

Quickly he made haste for the stairs to the cabin and closed the door behind him. As fast as the lightning came along with the thunderous clap, repeatedly, the cabin below was lit up from time to time through the little windows. He saw Rachel asleep on the forward berth while he laid upon the couch in the middle to wait out this light show with drums. Stay awake he told himself. Then another strike followed by a very big boom.

Eventually the booms became more estranged from the lightning. Yes. It was retreating heading to shore numerous miles away. A few more minutes and he would head back up to deck.

Seth reconvened up top, getting his instruments back on, lifting a sail back up and obtaining direction from his GPS. It looked like the third rig was fifty miles ahead. Because of the wind and swells they had to go slow but once the storm passed, they could go much faster. Seth estimated an arrival time tomorrow night at dinner time. Then again maybe the storm would take all the wind with it and slow them down on the other side. That is life. It could be twenty-four hours as in the day after tomorrow morning. At least the worst was over. The salt sprays were lessening and white caps diminishing as well. He noticed the rain stopping too. He looked up to see if the sky held any clouds. Hard to tell. Soon though, morning was almost nigh.

Seth was thinking about himself and Rachel and wondering if they had a future when a light shone on the mast. There was a hole in the sky and light poured in. Out ahead of his vessel he could see more light and calmer waters. He stood up to see better. Maybe, just maybe this was a Cat One and in front of him was the center. Seriously? He wondered if other storms had centers. He was not a meteorologist. He just did not know this. He sat back down and contemplated Rachel, this storm, and his life. And now she had a kid as in Patrick. He would like to get to know him and do things with him. Maybe he should investigate other work. This work had a degree of uncertainty to it. He was used to that. It is why a storm did not bother him, not one bit. Why did he like danger? Why did he like being on the edge? But mostly, why did he like the extreme of possibly dying? Was he fearless or stupid?

The calmness ahead of him struck him as unique as he sailed in that direction. He remembered that centers of hurricanes were about 20-40 miles wide. Also, that the right side of a hurricane was the worst. That means they just went through it. Wait until he told Rachel she sailed through a hurricane. Would she be mad at him? Hit him? Or maybe thrilled? Maybe he should not tell her. As he was deciding about what to do the door opened from the cabin. She appeared and smiled. Her bandage was a little bloody. Maybe she rolled around down there.

She stepped out and looked around.

"Incredible."

"I know, right?"

The water was calming right before them and one felt a circular wind die down to a stillness.

Seth stood and said, "I am going to make more coffee and breakfast. Be right back."

"Sounds perfect. I will just sit and stare at this enormous weather change. Heaven is looking at us."

Seth agreed and made way for the cabin.

Rachel noticed everything. The rain was gone. The sideways wind disappeared. The salty ocean sprays had completely negated and there were no white caps. She waited for a dolphin to appear. There was an aura surrounding them. Stillness. Calmness. Aloneness.

No need for gripping any handles, avoiding water on deck, or hitting sharp edges, thereby splitting open your forehead. She was lucky she knew it. It could have been far worse. The colors of yesterday and last night were history.

"Heaven's Gate, that is the opening. It must be what

sailors called something like this after being at sea and battling a severe storm."

"Is that how it felt last night, a severe storm?" He asked her when he came up with breakfast and coffee.

"Worse." She replied.

"I believe it was worse. I believe it may have been a Category One Hurricane surpassing a severe thunderstorm. Hence, this is Heaven's Gate we are in right now."

Her eyes became wide and she gasped, "That means there's more!"

Seth quickly assured, "Rachel, the worst is over. We are in the center for 40 miles, then a few winds and isolated storms on the western side but it is rapidly heading east out of our way."

He came to her and set down the breakfast and coffee tray next to her.

"Enjoy. We made it." She stared at him in disbelief. She felt shell shocked like hit with a wrecking ball but still alive waiting for the next hit when it swung back in her direction.

"Seth."

"Yes?"

"I was in worse danger than expected. Possibly, I may have died because of our lack of knowledge of the storm. Comprende?"

"I had no idea it was to be worse than a storm, no news, no warnings. And it might not have been except this opening makes me think it was. Storm trackers will know; we will know later."

"I am not sure that we should have been in more danger than you expected from criminals. You should know these things. Do not be so cavalier, with your life or with mine."

"I am so sorry. I know you signed up for danger but not catastrophic natural causes. I am sorry, I really am."

"Yet. It is over. We survived. And maybe it just did work itself up and get feisty for us out here. Testing both of us."

"A few more days Rachel. You are doing so well with the sketches, our find and only one more rig. Then it is back to land. I promise to keep you from harm as much as possible."

He set before her bacon, eggs, toast with strawberry jam and orange slices. She ate continuously until it was all gone. Then Seth brought out a large sketch pad and pencil. He began to draw her with the bloody bandage and hair pulled back. The face of a survivor with dreams and ideas for her future. She looked out beyond him and smiled at the calm waters repeating, "The worst is over. We made it."

Rachel held her coffee cup and sipped the contents. Here she was in heaven with Seth falling more and more in love. The job was almost done. Almost.

"Would you like anything else?"

"More coffee please. I do not want to let go of this moment."

"More coffee coming up." He set down his sketch. He had already sketched her face and body. It looked like her. She did not know about this talent or hobby. Pretty good she thought.

He returned and filled her cup.

"You are good, Seth. Do you paint as well?"

"I haven't but I think I'd like to try."

"Maybe you are an artist and didn't even know it."

"I suppose it's like singing, if you never try, you don't

know what you're missing."

"Sure."

"Do you have any talents, that you know about?"

"I steered a sailboat through a hurricane last night. I think that qualifies as a talent."

"Then, I will title this *The Sailor and The Hurricane.*"

The couple watched a seagull land on the bow of the boat. He stayed a very long time like he did not want to leave. Maybe he was lost in the storm. Seth gave Rachel an update about when he thought they would arrive at the third rig. After that it would be smooth sailing back down towards Sarasota. He asked her again about the festivities of the Fourth of July and could she make it with her son and friends? It would be a great time he said. Fireworks and food and lots of boats. She said it sounded like a great time. She looked forward to it and she knew the boys would absolutely love it. There was about two hours of complete stillness and the boat went nowhere. They both knew it would not last so they made lunch and dinner and set it aside. The couple took a nap below waiting for the winds to pick back. They were ready. Prepared.

The middle may be 40 miles wide, but it is a moving storm so the calmness did not last. But Seth decided he had to adjust the course and go more west taking in the counter clockwise winds coming from the northeast. This course lasted for several hours with gusty winds mixed with strong winds but nothing like the first day. They cruised along at quite a quick pace. It was fun and no sea sprays, no white caps, or large swells, just wind. The colors of the second storm were different, there was more light, good wind to go fast, and the sun came out through the puffy white clouds bringing them back to reality. Tonight, they would have a sunset. And by the next morning they would be very close to oil rig number three.

The puffy white clouds settled across the sky and made for a beautiful sunset. What is that expression thought Rachel? Red sky at night sailor's delight. One more day and then they would return to port and be off the water. She liked the sailing but enough was enough.

"I will take the night shift for sailing tonight. Would that be good, say one or two o'clock until morning?" Seth scheduled himself for duty.

"All right, so you go to sleep now and I come get you then?"

"That way we'll both have good sleep before the hit tomorrow at the rig."

"You think there's anything on this rig?" Rachel asked.

"Nobody has been out here, so I am not sure. I do not have any feelings for this one."

"Will you need to sleep in the morning as well?" She was just checking to know her time table.

"Probably like just two or three hours, then I should be good."

"The plan is set. We do not motor because we save the fuel for the trip home, right?"

"You are learning, sailor." He smiled at her. Then he headed down the stairs and retreated. She kept the boat afloat and headed northwest. Some gentle trade winds fell against her sails and propelled her forward. Tonight, she was thinking of nothing, nothing at all. One more day, then back to reality. She found peace out here and was thankful for that. How could anyone sail across the Atlantic? Her aunt did that once with her fourth husband. He was a seasoned sailor but the Atlantic? Never. She would never do that.

CHAPTER 25

After the beautiful sunset of soft oranges, peaches, pink pillows, and soft blue hues Rachel performed her duties. She sailed according to plan aiming for the 3rd oil rig, hoping to be there by morning or so. Tonight, she was enjoying the trip. In fact, it was like the sea had parted, and said, come here … we want you to come this way. No, the ocean was not glass, it was not angry either. She looked over the side of the boat, and occasionally, saw little eddies in the water. She remembered from living near the lake that eddies are swirls you can see just like a drain in your bathtub. Here they are in the ocean. One year she was a lifeguard and she learned about big eddies taking you out to sea from huge waves, they caused concern because someone could drown much easier when being taken out. Riptide is what they called those currents but they acted like eddies. The ocean was powerful indeed.

Valeria Dave sent Coyoti a message that he could take him out in his boat tomorrow. He replied that he would bring his daughter and a bodyguard. He would also pick up lunch for everyone. Valeria Dave asked him where he wanted to go and Coyoti replied with you will know tomorrow. He shook his head; this business was minute to minute. At least with the speedboat he could go anywhere in a very short time.

Meanwhile the man who visited the bait shop and loved to fish had decided to take his son out with him. Even if he was young, he thought it might spark some interest. They would stop and catch some bait fish and go out as far as possible. He had never been to the old oil rigs and heard sometimes a fisherman gets really lucky out there. The trip would take about six hours and the little kid could sleep down below for a couple of those hours.

Carlos thanked his grand daughter for putting him online to pull in further customers. She told him "No problemo." He sat down to have a serious talk with her and discuss business and what his plans were. She listened intently, pondered his reasons, and asked when she would see him again. He said he would write to her when he got to where he was headed. He did not know for sure yet. But he would send for her. He had faith in Valeria Dave to help with the business and look in on her. His sister was going to come for a while as well, so she would not be alone.

Finally, he said he had to get away from the business, the side business, he never liked it and now he saw a way out, thanks to Valeria Dave. She said okay not understanding everything. He gave her a big hug and said in a few days on the Fourth of July it would all be over. She asked him if he was the bad guy or good guy. He replied that he was always a good guy throughout his life but some guys forced his hand and he turned into a bad guy. He was making sure those bad guys were turned in and that is why he had to go away so they wouldn't know where to find him. Will they find me she asked? He said no because he had made it to look like he's complying with them and all will be good. Trust Valeria Dave. She said okay. She told him she would buy a car with the extra money he gave her for managing the business. And her aunt would help her and to not worry about her. "Grandpa, I love you. I will see you soon."

Around one o'clock in the morning Rachel went below to wake up Seth for the night shift. He popped right up and reported for duty. She fell asleep after eating some supper. The boat gently rocked her to sleep. Maybe she was getting used to this sailing. The more you do something the easier it gets. She knew one thing tomorrow she was going to scuba dive under the rig after they scoured it for drugs.

Time went slow for Seth up top. Maybe lack of sleep was catching up to him. Sure, it was peaceful tonight with a few stray wind gusts and misty wet conditions. He could handle this, almost asleep, he felt. Maybe tomorrow would prove profitable. But who was placing these drugs out here on the rigs? Maybe Valeria Dave would find out this valuable information. Maybe he already knew and had not told him. Maybe tomorrow afternoon he would sketch a fish after Rachel speared one. Then he could paint it in the future. That was a good idea. He took some deep breathes to help wake him up and continue his shift. The boat was slow moving but they were almost there. He started singing to himself to keep himself awake. What else could he do? Pushups, sit-ups? Maybe he would get all his exercise routine in on night shift. He admitted he looked rather funny exercising on a boat at three in the morning in the middle of the ocean.

At six in the morning Rachel popped up through the opening very chipper. Today was going to be a good day. This was the final rig, she would scuba dive again, maybe spear dinner and end this trip with a positive note that they were headed home. She had eaten fruit before she came up and some juice, made an egg and pepper rollup followed by a bagel as well. She brought those up to eat while Seth went back down for a few hours. He told her to wake him by ten and that probably she would see the rig even before then. No problem. The wind was almost nonexistent, so cruising was slow this morning. The sun would soon be up. It was already lit up everywhere. Seth retreated and was asleep in a short amount of time. He had checked his phone and there were no messages. Nothing is happening he said to himself. Okay, let us get any loot from here and go back. Sounded good.

Rachel smiled and approached today much differently from the previous days. She had a spurt of energy and was feeling like she had purpose. She felt strong. She wondered about this new energy. Why did she have it? Oh well. She looked ahead and saw the 3rd oil rig. It was a big, big rig. Unbelievable. She decided to not wake Seth as it was only eight o'clock. She had let him sleep until ten. No problem. She had this. She could even anchor by herself. She assisted him a few times. She went through the safety items for the mission. She knew where life jackets, medical care, water, guns, and smoke bombs were located. She even knew where a knife or two were for fishing, etc. They had not used hardly any gas for the small motor, only in the river on the way out. The Coast Guard had even checked them out so all was good. They still had food left and fresh water, likely for another week. She was prepping herself like a good sailor when she saw a boat moving way ahead near the rig. It appeared to be a fishing vessel. She got the binoculars out and could see two people on board. They were motoring about. Rachel picked out her spot to anchor on the east side of the rig. Then proceeded to go according to plan. The fishing boat maneuvered under the platform. She wondered if she should be on guard. Fishermen were a nice bunch, right?

The fisherman made it out to the big rig in good time. It took about three and a half hours at full speed. Now he was perusing under the rig checking his fish finder and seeing if this might be a lucky place. His little kid slept all the way out here and had just woken up. He was helping his dad set some lines while his dad had to motor under the rig. His dad had cut the ballyhoo into right size pieces for the lines. He was fishing with his dad in the ocean. He was a happy little kid this morning.

Rachel set the anchor down and Seth never woke up.

Meanwhile Valeria Dave and his crew had just taken off from the dock in town. They ate whatever they brought for breakfast and sipped on some coffee. It looked like a pleasure cruise. Nothing could be further from the truth.

Coyoti was packed with ammo today, him and his bodyguard. They had a purpose of finding their brother's money and drugs set out two months ago. It was worth quite a lot. Valeria Dave worked for him so this should go well. The speedboat would be fast and they would be back for dinner he suspected. Once they were out two thirds of the river

Valeria Dave asked where he wanted to go.

"I want to go to the 2nd and 3rd oil rigs, the old abandoned rigs no longer in use."

"For sightseeing, picture taking, or maybe you are going to get into the oil business?"

"You are good. You are funny. I like you. Just go fast. I have got something to pick up, like I told you."

"Are you expecting anyone else, any trouble?" Valeria Dave looked at the girl and back to Coyoti.

He took his time. Valeria Dave was right to ask. One never knew out here in this business. After all they killed his wife's brother's wife. Territories. "I've got my guy but just in case I fall you take Xochiquetzal."

He paused. "I will."

"How long until we get there?"

"One hour if the waters flat. Hour fifteen if there are waves. Looks calm today after the storm passed through."

"Perfect. Vamanos."

The fisherman was having a good morning. He had caught fish and his son had caught as well with his help. The oil rig was a good place to fish. He knew he could not stay long. After they had caught six good size fish, he decided to leave this rig and maybe find another spot heading back. He gave the boy a snack and began to head out slowly towards the sailboat. He thought he would find out what they were doing way out here.

CHAPTER 26

Rachel saw the fishing boat headed her way. She stared at them, then realized it was a man, and apparently, his son. He waved to her and she waved back. He took that as friendly and decided to continue in her direction. He approached slowly on her port side. Rachel was feeling rather welcoming and asked if they wanted to tie up. Why did she ask that? The fisherman thought why not? "Sure," he said.

He leaned over and tied up a line near the bow to her vessels cleat on her starboard side and she asked the little boy for his stern line. He did his best to hand her his line. It was so calm that it was easy to do today. They began chatting about fishing and what he had caught this morning. The little boy was talkative too about his first big fishing expedition. He showed Rachel with his hands how big the fish were they both caught. Rachel was impressed. She told them she planned to scuba dive and maybe spear a fish or two underneath the rig. The little boy was keen on listening to her. He had heard about scuba diving and wanted to know all about it. This went on for quite some time. She told the little boy she had sketches of fish she would show him she had seen under another oil rig. The pleasantries were just that. The fisherman thought he could use the break and relax for a while before returning home. The little boy showed her the ballyhoo in the back of the boat and told her how his dad had caught them early this morning. "Your dad really knows what he is doing."

"Let me catch one of these for you to see, okay?" he asked.

"Sure, I'd love to see the bait fish you have to catch the really big guys," replied Rachel. The boating parties waited for the little guy to catch one with his bare hands. The little kid starting laughing when he would get one and it would slip away. This went on for a long time. It was a game.

Finally, he caught one and brought it out and put it way above his head to show Rachel. Long and slender it wiggled and wiggled and dove out over the boat and landed in the water.

"Oops!" he exclaimed. They all started laughing, relaxing, and enjoying the moment.

"Please, get one more and I'll take a picture of you."

Rachel went to get her phone in the compartment where the gun was held. It was always ready laying there. She did not need it right now. She came back to the side of the boat and waited. So, the little kid started the process all over again. He struggled and struggled but after a while he landed another one. "You ready?" he asked her.

"Ready!"

He brought out another one and quickly raised it up again. She snapped the picture with him and his ballyhoo. She smiled and told them she would send him a picture. The kid felt proud of his hand caught bait and then placed it back in his father's container. Just then they were alerted to a speedboat coming right at them. They waited. Rachel replaced her camera with the gun while the fisherman and his son looked towards the fast boat. It came up right beside them making a big wave, then spun around and came very close for a second time. Rachel saw who it was driving the speedboat but did not recognize the other two men. Better safe than sorry she tucked the gun into her pocket. Ready. This is what Seth had taught her. Where was he anyway? He was missing all the action. Calm down she told herself, it's just a little fishing party and some sight seekers.

Coyoti decided he wanted to tie on the fishing boat. He had the fisherman take his bow line and instructed Valeria Dave to the stern for the same. Rachel did not know what to make of this. The bodyguard seemed on edge and Coyoti was acting strange, suspicious like. After a minute or two of small talk about fishing and the oil rig, Rachel figured out they are here to find what her and Seth are after. What else could it be?

Valeria Dave was helping the little boy to tie his line on the fishing boat. The kid kept looking at Coyoti's bodyguard. He thought he looked familiar. He had a puzzled look on his face. He spat out, "I know you!"

"What do you mean kid?" asked Coyoti.

"He picked up a treasure on an island."

"Treasure?" asked Valeria Dave.

"What treasure? What island?" Coyoti was livid and pulled his gun out pointing it at the boy.

"I saw him with a big treasure box."

Coyoti cocked the gun to scare the boy. The boy ducked when he saw the pointed gun at him. Coyoti pulled the trigger this time and fired. Valeria Dave swirled around to see. He could not believe his eyes when he saw the pointed gun. He pulled out his own gun and fired twice at Coyoti before another shot from him could be fired. Valeria Dave was a good shot and he did not miss. Coyoti went backwards after the double hit and landed on the boat mantle, then fell sideways to the floor. The bodyguard had been enjoying his sea scape and was underprepared for the gunfire. His eyes glanced from Coyoti to Valeria Dave. He shook his head-these guys work together, man. What is up? Thinking he was next he pulled his gun and immediately fired upon Valeria Dave hitting him in the right chest near the shoulder. He wounded him but still he stood.

Rachel taking all this in, pulled her own gun out and fired at the bodyguard after he shot Valeria Dave. There could not be a fifth shot that was not hers. She aimed with fierceness and took the shot but the bodyguard still stood. She had hit him in the head, dead center. Another shot took him down but who fired? Seth had arrived when he saw Rachel firing her weapon. He saw the man standing with a head wound but aimed and hit him in the chest. Two vital blows made life impossible. Then he threw two smoke bombs. One hit the speedboat floor near the bodyguard and Coyoti and one he tossed lightly on his own boat. The fisherman ran to his son who had escaped the gunshot directed at him. Seth approached Rachel but she could not see a thing. He took the gun and said, "Good shot."

"Smoke bombs."

"Smoke bombs."

"I was wondering when we were going to use those." She

held her hands over her mouth and nose and retreated away from the profuse smoke.

"Stay here," Seth instructed. He went to the fishing boat and climbed over then instructed them to stay put while he checked on the other boat. "I am the good guy. Everything is going to be fine."

Valeria Dave holding his shoulder checked on his boating companions, or guests, which were no longer alive.

Seth and Valeria Dave had a quick conversation. Seth checked his shoulder which was bleeding. He thought he aught to not drive the boat back-he could pass out or whatever.

"We need to get this cleaned up, or rather I do. You are in no shape. I think maybe the fisherman should drive the boat back. We will radio ahead the situation and have someone there to clean up this mess."

"Not the trip I was expecting, though, I suspected he was up to no good. I do not know what you've found but there's definitely more."

"I am thinking the same. So, Rachel and I will stay with the little kid and two boats. That is doable."

"Glitch."

"What glitch?"

"There's a little girl on board."

"Where?" Seth asked.

"Down below."

"Oh, for fucks sake."

Seth sat down applying pressure on Valeria Dave's shoulder while he thought. After a minute he stood and announced to Rachel, "Rachel, honey, take the passengers on board our boat."

She called back, "Okay, you guys come on our boat until we sort out this terrible situation."

"There is one more. Sir, will you come get her." Seth went below and found the little girl and brought her out. He lifted her up and over to the fishing boat. The fisherman took her and his son to Seth and Rachel's boat. He lifted the kids over and then climbed aboard himself. They all went below and once down there Rachel had to tell him something. All of them were looking and waiting for words from her.

"Seth is a good guy. Please believe me when I tell you he represents the good guys out on the ocean."

"I believe you. He is like the Coast Guard; they are there to help boaters in trouble and catch the bad guys." The little boy spoke like he had been taught right from wrong.

"Son, you saw that man before?"

"Dad, I'm sorry I didn't tell you."

"Tell me what?"

"One day when grandpa was guarding the big Coast Guard boat, I fell asleep on it and two big guys took it for a ride. They went to an island and loaded something from the island onto the boat."

"Oh, you were the one sleeping." Rachel recalled the story. She just did not have time yet to reach out to the little boy.

"Do you know about this?"

"She shakes her head. "I do. I have told Seth but we were leaving on this assignment-so we didn't have time yet to tell you. I am so sorry."

"No. No. You saved our lives today. I want to hear about the other story but let us get through today, first."

"Daddy, I love you." The little boy started crying. His dad hugged him.

The little girl put her hand out to the little boy. She spoke a few words in Spanish to say I am happy you are good. He replied in kind. Rachel offered the little girl a drink. The party below sat there in silence waiting for Seth to return.

Seth made some phone calls. Valeria Dave was in pain. Seth bandaged him up and helped him to lay on the back bench. He covered him and told him the plan. In his condition he just replied, "You're the boss at the moment."

The other two bodies were quickly assessed for absence of life, blood loss and blankets placed over them. Seth cleared the driver's spot and made sure the fisherman could likely maneuver the boat to a safe dockage. Of course, he could do it because he had to do it. Seth and Rachel would take care of the children and two boats. He looked over at the oil rig, but first they had a job to do. He would go scouring himself on the rig with Rachel watching the kids, then she could scuba dive while he watched the kids. Maybe they would have a fish fry tonight. Oh yah! Seth rolled his eyes as he had not expected a crazed killer to come so near to their boat.

"Tell Xochiquetzal, (sho chee ketsal) that I will see her after I get checked at the hospital. I will tell her the story. Coyoti told me to care for her. She has seen much tragedy lately." Valeria Dave relayed.

"I will. See you in a few days."

Quickly Seth made his way back to his boat. Rachel had everyone below. All was calm not like the scene on the speedboat. He asked to talk with the fisherman alone. He came up and Seth told him the conditions. This is one of those times that Seth had to break his code, not divulge all, but carefully contain and put forth the urgency and secrecy of what he did. The man understood, he really got it because his kid was fired upon. The man took it as his duty to support the Coast Guard. That is what he told him. His father sometimes does security duty watching their boat for short details. Seth took him over to the speedboat, showed him the ropes, also to look at Valeria Dave from time to time, make sure he was still breathing, etc. He instructed him that an ambulance would meet them and other people would take care of the cartel. Everything would be done within the confines of the law. "You are not breaking the law." Seth reinforced. The fisherman went back to the sailboat and spoke to his son. He said goodbye to his son and explained he had to run a boat for the kind man and get someone to the hospital.

He went back to the speedboat, started the boat, and said, "Thank you for watching my son and saving our lives today."

"It will take about an hour. The seas are calm, so no problems."

"We'll put your fish on ice!" He waved him off.

"You can cook them if you like."

CHAPTER 27

"Xochiquetzal, Valeria Dave is going to the hospital. He wants us to take care of you, okay?"

"Esta bien, si."

"Tell me what your name means?" Rachel asked the little girl.

"She does not speak English very well," the little boy said. "Let me ask her."

He spoke to her in Spanish and asked the question. She replied it means beautiful daughter in Aztec which he relayed to Rachel. Seth told them he had to go investigate the oil rig. Maybe everyone needed a nap he suggested. They all agreed. Rachel made lunch and Seth left. She made a rule that when up on deck each person had to wear a life jacket including her. They said after a nap that would be just fine. Maybe they could color and look at her sketches, too.

Seth managed to load himself and a few supplies in the dingy. How that mess just happened was not typical. Valeria Dave was going to need to give him more details. But that would not happen until after he was seen and maybe even hospitalized. He had heard the speedboat way in the distance, that is what woke him up. Next thing he knew Rachel was capturing a picture with her cell phone of a little boy who was tied up to his sailboat. He had a small fish in his hand and a great big smile. When he climbed fully up top and the speedboat was near, he saw Rachel pull out the handgun. Immediately, he went below and retrieved another gun. She must have seen something that alerted her to possible danger. That is all he had. Next thing he heard loud chatter, a banter back and forth, and retrieved the smoke bombs. What he heard was three shots in succession and saw Rachel's gun pointed at the speedboat. She fired. No hesitation. Her shot hit the guy in the forehead. She was out to kill wasting no time. Then he realized two lives had already been threatened, so she had taken her best aim to stop the situation before her own life be taken. The guy stood there not moving so Seth fired a shot aimed at his heart to make it permanent. Quick thinking after a split-second assessment proved to be the right choice. Her and the fisherman were next. Why? She did not know. But she felt certain and provoked. Because of all this he was certain this rig contained drugs, maybe even cash.

He climbed up the old ladder checking for weaknesses. His dingy was tied below. He had grabbed a sandwich and once he was at the top, he took a moment to eat lunch. He scoured the horizons looking for another boat. He did not want any more boats to bother them in any way. They had two kids out here as well. When he got back, he would call in and ask for two extra days, especially now that they had two boats to bring in. Maybe the Coast Guard could bring in the fishing boat or he could get it towed. He would work on what to do. He had to call and see how Valeria Dave was as well as the fisherman. He never even got the guy's name. The little kid was Jose around the age of seven. The little girl seemed to be two or three years younger.

Seth walked around and looked and looked for over an hour. Nothing. He stood outside and asked himself where would I hide drugs and cash? I would want it to stay dry and away from onlookers. I would go higher and so Seth climbed way up to the top. He reached another level and walked over to a small compartment which had a three-hundred-and-sixty-degree view. He called it the bird's nest. The door was stuck. He had to pull and pull. Probably from rain and moisture. He thought about breaking some glass but then he would have an injury to deal with. Better safe than bloody, especially with how things were going today. He pulled and it swung open sending him flying near the edge by the stairs. "Gotcha!"

Once inside he opened everything, looking up and down. Below one of the control panels he found a compartment. He opened it. Bingo. Cash. Cash and more cash. Then in a storage locker or coat closet he found bags and bags of drugs. He opened another and there was more. Someone went through trouble to load this up here. He thought maybe they should leave the area and not be seen. He would check on Valeria Dave when he returned to the boat with a phone call. He sat down on the floor and became overwhelmed. Someone wants a lot of people to die. This was big. How many other places held drugs? What other places? He tried to think like a gangster. His mind did not work like that. But what if you had something to hide-where would you hide it? Think like that Seth, he told himself.

He loaded the drugs in another bag with the cash as

well. Then he made his way back down the stairs, away from the isolated tower and back down to the main platform. He loaded the stash with a rope secured to both bags and sent the line down to the dingy. Once he hovered over the boat, he dropped the load and placed it on board. Then he began the job of lowering himself via the iron metal stairs. Carefully he maneuvered down. He looked towards the sailboat he supposed to check on the precious cargo. Then he mis-stepped, he caught the next bar but with his impact it broke free and Seth went plunging downward straight to the sea below. It happened so fast he could not stop the rush to the ocean. He descended below from about thirty feet missing his dingy and went down, down, and down. He held his breath, used his arms to slow and tread water until he made his way back up. How could you do that Seth? Mistake. Do not make any mistakes. It is a good thing you did not hit your head. His dingy was tied to the stairs and was four feet from his body. Not a big deal. Get aboard and be gone. Tonight, all of them could relax.

Back at the sailboat the crew was just waking up. He had Rachel help him with the stash. They placed it out of view, hidden and untouchable from the two littles aboard. Now it was Seth's turn to watch the kids while Rachel went diving. "I have an idea," she said. "Why don't we all go out on the dingy for a ride under the rig and I will snorkel around. Because you cannot snorkel and watch me while watching these kids. We can eat the fish Jose caught this morning and I do not have to dive and spear."

"I think that sounds fantastic. Let me make a couple phone calls first."

Rachel gave the two kids a lesson on the life jackets and how to properly put them on. She also explained about the motor and where to not put any body part when outside the boat. Even though it was a very tiny motor it could cut you she explained. They had their swim suits on so maybe they could swim under the rig. That pleased them. They wanted to go swimming. She wondered if their parents would mind? Well, she decided she would treat them as her own. She would let her own child swim for a short time.

Seth called his contact to check on Valeria Dave. He was in surgery. The bleeding in fact was from a cut artery but the pressure dressing had formed a tamponade and stopped the bleeding during the boat trip but once he was moved it gave way and more bleeding persisted. The other two were taken to the morgue and identified as John Doe times two. This catastrophe could not be exposed until after the Fourth of July. It was kept hush. The fisherman sent a message to call him. Seth called him. He said he was fine and asked if the boy was okay. Seth asked him if he could stay out two more days and return. Seth told him he would put him on the phone letting him tell him about staying. He thanked him. Seth told him he would find out about the day his dad, the boys grandpa, was watching the boat. He told him they likely drugged him to pull that off.

"Now, I am doubly lucky, I would say. I think I need a couple days to unwind after this traumatic fiasco."

Seth assured the man this does not happen all the time. "The seas are safe but we are experiencing increased drug running from the open border. The party in charge wants it open and the other side wants it closed. Hence, nothing is being done. The cartels are looking for new ways to bring them in. It is a tragedy killing young folks quickly. We are on it he told him. If you see anything you can call me."

"I will. Thank you." The fisherman talked with his son and explained how these two had in fact saved them. He was glad he went to her boat that day and she was friendly. He told him to trust him and pretend he was on vacation at his aunt's place. The kid told him he would help with Xochi because she talks little English. Great his dad said.

"Okay, let us go navigating under the oil rig! Ready?" Seth was treating this like an adventure. He switched off his work mode to play mode.

"Aye! Aye! Captain." Rachel and the kids said together, then smiled. Smiles. That was good. Let us move on. Hey, she thought, the job is done. They had achieved what they came for, drugs and lots of cash. What a bonus.

The dingy made its way under the huge oil rig. Tons of steel above them gave shade and a few sounds now and then from wind or something loose swinging made it real. For the kids it was like a giant fort. They wished they could go up but for now underneath was cool.

"Captain Seth, what are we to call this rig, rig number three?"

"Well, I had an idea. It is more of a clue. Do you want to know?"

"Yes, tell me the clue." Rachel anticipated.

"Three B's."

"That is not much of a clue. Give me more."

"Way up there are quarters which contains a birds eye view."

"So that's one B."

"Yup."

"I'll take another clue."

"Something that happened today," he whispered.

She winked at him and stopped the game. Kids did not need to hear this. Hopefully, they did not see much, smoke bombs and all, and the little girl was below and saw nothing. The little boy ducked, so he saw something. He saw the bad guy and he had seen him before. What are the chances of that happening? None.

They assisted the kids out to swim after they tied up to a post. They had life jackets on and swam around showing each other some fish below. No one gets to do what they were doing. It was thrilling.

Seth went near Rachel in the water and asked if she had enough clues.

"Yes. It shall be called Bloody Bird Bath, the third rig."

"You got this. You got this spying, recurring themes of a drug dealing life with an occasional murder thrown in to test your aim."

"Oh Seth."

"I am sorry. You did what we taught you. You were going to be dead, just know it. You beat him."

"Yeah, I am pretty calm in a storm."

"Yes, you are. That is why they said yes, you can come on board and do Operation Lexi."

"This was my test?"

"Yes. But they already knew you were fit and ready. But now you got this. What do you say, a few more jobs?"

"And then what, retire?"

"You do have the boy." Seth reflected.

"I do."

"We could do local jobs on a weekly basis together."

"I would like that. But then I would have three jobs. Oh boy, and being a mom is a big deal."

"It is something to think about. Scarlet will help us. She has been given lots of authority-it is not the drug deals of the seventies or eighties. She likes you, too."

"And I like her. And I am looking for a different path. Nursing is great but there is no advancement. Doctors can do this and that, work for drug companies, businesses, etc., and they still think a nurse is purely bedside like we have no brain."

"I am so sorry. With your skills you can be on the frontline in dealing with these deathly drugs which are poisonous."

She smiled at him. He got her. "I always did want to do helicopter nursing. Seriously, I mean it."

"I remember."

CHAPTER 28

The oil rig fort idea and execution were the hit of the day. When they circled back to the dingy the kids had big fish stories to tell. "I'm sure it was a dolphin."

"No, esta es shark!" Xochi screamed.

"You think you saw a shark?"

She raised her head up and down while Jose said it was a dolphin.

"It swam so fast and circled around. I think it was a dolphin because of its nose."

"Guess what?"

"What?" They asked in unison.

"In the boat as fast as possible."

Rachel climbed aboard swiftly and pulled them up into the small craft, while Seth pushed from the water. Once they were all in, he climbed aboard as well. He looked around. He had not seen any shark but that did not mean they weren't around. He would check his shark spotter on his phone. Maybe he would show Jose his shark app, he would probably like that. He turned on the small motor and away they went to the sailboat. What a day he thought. He might take a small nap to really rest.

Back aboard the sailing vessel Rachel showed them how to use the shower off the back of the boat and explained how to not waste water as the boat only had so much. Once they ran out, there was no fresh water. The kids looked at each other. They knew you could not drink salt water but maybe if you ran out you could. She said no you cannot, so use the shower with the least amount of water used. If you want to have a water gun fight then use salt water. They smiled.

Seth went to the fishing boat and retrieved the fish from the morning catch while Rachel brought the kids below to make cookies. Make cookies they asked? She captured their attention and showed them how they would cook on the boat. They cut up the premade batter and put the pieces on a tiny pan, then placed it in the small oven and set a timer. She found some kids books from the previous boat owners and gave them to the kids while the cookies baked. She was saving the coloring and paper fish making for the next two days. Tonight would be casual and a big glass of wine after dinner to wipe away the day.

Seth scaled and fileted the fish caught by the fisherman and his son. He put them back on ice and into the fridge. He was relaxed, calm and void of thoughts just enjoying being in the sun at evening time. Rachel came up top and spent a few moments with him watching with curiosity. She turned the radio on for some background music.

"What shall we make for dinner tonight? We had not a moment today to think about tonight."

"I thought we were having the fish."

"We should save that for tomorrow night when we get

out of here."

"I could make hamburgers and hotdogs, all of them, then we would have lunch the next couple days just in case these kids eat a lot." He remarked.

"I think that is a great idea. We will make macaroni and cheese, cut up veggies, and open some chips n salsa. I can make a potato salad as well for the lunches. Sound good?"

"Yes, perfect. When we go to the new place tomorrow, we can plan a fiesta and make something to go with this fish."

"Sure, we will plan it while sailing tomorrow and start after we arrive. I am going to have them make paper fish."

"Cute."

"Yeah, right?"

"I think with all the sun and being out here today they may go to sleep early. We always did as kids it seems the first night we went to the beach."

"Seth, you think we are okay staying here by the rig tonight?"

"I think we are in the clear. I sure hope so. But always be ready out here, okay?"

"The timer is going off," shouted Jose.

"Coming."

"Cookies are ready."

"Cookies?" Seth asked.

Rachel took the cookies out and the kids were amazed that such a small oven cooked them good. Next up was the macaroni and cheese and a potato salad for tomorrow. She grabbed the raw vegetables from the small fridge and placed them on the cutting board. As soon as the cookies were cool the kid's eyes went big and each asked her for two. The kids ate cookies and watched Rachel make the potato salad and cut up veggies.

Dinner was up top at the table. Hot dogs and hamburgers cooked on the grill, a few with cheese, buns, macaroni and cheese, raw veggies and ranch dip, milk for the kids, a rum and coke with lime for the adults, more cookies for dessert and a big thanks to their families, friends, and God, and lastly, the big ocean and sailboat.

Rachel showed them where they would sleep. There was a room that they had not even seen below and it held two bunk beds. Jose took the top. She placed the pillows and a blanket for each and said goodnight. They knew where the bathroom was and where she would be sleeping. They could come and get her at any time. No one was allowed up top unless she was up there as well. "This is the absolute rule. Understand?"

"Yes. No problem," said Jose.

"Si, Ms. Rachela," said Xochi.

"Goodnight Jose. Goodnight, Xochi. Sleep well."

Rachel and Seth cleaned up putting the extra burgers and dogs away for lunches. What a day thought Rachel. She would sleep very well tonight. Thank goodness it was not raining like a few days ago. Seth changed into his sleep shorts and Rachel prepared for the night too. She wore a knee length pajama gown grabbed a pretty scarf and found a bottle of wine. Seth had the glasses and both ascended to the top after opening the wine. He turned on the music and she poured each of them a glass. How peaceful it was tonight. It would be a busy couple of days with two kids aboard, which neither of them was use to. They admitted both seemed like well-behaved little ones. Then again maybe kids were perfect for strangers. That had to be it.

"Maybe we would be good parents, did you ever think of that?" Seth asked.

"Well, doesn't matter anymore because now I am one, good or bad," Rachel offered.

"You have a point. I wonder about this Xochi, if she has parents."

"Did Valeria Dave say anything about that?"

"He said Coyoti was the dad and that she's been through a lot lately," Seth continued.

"Must be why he brought her on board the boat. He could not leave her." Rachel added.

"Except, she didn't even ask for him or anything about him."

"You will have to find out when we return. She is a lovely child. She had no place out here with a trigger-happy father acting bizarrely."

"And looking for drugs that kill."

Rachel poured them another glass and turned down the music a little. Then she went and sat right next to Seth and put her body next to his. She leaned into him some and closed her eyes. She felt dreamy. Maybe in love. Love, yes.

Seth put his arm around her and held his wine with the other hand. He brought her closer and kissed her forehead. She had her eyes closed. "Dreaming?"

"Maybe."

"What of then? Tell me."

"Do you want to know?"

"Yes, please."

"I love you, Seth."

She took a sip of wine and straightened up some and turned her head and looked at Seth. She repeated, "I love you Seth, I really do."

Seth felt comfort and joy all at once. Is he really getting so lucky to have this good woman sit beside him and be so sweet? Unbelievable, but true. He never planned on this. He needed a business partner but this?

"I love you, too." He reached over and kissed her, longingly, and with fervor.

He reached for the bottle and finished the bottle into their glasses. A couple of swallows and the wine was gone. He set down their glasses. He kissed her ardently and with abandon. He knew he could not make love tonight but he wanted her and he wanted to show her how much. She returned the amorous affection like there was no tomorrow. Beautiful kisses and reaching grasps to beckon one another for the next time of togetherness. The night needed no mending as they were one.

All were calm. Everyone on the boat that night slept soundly and did not wake early even though the sunrise on the ocean is brighter than bright.

The fisherman got his friend to drive him out to his boat which let him bring it back in. He made up an excuse of a broken arm by another passenger on another boat and he had to help escort him to the hospital. Very early before daybreak the two sped out to the third oil rig and retrieved his boat without interrupting anyone asleep. They had had a terrifically awful day and he wanted his son to have a nice time, hopefully, forgetting the man with the gun and enjoy sailing. Seth told him he was going to teach him how to sail today. How wonderful! They would be much better off without the fishing boat. No problems. He boarded his boat and started his engine. Then as quietly as possible he drove off towards home, back to Sarasota. His comrade was going fishing so he set off straight south. The fisherman thought he might fish closer to the islands today near the river. He would catch fresh bait fish if needed. His wife was off with the other kids visiting her sister in Tennessee and was gone for a week. He did not even want to tell her about his misadventure that occurred yesterday. Maybe he would just forget about it like it did not happen. That is exactly what needed to be done. Seth was hinting as such. But he would be there for his boy and the Coast Guard. They must be told. But first he had to clear everything with Seth. That much he understood. The less people the better.

The crew woke and had breakfast below. Today was going to be great Seth told everyone. They listened as he spoke about the coming events. "We are going to teach you all to be sailors today. "Are you in?"

"Yes."

"Si."

"Yes, Captain."

"My first mate will be Jose. My crew will be Xochi and Rachel."

"Cool," said Jose. "Aye, aye, Captain!" exclaimed Jose. Jose made the salute to him. Seth had no clue where that came from, maybe cartoons he thought.

"First up is what to do if a man goes overboard." All eyes were on Seth. "After that drill comes the rest of the training." He pointed to Rachel and told her where the round life buoys were located up top. Then he ran out of the cabin, up the stairs and went and jumped overboard. She followed putting her life vest on, they followed after putting their vests on.

They looked around and Rachel found him kicking and yelling help. "Man overboard, "she screamed and pointed to him in the water, then she showed them where the life buoys were kept. She had them grab one. "Guys take one of these and toss it over to him in the water. Keep yourself on the boat. Hold onto something. Go ahead toss it."

Rachel's toss made it right next to him. He grabbed the ring and with his other hand made his way to the two other rings. He wanted to show them the importance of knowing where these rings were kept, how to toss one and save someone's life. Mission accomplished. First lesson done.

After Seth dried off, he assembled his crew up top and gave them all basic information. "Sailing is all about the wind.

Can you tell me what direction the wind is coming from?"

The crew looked around at the ocean for any waves since no sails were up. Xochi tried to determine if her hair was blowing from the wind. No, she figured out. Jose looked at the ocean, since there were no trees out here. He looked at Rachel's hair and a few pieces were blowing over her eyes towards the horizon and away from the oil rig. He pointed out in that direction then looked towards the oil rig.

"Do we know what direction is that way?" Seth pointed to the rig.

"No," they said.

"It does not really matter what direction, be it north, south, east, or west it is. If we know where the wind is then we can sail. If we had a map then we would know that that way is west, where the sun sets. So, the opposite way is east." Seth pointed to the east and said, "the shore or land is that way as well."

"The north is that way and we need to head south to return to Sarasota."

"Now when we lift the sails up, the wind will hit the sail and move us along, you will see when we are going. We do not head into the wind or with the wind behind us as we would move to slow. Heading home will be perfect for sailing with the winds coming from the west."

They listened but were not really grasping.

"Important features are next. The mast is the tall pole right there, it holds the sails." They looked all the way up. "And the boom is there and it lets us put the sail out or in for more wind to make us go. You will see. Back here and under the boat is the rudder. That is how we steer using this wheel.

We go with wind movement, sails, and steering. Very simple really. Now how are we staying in the same spot for hours and hours?"

"The anchor." Jose said quickly.

"Right. Do we have one or two anchors?"

"Two, one in front and one in the back," stated Rachel.

"Perfect. Jose, you will help me lift the stern anchor while Xochi will help Rachel with the bow anchor."

Each went forth walking carefully and holding on when able. After the anchors were up Seth started the small motor to turn his vessel around. He instructed and showed Jose about lifting the sail and keeping clear of the boom at all times. Once turned the crew sat on the benches and saw Seth raise the sail and let the boom out so the sail could catch the wind. It was not very windy but a nice breeze set them on the path back towards Sarasota. He showed them how he could change the direction of the boat with the rudder and how the wind would flutter the sail. "We are aiming for a good spot that keeps us moving in the right direction and flowing over the water." Both kids felt accomplished by helping bring up the anchors and make the lines go in a circle.

He quizzed them on the name of certain items keeping it simple. The kids sat still and just looked at everything as it moved. They were sailing.

The crew sailed for over two hours smoothly over the Gulf of Mexico heading southeasterly. The weather remained perfect, no storms, no choppy waters, and no hurricanes on the horizon. What a relief thought Rachel. Seth had her take over. He went below to retrieve his sketch pad. He came back and sat opposite of his crew and began to draw. Xochi and

Jose sat very close watching the sails, the ocean, and the wind but most of all watching Rachel. She was using the steering wheel, her hair was blowing, she was smiling and enjoying the day. The two kids were intent that if they had a turn, they might know what to do. After he had sketched them sitting on the bench with her in the back, he had them go sit on either side of her. Perfect. Yes. This will be nice. He made another print with all of them at the wheel and the beautiful water left behind as they sailed on and on.

He would like to get farther south than the second rig to make for a lighter day the next day and maybe save some time for an island walk. He told Rachel his plan and she agreed. He sailed on and on while they went below, made lunch, and planned the fiesta for tomorrow. She had the kids make paper fishes of different sizes and give them names and stories of how they were caught. They also made a Xmas tree but in the shape of a palm tree. It was her idea to have a Christmas in July party for their fiesta tomorrow. The idea seemed utterly crazy but they got into it making decorations for the palm tree which was cut out of a cardboard box. Did she have any lights, or Christmas music? She would have to look she told them. After all that she decided to make a big salad, a cowboy salad, for their fish dinner tonight. She told them they would love it. She knew of no one that did not like cowboy salad.

"He is going to be so surprised about our decorations." Jose expressed.

"He will be. I wish we had a couple presents to wrap." Rachel lamented.

"Si, si." Then Xochi told Jose in Spanish they could wrap up vegetables. Both giggled.

"Maybe we could bake a loaf of bread and wrap it up. I bought a frozen uncooked loaf. Let me find it. It could rise while it is wrapped." She sifted through the supplies in the freezer which were diminishing and found it.

After making decorations, a palm Xmas tree, a cowboy salad, and a wrapped uncooked loaf of bread waiting to be fresh bread the crew went to their bunks and Rachel laid down as well. Seth, the Captain, stayed up sailing for hours, after he had passed the second rig and it was out of sight, he dropped anchor. He felt safe in these waters, this territory, as Coast Guard was always coming and going around here. Almost home. He let down the sail and headed below for lunch, though, it was almost dinner time, and then shut his eyes and rested until it was time to cook dinner.

Much later he awoke to find it dark outside. His crew had pulled out more leftovers and told him tomorrow was the fiesta, or Christmas in July party at the island. He did not have to cook tonight. Good. But he should leave early to arrive in time to play on the island and cook the fish and celebrate Christmas. They told him to figure out what time he had to leave to make it to the island. He was the captain and should know how to do that. He replied, yes, he could absolutely figure that out. That lesson was above their learning for the very first voyage.

Before they went to bed Seth called his dad so Jose could speak to him and maybe receive a message from Valeria Dave for Xochi.

He handed his phone to Jose. "Dad?"

"Jose, I miss you. Are you okay?"

"We are having the best time and tomorrow we are going to have a fiesta, a Christmas in July, and we will eat the fish we caught."

"Wow, sounds like you are having a fun time. That makes me feel great. Can you tell Xochi that I saw Valeria Dave, her dad's friend, and he said he will see her in a few days around the Fourth of July. He has been trying to contact her family in Mexico. Tell her she has friends here and we will take good care of her. Give her a big hug he says."

"Okay, dad, I will do that. She is much fun and we have been busy learning how to sail a boat. We both pulled up an anchor and learned about the wind and which way the wind comes from."

"You learned how to sail. Awesome."

"Yes. And the sail takes the wind and pushes us forward. It is connected by a big tall mast and held together by this heavy boom."

"You are learning. Okay buddy. I love you. Hug Xochi from her dad and friend, okay."

"Bye dad. I love you, too."

Jose went and gave Xochi a big hug from her dad and his friend. She hugged him back and said, "Gracias, mi amigo."

Seth went to work on his timing. He did want to get his crew there early for a fun filled day. Tomorrow was no drugs, no cash, no speedboats, no calls, and lots of island fun. They wanted Christmas music. He better look for that, or maybe he could find it on his phone.

They had come out rather slowly, in cruising speed, then got hit with that storm or mini hurricane. They had to cover two abandoned oil rigs and a romantic interlude. Now would go much faster. He could motor some in the wee hours before the wind kicked up. He calculated about nine hours of sailing and it would be nice to get to the island right after lunch. That meant up at four am. He set his clock on his phone and retired very early. Rachel handled the rest of the crew. They sang a few songs rehearsing for tomorrow. This parenting thing was going well.

In the darkest hours of morning Seth set sail for the island of Egmont Key where they would have their siesta and final day at sea. He texted Scarlet to give her his whereabouts as he always did when finishing up an operation. She texted back she was in town and would be visiting someone in the hospital tomorrow. She looked forward to seeing him on July 5th at his house. He sent her a smiley face. He did not know who she was visiting in the hospital. She had friends all over the place. He could not wait to give her the report on how well Rachel performed. Maybe there was a future for Rachel in the business, he thought. Finding these drugs just saved numerous lives.

CHAPTER 30

Scarlet was back in town at her second home in Sarasota. She had a lunch date today over at St. Armand's Circle but first she paid a visit to a friend in the hospital. She went to the front desk after parking in the garage parking lot at Coastal Memorial Hospital. The new additions looked fabulous. She must take a tour very soon. Maybe after the Fourth of July she would do that. She had donated a large sum of money for the renovation, an undisclosed amount. I need to see Parker Faith she told the front desk.

"Let me find that patient for you."

Scarlet waited and looked around. The volunteer found the patient and told her how to get there. Scarlet followed the directions and picked up some flowers on the way from the gift shop. Today she was dressed in a floral sundress, sandals and carried a sweater just in case the air conditioning was set too low.

Scarlet rather liked this 7th Act of hers. She followed her hearts desires and lead a decent loving life. What more was there than helping folks, disseminating justice, and appreciating the arts? Her missions were fully approved from the top and success was imminent with this latest operation. Poor Lexi, the girl who wanted to stay up all night and study. Normally, even taking one of the speed pills would not have harmed her but now somebody is lacing them with a powerful pain killer ten times the normal dosage. Good grief. Will it ever end? Evil. It should. It made her feel good that she was doing her part-even if in secret. Success tasted delicious she thought. Maybe she was hungry. Maybe she would not die after all.

What is the purpose is the real question? Why kill a student? She browsed her brain for answers as she walked through the hospital hallways passing nurses and doctors. Lovely place. Everyone is so kind. Her friend had been moved out of the ICU earlier this morning. She looked at the nurse's station. They were all busy. Good. She entered alone and shut the door behind her. Quietly, she said hello and walked over to the bed. The patient was covered in soft blankets and turned towards the window. She set the flowers over on the bedside table and walked over to the chair greeting Parker with a soft hello. Scarlet sat down and began talking, asking, "How are you doing?"

Her friend's head was covered as well but his eyes opened and he said hello back. He reached his right hand out to touch Scarlet's. "I have been better. They tell me surgery went well and I should be out of here in a couple days."

"That is great news. Tell me more."

"Scarlet, two kills, sorry about that but these guys were evil. I am not even sure that was his daughter, please check that out. Though, I did not expect it to go so wrong. But maybe it is for the best."

"Valeria, you did what you thought best. Sounds like you saved three other lives besides your own. I will check into this daughter thing and find out more. Everything is hush-hush waiting for the sting two days from now."

"What did Seth find?"

"We will know tomorrow night or the morning after. He will be back then with the two kids."

"His girl saved my life. I had another shot maybe for a second but she fired first. I was hit in the left shoulder and I am a leftie, so not sure I could have saved myself. Rather quickly, she acted with impulse. Good thing."

"Rest now so you get out and heal. Who will go in your place to the storage unit?"

"I can send his daughter." Valeria said his thoughts.

"The boss probably gave this guy some time to bring back the cash. They might not even know he is missing yet."

"He will not suspect me when the sting happens. He will think Coyoti got taken in or is dead."

"Wonder if he'll send someone else to check out the rigs?" Scarlet stated her question aloud.

"At least Seth and Rachel cleaned them out."

"Let us celebrate that and you getting better. See you after the Fourth if you get out."

Scarlet stood and said goodbye to Valeria Dave, her double agent and spy. He waved to her with his hand, said thanks for the flowers and carefully turned back over to his back. That left shoulder was still painful. He rang his nurse call light. He needed a pain pill or two to recover, that way he could move better and get out of here on time.

Parker called his roommate on his cell phone. He was

going to need some clothes and likely a ride home in a day or two. He would explain his surgery as a torn rotator cuff repair. It had been an emergency, and hence, the hospital stay.

"Hey, I will bring you something to eat tonight. What do you want? Are you eating food yet?"

"Yes. Today I can eat regular food. I will take a gyro and fries and bring Greek sauce as well. Thank you. I appreciate the favor. See you tonight."

He also needed to reach out to Carlos's daughter and ask her a favor. He went through the drill, he had to be certain he was not endangering her life. Only then would he ask her to participate.

He called Margarite Mendez to invite her to the Fourth of July festivities.

"Hola, es Margarite."

"Hola, es Valeria, your grandpa's friend."

"Si, como esta?"

"I have a favor to ask of you? Would you come to a party with food and fireworks, the celebration for The 4th of July on the river?"

"That is great as I have nothing to do. I will bring something, too. My aunt is here-can she come too?"

"Sure. I will pick you guys up at say four o'clock. Bring some chairs if you have them."

He hung up. He'd have her drive him to the storage and open it, send the signal and wait for their arrival. Once they arrived, he'd open the unit, take the money and depart after they saw the drugs and Margarite's face. That would work. He wasn't sure how many were showing up with vehicles to take part in the split. He tried thinking if there was anything else on his agenda but the pain pill kicked in after he took a drink of his ginger ale. He fell asleep. He slept until his friend arrived. The nurse came in at the same time and assisted him up to the chair. Surprisingly, it went well. It felt good. He was getting better after all. He ate his entire dinner brought to him by his roommate. They talked. They laughed. Then he asked him if he got out tomorrow would he pick him up, or even the morning of the fourth? He would gladly do that for him as he had given him a place to stay. When his friend left he said, "I'll tell the nurse they don't have your name right, I'll give her your correct name." He waved bye.

All was set. He just needed to open the storage unit for the drugs to be placed in and then open it later for the buyers. In and out, then arrests before anyone escaped. He needed Margarite to assist him to drive there before the fireworks. Seth would meet him in the morning to place the drugs inside, whatever drugs he had found. He would have Seth pick him up and bring him back home. By four o'clock he should be feeling better, he hoped, and could drive to pick her up. Bad timing on his surgery, though, he felt lucky to be alive. This business is crazy. Very crazy. He knew about Operation Lexi, her death as he had been to the funeral. Who alerted him to her death and cause? It was the police officer at the hospital. Two years ago, when he came here to score big money with the cartels he almost died. He was shot, left for dead. Almost starved from his own people. He saw Carlos's wife taken down and Margarite's parents. It left him devastated.

He was angry. Then this cop introduced him to someone. Someone wanted to friend him and work with him. They saw his skills. Skills? Those were just life habits that became part of him. Do or die. They told him he had the look, the look of death and evil. Except when he smiled, then his heart poured out. This look can help us to stop these drugs. He met Scarlet and her organization. He met Jesse and became connected to Seth. Now he had purpose by making amends for Carlos and those he lost. He would work and make a new life for himself. He was tattooed with eyes of death stoking fear in those that looked at him. Dave was extremely muscled and lean, and just this morning the nurse shaved his head at his request. He looked even more evil. Except when he smiled. He was getting to where he wanted to be. He was close.

His surgeon stopped by late that night and cleared him to go sometime tomorrow, the later the better. If he had any problems, he told him to call him. He gave him some prescriptions, his cell phone number, and instructions to come to the office in ten days. He told him he was lucky, that the bullet only nicked the artery not severing it which could have been fatal.

He thanked him. Yes. He would take it easy for six weeks or longer. No lifting he said.

Valeria called his friend and asked if he could come by tomorrow in the afternoon say three o'clock to pick him up. He would be good to go.

Valeria had been working with Scarlet and Seth, though Seth did not know for sure he was a double agent. He wanted to continue but maybe he needed to hire a new hit guy, bodyguard tough guy man, to replace some of his jobs. Maybe Valeria Dave needed to put a suit on he thought. Hey, it would not hurt to ask. He was going to ask Scarlet when he saw her this week.

Margarite went to the store to get some supplies. She knew exactly what she was going to make for the picnic. She laughed.

Scarlet went on her lunch date. Driving over the beautiful bridge in Sarasota was so lovely. Both sides held aqua blue water and the shoreline of the whole city behind you. She especially liked it at night when it was lit, she thought of the fireworks. It made for a fabulous night of patriotism! Maybe she would make Jesse a spectacular dessert for their own picnic. She would have to look that up. Something about whip cream, vanilla pound cake, strawberries, blueberries, and French vanilla all in a clear glass container. Her friend called her and said the circle was too busy. She said to meet her at an outside café near The Mote.

"Sure, I will be there in a few minutes. Save me a spot."

"We can watch the tides out here, coming and going. The afternoon tide will be going out in an hour or two."

"I'll be there in five, order me a glass of white wine and an umbrella for shade."

"Will do."

Scarlet joined her friend and they chatted about the old days when they toured the world singing and playing instruments. Life was good. Her friend Lucille asked her if she had seen the papers lately with the southern border wide open like we do not have a country anymore. She heard dangerous folks are walking right over and that people who are running from their country pay cartels to get them across. Unlike our ancestors, she told her, when we were shipped over at anybody's whim for money only to become a workhorse or slave. Times have changed and the country fought itself to undue slavery and bring freedoms and prosperity. We should preserve it they both said. Scarlet smiled. She was trying to do her part. She asked her friend what else can we do? Vote, she said and now that is under fire with each side claiming fraudulent voting machines, counting, etc. Both, exasperated, conceded when will we have true peace with happiness loving each other and the government being fair to both sides? Lucille told her she should run for office. She was sure she would get many votes.

"Do you think? If I was younger, I most definitely would consider. I am looking forward to great grandchildren, and maybe, I will even get married and have a wedding. Honeymoon, too."

CHAPTER 31

"Oh, Scarlet, I love that idea!"

"Do you?"

"Yes."

"I do too. I do not have much time so I better be planning it out."

"I'll be there, you can count on that."

Seth left early in the am right on schedule. The wind was mild but doable. He could probably set the course and sit back, let the ship run itself. He did not like to do that because he was afraid of falling asleep and hitting something. But he could get a coffee and be in cruise mode. And so, he did.

Two more days and this trick was done. Successful thus far. He needed to get the drugs off the boat without being seen, cash deposited into an account set for Margarite as damages for the death of her family two years ago. Then he would go to his house, and rest, clean up and buy some groceries for the Fourth of July and the small party at his place on the fifth. Maybe he should make his grocery list now, get it out of the way. Good idea.

Today they would eat leftover burgers and hot dogs for lunch then cook the fish for dinner. The kids were planning a Xmas in July party. That sounded fun. He needed some music. Maybe he would blast it out on the beach from his lone speaker-that would work. They could have lunch on the boat and dinner on the island. Sleep there that night and go back to the marina on the third. Followed by festivities on the fourth and fifth, and finally, nothing to do on the sixth. Maybe he would start painting then after he drew more. Scarlet would pay them and let them know when the next trick was up. She had her sources, found out specific knowledge, experts gave her tips, then she told him, her special few went forth with the plan.

Sailor Seth passed the time and then suddenly it was daylight. The crew came up top and meandered around looking for a place to hang out. Rachel brought him breakfast. Jose and Xochi were super excited for today. They were having a party starting with cooking the fish he had caught and then escaping to an island which could be explored. Around eleven or so Seth asked Rachel to cover for him for a couple hours. Could she do that? Yes. Of course, she said. The kids went below to color more items for the party.

Rachel spotted the island and headed that way sailing. She would anchor and lower the sails on her own. She was a one-man team today. If she needed Seth, she would call him but if not, then alone it was.

When all was done, she headed down below for lunch and drinks.

"We are here guys! Land ho!"

Seth was up and turned on some Xmas music. He got

the party started. The kids emerged with the same outfit, swimsuit, and shirt with hats on.

"Ready!"

"Let us eat lunch before we go exploring. It will be quick as it is already made."

It was a fast lunch.

The kids poured into the mini boat with life jackets on and Seth took them to the island. Rachel stayed aboard to prepare anything else for the dinner and to clean up lunch. She just might swim to the island she had told him.

Rachel brought the Christmas tree up top. It was paper with paper ornaments. She placed it next to the mast and tied it up. She had a couple boxes with makeshift wrapping paper and placed them under the tree. She wondered if there were any light aboard the boat. At night she could spotlight the tree. She prepped and set place settings on the table and held it all down with a tablecloth and a couple pans to hold. They had thought about cooking on the island but were uncertain if that was allowed. So, they made the plan for the boat. After all who ever has this big of a boat out to sea?

Sailors, all four of them, celebrating the best holiday in July for fun. She put her swim suit on, jumped in and headed toward shore. They were still on the beach collecting something, shells, or wood, she supposed. She had forgotten her life jacket, not a big deal as she was an excellent swimmer, but the kids would give her grief. She disobeyed a rule. Darn it. Halfway there, she noticed the current, as in a big current. As she swam towards the beach the current was taking her sideways. She stayed steady but became way off course and passed them by on the beach. By the time she got to shallower waters she was way west of them. She had a nice walk on the beach back to their location. She needed the exercise anyways.

"Miss Rachel, you didn't wear your life vest," said Jose.

"I know. I forgot and realized as soon as I entered the ocean. Then a strong current came from the east to the west and dragged me some. But here I am."

"Seth would have saved you, ma'am." Jose said with a smile.

"Captain Seth, yes, would save you. Muy bien!" Xochi added her excitement and gave miss Rachel a hug.

"Come see our pile of shells, Miss Rachel."

"Sure. Show me."

She followed Jose leading the way.

"Bano. Bano," yelled Xochi.

Seth looked at Xochiquetzal.

Jose said, "She has to go to the bathroom, like right now."

"Let us do that. We will take a little hike in the woods." They followed Seth up the sand hill to the woods in single file. He made his way looking for a clearing. Surely hikers and boaters came in here all the time. He knew that. The followed behind one by one. He turned back around and said, "Once you're in the woods, go ahead and go, and we'll wait for you just up ahead."

Xochi stopped and Rachel went around her and kept walking just a bit. Jose was with Seth way ahead but visible. When Rachel turned around, she saw a large snake dangling from a tree near Xochi and she did not mean to but she screamed.

"Snake!"

Xochi looked up. She stared at the snake. She had seen its

kind before. She did not like snakes but she had to finish her business. As soon as she was done, she pulled up her swim suit and took a new path away from the snake. Rachel held her mouth for fear she would scare the girl. But Xochi did not scare.

"Es no venenosas!"

Rachel looked at Xochi. She understood. How did this little girl from Mexico know that this snake right here was not poisonous? She would know because she has seen them before in the wild likely.

She mumbled, "Learning from a four or five-year-old."

They caught up with the guys and explained the scenario.

"Bien Xochi, you heroe!"

"Si, si."

Seth shook his head up and down and decided to put Xochiquetzal at the front of the line. A hero blazes the way. Yes, they do. They followed her through the woods for a good while. She made it to the other side of the island and then said, "Vamos a la playa."

They followed the beach back to the pile of shells already collected. For a while they laid on their towels and the kids swam in the ocean. Seth and Rachel talked about the history of this island. Seth knew it all. She did not.

"The current picks up later in the day. I should have warned you. It did not bother us as we were in the dingy and it was early."

"Dingy it is. Dingy back for me."

"Remind me to get on the shark app. I want to show Jose."

"He will love that. Show me too since I am done

swimming. I forgot about sharks-do not remind me, please." Rachel laughed. Once she thought about sharks, she could not stop thinking about them.

Much later and before the kids got bored or tired, they retreated via the dingy and came back to ship. They rinsed off and got out of their wet suits and put big shirts on for pajamas. They saw that Rachel had put the tree up. Seth searched for some little lights and found some below. It added that Christmassy feeling. He turned the music on and got the grill going for the fish. Rachel poured drinks for everyone and Seth pulled out the shark finder and showed Jose the names and size of a couple sharks in the area.

"Oh, my god. I am never swimming in the ocean again!" Rachel said very loudly.

"I bet you will."

"Only if I am stuck out on an island like Gilligan's Island. Then I might."

"Who is Gilligan?" asked Jose.

"A TV show with lots of reruns we watched when we were kids. Our parents even watched it. I always thought it was real but it was made for entertainment."

"Gilligan goes off with a skipper, a scientist, a rich couple, a movie star, and a girl. They go boating but a storm comes. Then they crash on an island where they live for the next seven years. They never get off the island after their three-hour tour."

"I wouldn't like that." Jose chides in.

"It was funny though and very real like. Like we are right now if we crashed into that island from a storm. We would be eating snake tonight." Rachel played along.

They all laughed. They were going to eat fresh fish, cowboy salad and whatever else Rachel cooked up. And they were going back home tomorrow, not staying on some island for seven years.

She had wrapped up the fresh bread earlier in festive paper.

"Grills ready."

The fish was put on, kids helped bring up the rest of dinner, music was playing and it felt very festive. After dinner they would open the gifts, except for one gift for the captain which they wanted him to open right now. Xochi took the gift for Seth to open. He tore at the paper, smelled it, and said, "Perfecto."

"Do you want to know what it is?" Xochi asked.

"I know what it is?" he retorted.

"Yes, but you don't know we made it today!"

"You made fresh jerk seasoning today?"

Seth opened his arms asking for a hug. Xochi came and hugged her sailor friend.

"Thank you from the bottom of my heart. Our fish is going to be super delicious, thanks to you." She smiled bigly.

Margarite returned from the store and baked two batches of brownies. One would be for any kids around and the other would be for the adults. She was baking pot brownies. She could not wait to taste test her own concoction tonight. She had little containers for them. She did not want to mix them up. She had a green container and a red container. She put the pot brownies in the red container. "Now remember that honey. No confusion." She wrote on a piece of paper pot and put it in the container. Then she placed a note with the word kids and put it in the green container. No mix-ups now. She missed her family who died two years ago. It seemed like whenever she was having fun that is when she missed them the most. She got a few tears in her eyes and they ran down her cheek. She wiped them away. This was going to be the first date she ever had. Her aunt was here to witness it. She wondered what her aunt would think of Valeria Dave as he was quite colorful, full of tattoos, but a kind gentle soul underneath. Her grandfather trusted him completely. She did too. What should she wear? She had just realized it was a date. She went upstairs to find something attractive. He was older but not too much older. She was sixteen and he was twenty-four. Was that too old? Maybe. But they could be friends first for quite some time.

She had no problem with it. He was going to help her run her grandpa's business anyway. They would rely on each other. Her aunt was going to live with her until she turned eighteen, maybe longer. Her aunt said she would take her on a cruise for her 17th birthday. She could not wait for that. She sat on the sofa and waited for tomorrow. She had a 4th of July date.

CHAPTER 32

On the morning of July 3rd the local police department including the sheriff's office who were working on Operation Lexi held a meeting. They invited the DEA, Coast Guard, FBI, and security business employees involved in 4th of July Manatee River activities. The police wanted all hands-on deck in preparation for the fourth to keep everyone safe. They felt it best the officers work as a large team and know many others are out during the whole day and night. The sheriff had a special video to show them of the drugs seized off shore, under the water in containers and on an island nearby. What was not shown were the undercover operatives including the lady behind it all. Operation Lexi was not mentioned. Only that the newest drug on the open market was deadly. Narcan was dispersed to all in attendance. It was shown how to use via nasal airway and IV use for the paramedics or someone trained in IV use.

So that it would never be talked about or escape via reckless conversation, only one person knew of Operation Lexi and that was the captain. One IA operative knew and a federal judge. In total only three persons knew of this secretive mission in this most deadly of businesses outside of Scarlet and her team. The cartels and their mission to infuse the states with deadly fentanyl was a top priority but handled differently. The war on drugs was hardly working and a new approach had been initiated. In fact, only three places in the United States were attempting this trial and Florida was one of them. Some of the police this morning would find out tonight when pulled away that they would be involved in the sting right before it happens. Why the secrecy? In order to capture any of their own, or friends of friends, one must not let on.

The sheriffs under water unit had done a fabulous job of scuba diving and finding sunken cargo from a lowered life boat that no one expected to drop drugs to the ocean floor near an island before coming into port. Later these were transported to the nearby island at night by nefarious individuals and picked up when no one was watching. Filled with drugs, later to be laced with fentanyl right here in America. Why in America? Because many illegals were working for the cartels. Once they escaped over the border, they reported to their next guy here in America and worked for him to pay for the 15K owed to the cartel. How long does it take to pay off 15K? The police estimated two years or more. They fed these people, gave them quarters to live, and demanded they work either selling, distributing, and even making the laced drugs. The captain thought to himself, it is amazing these drugs are even being manufactured or altered right here in the states.

Scarlet and her teams were never seen and remained unknowns. Valeria Dave would disguise Margarite tomorrow night when at the location. Margarite held the key to the storage unit. Only those that showed up to buy the drugs would be taken down, and of course, any additional cars that had folks waiting on them to load up doing their dirty business would be found out as well.

A perfect sting put on by Margarite's grandfather who was a trusted man in the business and unbeknownst to the cartels to have turned, as well as Valeria Dave. Dave would blame it on the young dude flashing all his money, power and little girl around that a cop found him and a shoot out ensued. He is in the morgue he would tell them-go see for yourself he would tell the cartels. Then Dave would talk to them about future operations. He needed the money, knew many people, and wanted some action. The cartel respected Dave, he had survived the blast when most of the family was murdered two years ago. They thought he held a superpower if you will. Plus no one knew that his grandmother and grandfather had a huge ranch or plantation in South America that produced all kinds of goods. He kept meaning to get back there someday but had not made it yet. He wanted to do something on his own. Thus far, things had not worked out until two years ago when Margarite's grandfather saved his life. His life now had some meaning, he was discovering what he was made of.

After a small break the Coast Guard told the officers how they were handling things tomorrow night on the water. They were prepared for burning watercraft, fireworks getting out of control and mishaps by boaters on the river. They would have three small watercraft cruising around up and down the river, one large craft near the fireworks and another up river on standby. Two more large watercraft were on standby from the north and south, along with the fire department. They felt prepared and ready for fires, disasters, drownings, explosions, as well as drunken captains of private boats, etc.

The police boats would be ready as well. They had four such boats that would be out scouting for any unruliness and reporting as such. Many a year the fireworks and fun on the river went off beautifully, but one must be prepared especially for an emergency like drowning, heart attack, intoxication or even a birth. One never knows. Of all the nights to have a drug bust, which they did not know where it was happening as yet, this was definitely not ideal.

The captain said hello to everyone and assured them everything would likely go as planned and he appreciated their support and confidence in this important endeavor. The meeting was over. July Fourth was tomorrow. Most people prayed it would not rain. Picnics, fireworks, and songs of pride for the USA were in order.

Carlos texted his business partners. One was a pharmacist he had known for quite some time. He wanted to make extra cash to purchase a second home. Carlos informed him he had a way and exposed his proposition. A businessman was looking to expand and kept after Carlos, knowing he had deals with the cartels, to give him something to do. Carlos liked the guy, knew he was a family man, and did not want to give this guy anything. One day he asked again and Carlos thought if he did not give him something somebody else would trick him and likely kill him. So, for his own good he said yes. When the murders occurred two years ago an IA agent, always looking to make a buck, and sometimes doing wrong things like blackmailing drug dealers, approached Carlos. He wanted nothing to do with this guy. He had already lost his family except for his granddaughter. The agent made a pass at Margarite one day out front when she was mowing the lawn. Carlos saw it from the garage. Hell hath no fury. This dude was not going to leave him or his one family member alone. Carlos called him and told him he could make a quick buck on some drug bust going down. Others were in on it too. He told him you just show up, take some drugs, and sell them to whomever you want. You know lots of people in your line of work. The IA agent said, "I am all in. When?"

Carlos smiled at that one. If you are going to play dirty, then you deserve it. Carlos had friends that were IA agents he had met after the killing. They befriended him. They truly wanted his help. He had been on the right side of the law since the gunfight two years ago. He had never killed anyone and since coming to America had been getting out of the business. Now he was doing his part. He liked America. Maybe one day he would come back but for now he was doing his part. His granddaughter was being looked out for as well. His sister, her aunt, would bring her to this island via a cruise on her 17th birthday. It would be a surprise. He smiled.

The fourth and final guy Carlos let into the operation was a drug company executive. As if they already did not make enough money thought Carlos. He wanted more. Carlos shook his head. He never met this guy and did not know much about him. This dude knew about the fentanyl and he knew someone who could make fentanyl on the side. The cartels wanted this drug badly. He would get the guy to make fentanyl and he'd purchase the Adderall and other street drugs himself. But Bingo! Carlos had the fentanyl for purchase. Even better. He could not wait to get his hands on it never thinking Carlos, a Mexican, would be his enemy or turn him in. How dare he? But no, hey, some people like America and want it to be safe you fucking scumbags.

Four guys in one sting ready to buy fentanyl, cocaine, and personal use marijuana. Show up with your truck or SUV and bring a guy to load it up and you will be in and out and home before the fireworks end. Carlos charged these men no money for this information. It was just fish feed he called it because he had been in the business and the cartels were still drug running. Carlos would give them the location five minutes prior. He had them wait out near I-75 at a gas station or two. His daughter had the key and would open the storage unit. All the cops would be on the river for the Fourth of July. Carlos had a special message for his daughter to give to the business man he liked.

Margarite doubled her homemade brownies. She did not know how many were coming to Dave's boat for a picnic. Red equaled marijuana and green signaled kids. Do not mess it up, baby, she told herself. In addition, she decided to wrap the adult pans in foil, a further protection or safety. She was excited for her date, even if he was twenty-four. That is like an older brother she thought. Well, that thought made her feel good-he would look out for her like a big brother.

She sat down and turned the TV on to a Spanish soap opera. Then the phone rang. She answered it. "Hola, es Margarite."

"Hola, es Dave. Como esta usted?"

"Dave. I am doing very well. I am super excited about tomorrow!"

"You are?" He did not expect that.

"Yes. I am. Are you?"

"Oh yes. Me too!" He could never tell her what is really happening. He would get her out of there in a flash. Maybe he should call an extra body guard. Or should he tell her, then she would know. She might not mind. He would tell her right before-then she would not worry all night long.

He would tell her when he was picking her and her aunt up in the car. The boat he had is very comfortable and it has a bathroom on it. "Great," she said. "See you tomorrow."

Valeria Dave said a prayer before falling asleep in his apartment. It was for the safety of little Margarite. He felt God's touch on his shoulder that all is super fine, you are doing good work, keep it up.

Scarlet and Jessie were busy making their menu and preparing for a quiet evening with just the two of them in her large condo. Jesse strewed some crepe paper and balloons around to give it the festive flair while Scarlet made a special concoction for the dessert. They would go super basic with hotdogs, two side salads, potato and macaroni, baked beans, carrots, celery, and broccoli with ranch dip and a cherry pie with ice cream. Scarlet decided they would be eating Fourth of July foods for days. Oh well. Jesse pulled out the good china which surprised Scarlet.

Once all the preparations were made, they went down for a walk outside near the water, and looked at the boats and other revelers walking, holding hands, strolling the downtown boardwalk. The couple dressed in red, white, and blue looked in love.

CHAPTER 33

The morning of the Fourth of July Margarite received a phone call from her grandfather. They talked and talked. Then he had her write down a note that Valeria Dave was to give to a businessman later tonight. She did as told and put it in her pocket. The note was signed and said, *Go now to your wife, it is urgent. Carlos.* She also put a key in her pocket. Carlos told her Dave needed the storage key to load something in the storage unit. Sure, she thought, not a big deal. Her grandpa used it for all kinds of things.

Dave slept in but quickly assembled for the day once he woke. He looked out the window and saw the weather was gorgeous, a perfect day, not too hot with no showers in the forecast. His roommate headed out early for an all-day picnic with his coworkers. Dave showered and paused to look in the mirror as he dried off. His shaved head threw him off guard not realizing what he had done in the hospital. Maybe he should wear a hat today. Dave was slender with defined muscles. He was cut for sure. He smiled. He had to remember to smile for his date today. He looked friendly when he did that. There would be no goings on with Margarite-she was sixteen. He intended to act like a big brother, very friendly, watchful and such, but he did kind of like her. She was beautiful. He told himself prepare for your future, be ready as two years will be here and gone. And what do you have to offer anyone?

Valeria Dave needed to prepare for the future. And he must talk with Scarlet. She held the key; he was certain of it. Dave ate scrambled eggs, bacon, and strawberries with kiwi chunks. He would pick up Margarite and her aunt at one o'clock and take them to his boat. She would have the key. He had already met Seth this morning and transferred the drugs into the storage unit. The day would be spent with a picnic on the dock next to his boat. Around eight o'clock he and Margarite would go and open the unit, make the transaction available to four men then leave. Margarite was needed as an alibi and her association with her grandpa sealed the deal. These guys going down were here on US soil making a buck. The unknowns were who put these drugs on the oil rigs? They were to be targeted next. Operation Lexi needed the drugs off the street asap, then find the sources and execute, as in kill, the fentanyl business, if possible.

On the way Dave stopped to get some flowers for Margarite and her aunt. The morning parade had finished but left many patriots sitting along the road waving their little patriotic flags. Many were dressed in red, white, and blue. He drove out to pick them up as they lived east of I-75. Later today he would be driving Seth's new car when he needed the speed.

Seth and Rachel had returned in the rented sailboat with the drugs on board. Rachel helped clean up while the kids played on the dock. She packed up her and the kids' belongings and drove them all back to her place. For not having any children a couple months ago she now had two in the car and one back at a friend's place. Life was exploding for her in good ways. Today was the Fourth of July and tonight they would meet on a different dock and watch the fireworks. She stopped at a drive through and ordered sandwiches and fries for her lot in the back. She couldn't wait to see her son Patrick and give him hugs, then take a real shower, dress for tonight and lie down. What a great ending to the sea escape they had just been on for weeks. Having the children aboard the last two days mellowed the whole trip. It was almost too much to think about. She bet herself the coming days might rouse in her what actually transpired.

Henry and Patrick were waiting for her in the parking lot. She opened the door and gave Patrick a big hug. He hugged her back. Henry smiled. And said, "He missed you miss Rachel, we're both glad you're back."

"Thank you."

"What happened? Did you pick up a couple more, huh?"

Rachel introduced Xochi and Jose to the boys and invited everyone into her place. She asked if the boys would keep an eye on the two littles while she showered and got ready for tonight. No, they would not mind. They took them to see Henry's mom because she loves kids. Rachel unpacked as quick as she could, showered, got in her robe, and laid upon her bed. It felt so good. She went to sleep.

Meanwhile at Henry's place, his mom called up Juan, as she recognized the little boy, Jose. He said he would be right over to pick him up. She did not know who was Xochi's mom or dad. Juan said that Rachel was watching her for a few weeks. "Oh, okay. Perfect."

The kids sat at the kitchen table and ate the sandwiches and fries. Henry's mom gave them their choice for a drink. Xochi said she needed a nap too. Henry said they would stay here and let miss Rachel sleep for a while. Henry's mom had made deviled eggs and jerk chicken for the picnic later today.

"Did your mom say what time we are going to the docks?"

"I think she said around six o'clock."

Earlier in the morning Valeria Dave met Seth out at his boat. They went below and talked.

Valeria Dave gave him a high five. Seth was surprised but high fived back. "I'm just very glad you made it back without any injuries," Dave stated solemnly.

"Valeria, I am the one that is extremely happy you are alive. I got the report from the hospital. You almost died, man. The artery was nicked but it held from bleeding due to your position on the boat, it formed a tamponade and at any time on the way back, man, you could have bled out. God was looking out for you," Seth lectured.

"I know. I am blessed."

Seth smiled. "By the way, are you working for somebody I know?"

"I could be."

Seth smiled again. He likely was not supposed to know for sure but privately he knew Valeria Dave was a double agent and working for some retired opera singer that he also knew.

Valeria Dave smiled back. "Here is the deal man, I need some drugs so I can sell them tonight. You got 'em?"

"Sure do. Cannot wait to get rid of them. I got a big family date tonight. Rachel, her friend, and a bunch of kids. See you there on the dock."

"Yes. I invited Margarite, Carlos's granddaughter, and her aunt. Some down time is needed. It will be fun."

The pair unloaded the drugs into Seth's car in the trunk and back seat and Dave sped away. Seth finished cleaning up the boat and took his drawings, belongings, and extra supplies to Dave's car. He needed to get moving to get all the way to his place and back to Rachel's and then to the dock. He was weary. Maybe he should just bag out of the picnic and get his place ready for tomorrow. He phoned Rachel. Would she mind if he did this? She was so kind and understood completely. His energy was low and he needed some time to recoup. It had been a big job, maybe more stressful than he realized. So far, a success. Tonight, would end Operation Lexi and move onto the sources. Tomorrow it would be in the headlines, not naming the operation, but results of bad drugs and bad people. He thanked Rachel, kissed her over the phone and drove to his place, unloaded, and ate something.

On Anna Maria Island where Seth had his cottage, he was out front putting his flag out when a group of little tykes on bikes strode past. They had decorated their bikes and probably had been in some parade in the morning. Now he got to see firsthand a parade just for him. He waved. It was quite a site. He thought about Rachel tonight, she was going to have a blast. But he would be ready for all of them tomorrow. He texted her. Rachel. Job well done. Almost finished. Tonight.

When the fireworks are over, it will ALL be over. Thank you. Seth.

She fired back. Seth. We just got to Dave's boat. Kids are so excited. I will send a picture tonight. Sleep well. You did great. Good job Captain, First Mate, Rachel.

Meanwhile, Valeria Dave unloaded the loot into the storage unit dividing it up into four segments for the four buyers. Later he picked up his date and her aunt. He had company. They loved the flowers and insisted he put them out on a table on the dock where they had placed some chairs. Her aunt enjoyed a cold beer while Margarite had lemonade. Valeria Dave opened a beer. He put her red brownies away in the boat. He had burgers and buns for everyone later at seven. Why did he squeeze this bust in tonight's activities? He shook his head side to side. Better planning next time. Then again, he had not planned on any guests, or a date, even. So, he could not have planned better as he had not known.

When he came out of his boat her aunt was blowing up balloons and tying them to a string for decorations. That is a cool idea he thought. She will be good for Margarite over these next two years. Carlos would be pleased. In a way he wished it was midnight then the risky business would be over, but then his night with these two would be done as well. And he did not want that over yet. He told Margarite he had an errand to run at 7:45 tonight and he asked if she could come with him?

"Sure, whatever you need I am here to help. My aunt will help watch all the kids with what is her name, Rachel? Grandpa said you would need the storage key today-so here it is."

Boats had already assembled in the river in groups. They had anchored off to the sides in anticipation to watch the fireworks set off from the old bridge halfway across the Manatee River. Police boats were already out in force patrolling here and there keeping everyone safe. Parking lots were full and people were going to picnics and relatives' homes for an evening of fun. Around six o'clock the traffic died down and most people were where they wanted to be.

A calmness followed the day's bustling activities, parades both on land and water, and Americans jubilee for their country's birthday celebration. On the lawn next to the docks a group of young people were having a water balloon contest to see which partners could toss it the farthest without getting splashed from a broken balloon. Another contest was for eggs on a spoon racing to a partner and then to run back with it. One big massive celebration across the country brought much happiness for those participating. Young and old would have their enjoyment today on July 4th in the land of freedom called the United States of America.

CHAPTER 34

Henry's mother arrived with Rachel and all the kids. She asked Dave where to put her chicken and egg appetizers she had made. He directed her to the table near his boat. She placed it there. The spread looked great. Rachel brought baked beans, drinks and paper plates and cups. Dave made burgers and provided buns and sauces while another guest of his brought cut up watermelon and strawberries. Margarite made brownies and her aunt brought loads of chips. The party was set!

Henry's mother told Dave she made Jamaican jerk chicken. He looked surprised. "I love jerk seasoning, let me see."

She uncovered the foil from her chicken and he took a piece to taste test. "Mmm..."

Henry's mother's jerk seasoning
bonnet peppers
yellow onion
½ cup brown sugar
green onions

garlic

allspice, 2 tablespoons

thyme, 1 tsp

nutmeg

cinnamon, 1 tsp

salt

pepper

ginger root ,1 tsp

cayenne to taste

(From *Taste of Home* by Candi Rookwood-Clark of Jamaica)

Multiple folks sitting on chairs were scattered from the front of Dave's boat to his stern on the dock. The adults he let on his boat but children had to be accompanied. That was his rule. Margarite asked him to come aboard while they had started eating. They walked in the cabin cruiser and she asked him where he put her brownies. "I thought we should eat one of these now before the picnic."

"Oh really?"

"Yes. Because they are flavored. These are for adults and that batch out on the table is for the kids. Their flavor is chocolate and ours is well, for adults."

"Margarite, you made pot brownies?"

"Yes." She giggled. "Is that okay?"

"Of course, but do not tell anyone else. Let me do that." He snatched one and ate it quickly.

She took one, a big one, and ate it. She took the kids 2nd batch of brownies outside and placed them on the table.

With all the kids here, there would not be any leftovers for sure. The time was seven o'clock and they would not leave for a while. She heard music playing. This was fun to be near the water on a dock waiting for the fireworks tonight and enjoying a picnic. She watched the little kids, as she laughed, and talked with the older ladies. She helped kids make their plates and offered them drinks from the cooler on the dock. Her aunt's balloons floated from the dock post to the boats. Valeria Dave came and said they should eat so they could leave to go to the storage unit and get back for the fireworks. That sounded like a perfect idea.

Margarite was so happy she could not stop smiling or laughing. Pot did that for her. She did not do it but once a week, and then not even that. But she liked it. She did not let it mess with her. She had not tried alcohol yet and had no desire to do so. Valeria Dave, her date tonight sure was cute. She wondered if he was available. She knew him to be older so she would have to wait but that's okay she could still have fun and go out with him. Perfect she thought. She smiled again.

Margarite made her plate of jerk chicken, a burger, baked beans, chips, and fruit. Later she would have another brownie and watch the fireworks with her aunt and Valeria. But first they had an errand at 7:45. She checked her phone. She had time. She put it on camera and took some pictures of the boat, dock, and river. Many boats were floating in the river with party revelers. While she was snapping pictures, she heard the little girl Xochi scream and point to the river. Everyone looked in that direction.

Looking westwardly towards the setting sun where the

ocean met the river was smoke. And as they say, where there's smoke there's ... fire! The adults stood up and jaunted to the end of the dock where they could all get a better look. Xochi, who was wearing a lifejacket, went with Rachel to see better. Small amounts of smoke rose and then, suddenly, a large explosion occurred followed by a huge upwards moving black cloud. Black smoke overtook the entire area where, apparently, a boat had caught on fire. Everyone was watching and waiting. They hoped the people aboard were okay.

Not long after two large boats hurried towards the fire. One was the nearby Coast Guard boat and the other was a Fire Department boat. Both raced towards the explosion and fire. Once they arrived, a large hose of water was directed at the boat from both, while the immediate area was scoured for any passengers hurt or in the water thrown from the explosion.

Fairly quickly the fire was extinguished and sirens were turned off. Horns blew and directions were given to boaters nearby to look for passengers that may have been ejected during this explosion. Now it was a search and rescue operation post blaze and smoke. This would take awhile and patience was needed but also quickness in case someone was hanging on for dear life. They made an assessment to see how many were aboard by asking nearby boaters. A couple of Coast Guard employees boarded a dingy looking for bodies around the boat and on the rest of the boat which was still afloat.

Two people emerged from the cabin, unbelievably supporting one another. The fire had been in the back with the engine and surrounding areas. The front of the cabin cruiser was still intact and unharmed. The couple waved and said four more people were on board. Another couple was in the water floating towards the rescue boat and they assessed them for injuries. Two others were still missing. All four rescued persons were placed on the rescue boat and would be taken in for further treatment. Divers were needed and the sheriff's team was called. Every boat in the vicinity was alerted towards the missing couple. The explosion may have killed them, or possibly, they were on the beach or visiting another boat, maybe even swam away knowing it was going to explode.

Back on the dock Margarite and Valeria Dave told their partygoers they would be right back after a quick errand. "No problem, see you back for the fireworks."

Margarite was still smiling when she and Dave departed for the storage unit. She reached in her pocket for the note she was to give to Dave, she had already given him the key. "Here this is for you," she said. "Don't ask me why my grandpa already knows someone is not well, before the event happens, but here you go."

Dave read the note out loud. "Go to your wife, it's urgent, Carlos." He looked at Margarite. He debated but instead kind of lied to protect her. "Your grandpa must have changed his mind about including someone in the family business, the landscaping. So, he made up an excuse to get him away. Your grandpa is a thoughtful guy."

"He lost everything. He is working to rebuild his life, even at his age. I appreciate his generosity in helping others. I just hate this guy is going to think something bad has happened and later find out he worried for nothing."

"Oh, Margarite. Maybe he is helping him by not getting into an outdoor job when he's an inside kind of guy. Let us think he did it to save him."

"Ok, I get it. That is good. Some people can not stand the heat down here in the swamp. For sure. My aunt told me she went to get a job delivering and the boss took one look at her and said she would not like it because of the heat. That made her mad."

That settled her. He would have her hand out the unit number and buzz them in through the gate. Then he would meet them, take the cash, alert authorities and later they'd do their job. He would pick her up at the gate and quickly they would leave. The undercover cops and agents would tale the bad guys and pick them up away from the storage units. Thus, no tie in for Valeria Dave or Margarite, only as drug dealers, not snitches. It seemed like a perfect plan. And it was. They would be less one, one businessman that Carlos was saving. He knew he was not suited for any of this. The guy was a straight up preacher type-never has done wrong, only helps people. Therefore, Carlos decided to help him. This suited Carlos. He knew he would get lots of thanks on this one. The other guys were bad to the bone, always on the take, looking to make a buck and skin somebody in the process. Ethics, they had none.

Margarite sat in a chair near the gate which was far away from the unit. One guy showed up extremely early, like ten minutes before he was told to be there. She directed him to unit 434 and gave him directions. He seemed friendly. She wondered if that was the businessman, his skin was pale and very white. He did not venture outside much. She sat there waiting ten more minutes wondering when the next guy was coming. The time was eight o'clock and she wanted to be back on the road by 8:20 to make sure they did not miss the fireworks. Plus, they closed the bridge at 8:45. She saw another guy drive up. She noticed he had a badge sitting on the passenger seat-she could not see what it was for. She told him the same and gave the same directions. When he drove past her she saw a police emblem on his bumper. She thought he might have been a cop. It did not matter, her grandfather had friends everywhere. Then she remembered, this guy used to drive by and talk with her when she was mowing the lawn. She felt creeped out because he was so old, had a ring on his ring finger and his kids went to her school. She'd heard a rumor about him that he stole from the bad guys and used it for himself. That pissed off many a felon as well as drug cartels. People in the business of drugs said his head had a price on it. More creepiness.

As he passed, a car from the back came up to the exit gate rather fast. It was the first guy. He exited and sped off spinning stones airborne making a dusty wake behind him. Margarite smiled. He must have been the business guy who got grandpas tip to go see his wife. The third guy to emerge was clean shaven and very nervous. He was shaking like a lot. He wore his work clothes and a white doctor's overcoat. She could see his ID badge sticking out pinned to his shirt underneath. He was either a doctor, pharmacist, or lab technician. She gave him the same instructions. He looked at her above his glasses after he leaned his head down. Did he know her? She did not think she knew him. Get going she thought. This sure was a weird bunch going back to the shed, as she called it, from time to time. Were they buying lawn mowers, weed whackers, or what?

Her phone dinged. Valeria Dave texted. One more and we are out of here. Be ready. Dave.

Got it. Margarite.

A very fancy black SUV pulled up. Oh, no. This looked like the mafia, the president, or a funeral procession. Margarite got a case of the nerves, then remembered her grandpa knew all these folks. He did, didn't he? Shiny and black with a rack atop it glided steadily towards her and then quietly the window rolled down. A well put-together man with aviator sunglasses, suit and tie put his left hand on the window rim and tapped his fingers slightly as if to say do it now ma'am. She complied.

"Are you with Carlos?"

"Yes. Who are you?"

"I am his granddaughter. I run his landscaping business." Ooh, she said too much. None of the others asked any questions. Shut up Margarite. He looks suspicious. He reminded her of a mob member from a movie she watched. Oh, no.

"Is that right? I am Izan Mendoza and you are?"

"Margarite." Oh, for fuck's sake, get going sir, she said to herself.

"Directions?"

"Unit number 434, go left, circle around to the right then take another left and keep going."

"Thank you. Happy Fourth of July, Margarite."

"Happy Fourth to you too." She had to admit he was polite. What could he possibly want back here from grandpa's shed?

She gathered up her phone and purse, and put the folding chair back by the building. Come on Valeria, let us go.

Five long minutes later he arrived. She wanted to kiss him. She felt saved at this moment and had no idea why.

CHAPTER 35

Valeria Dave drove away fast. He went the opposite way that he came in. This puzzled Margarite.

He looked over at her, "Trust me," he said and continued a very fast pace. When he turned the corner, the tires squealed and left a mark on the road.

Suddenly, Dave turned into a mobile home park and drove slowly around the large block. He stopped near the cove that met the water. She did not know it but he could see the storage unit and if anyone was still there. He watched for a couple minutes making an important phone call. He called the officer in charge of Operation Lexi to alert them his part was complete. The chase would begin now to capture them, it would take all night and place the story in the paper tomorrow or the next day. Next up was to find the cartels that used the oil riggs in the Gulf of Mexico west of Tampa.

Six officers in three cars, all undercover, were alerted to three separate buyers. They did not know what to expect but overkill was in order. They needed arrests by morning and away from the storage units, closer to their homes or where they were going to sell the drugs. The whole operation was now depending upon them. Get it off the street and find the sources putting the second phase in place. Everyone wanted to keep the community safe from these drugs that normally would not kill, but now laced with fentanyl, a potent pain killer and narcotic, used in hospitals under therapeutic and anesthesia type settings with nurses and doctors administering via intravenous method would kill hundreds if not thousands.

Valeria Dave and Margarite drove back and reached the bridge before it closed for the evening. The river was lit up and festive. Margarite was still smiling. Dave was waiting to hear a few sirens go off towards where they just came from or maybe a car chase. Maybe he'd get a call with good news while the fireworks were ejecting into the sky performing a spectacular light show. He pulled into his parking space, jumped out and came around then opened the door for Margarite. She exited and he gave her a big hug. She hugged back not knowing what it was about but it felt good.

Everyone in the group was talking, laughing and waiting for the light show. Any minute now it would begin. Then the music started!

Meanwhile, the businessman with the white pasty skin looking to make extra money to take his wife on a surprise cruise for a special anniversary drove to a remote restaurant where he found his wife out on a date. Much to his surprise his thoughts wandered aimlessly and this shook him up. Unbeknown to him she was trying to get a part time job at a restaurant near downtown to make money for a special surprise for her husband. She sat in the bar area at a high-top table talking with a gentleman who was asking her questions. He offered her to be a hostess or a waitress, as she had experience in both areas.

"I would love to accept. I can work three evenings a week."

"Perfect, I will have the hostess sign you up. Nice to meet you." He left the table as her husband walked up and stood there wondering what she was doing.

"Hey, honey, what are you doing here at our favorite restaurant?" she asked him.

"Well, I am just following you. Our daughter said you came here tonight."

She smiled. "I thought you were busy tonight, so I made other plans. I thought I would dine and then watch fireworks tonight on TV. I know boring but, hey, it is okay."

"Let me join you. Let us make it festive."

"I would love that. And you are here with me, even better."

"We could eat, then go to the bay and watch the fireworks. I am sure there will be tons of them." She got up and went over to him and kissed him. That is all she wanted was his focus on her just for a night or at least once a week. He was always so busy with work and his dog it left no time for togetherness. The couple in love a long time ago began again.

Of course, the cops knew where the IA agent lived. Everybody talked about him and his wayward ways. When would he get caught? His boss said to some of his crew, "Next time, record it, write it down and I'll discipline him." But it never happened, until now. It was time to take him off the streets and these guys and girls were going to do it. He would bother younger girls, like it was his right, to haggle them and make them feel uncomfortable.

The agent got the drugs and frankly did not know what to do with them. His wife was out of town with his two kids for the holiday. He did not go knowing he was getting the loot. He pulled up to a local bar and went inside. He sat down, ordered a beer, lit a cigarette, and played with his phone. He thought about his options. He could sell the drugs, he knew a few addicts in town. He could plant them on a speeding bust when he accompanied an officer from time to time. The thought of seeing the guys, or girls face when he pulled drugs from the back seat of their car, well, that was pure joy. He laughed out loud, then took a swig of his beer. But maybe the third choice might be the best. He could turn into a dealer or get a warehouse for storage. That was the big time, payments were large as in the millions. He might be able to do it and with a partner would be a better idea. He saw the last guy pull up tonight when he had just finished loading his car. He dreamt of big cars, a nice mansion, and vacations to exotic locales. Maybe young gorgeous blondes in bikinis around the pool took over his mind. He shook his head. Until he could make that happen, he needed to sell a few bags of the blue pills. Speaking of blondes, a fully clothed blonde came and sat next to him. He looked around. Yup, she was alone. Maybe she was lonely. Heck everyone in his world was lonely. He bought her a drink. She asked to borrow a cigarette and they began talking and laughing.

Fireworks were exploding on the TV in the bar which was not far from the river. He forgot about everything and focused his attentions on this pretty lady. She played some tunes using his dollars, then asked him what he was doing for the holiday weekend. She was new in town and needed to find some pot or something. He told her I have got that and a few other recreational pills, forgetting he was an agent responsible to the United States Government. She laid down $400 dollars in hundreds. And looked at him as if to see if he wanted more. Since she was doling out hundreds, he asked for $700. He was feeling bold. She said yes and laid out more with an extra hundred. She excused herself to the bathroom while he went to get the drugs. When she came back, she got a table instead of sitting at the bar after ordering a fresh drink.

She loved this part of her job. The capture of a sexist pig made her smile. They told her to get him and get him tonight. We want him off the streets. He is messy, implicates ordinary citizens, racks up charges on people who don't deserve it. He makes us look bad and we are done with it. We just had not been able to do it since we found out from whistleblowers two months ago.

In walked the sloppy IA agent that did not have his priorities straight. He forgot the code of ethics and working with the public. His conscience was deleted, as in not there. He smiled as he approached her with the goodies. She smiled back. Silently, she said gotcha, bad guy.

She left and let the bust happen outside. The establishment did not deserve a bust tonight and the undercover lady was gone. Her disguise would keep her undetected. All good.

The pharmacist went straight home and began to make phone calls. He had been given a list of other pharmacists who wanted to make some money selling drugs from time to time. His list was short with three names on it. The first guy said sure, he would be over in an hour. He wanted to buy all of it. How much? The pharmacist had to think about this motherlode he had. It contained two methamphetamine type substances, stuff kids took to get by and be more focused when test taking, and a muscle relaxant used by many folks. Also, small amounts of marijuana in bags as everyone wanted that for personal use. He should keep the marijuana he thought as he might need that for himself or friends. He laughed. He was going to make some big bucks tonight. How much? The guy asked again. He had four blocks of each drug containing a thousand pills each he was told. "Twelve thousand pills for $120,00.00 and that's a bargain as you can sell each pill for upwards of $20/pill, almost $60/pill." He replied that he knew and he would see him in an hour.

His mother called, "Are you watching all the fireworks outside. They are all over the city."

"I know, mom. I know." He could hear the sirens going off near her house. It jarred him a little but he shook it off.

After a few minutes the sirens continued and continued until they stopped. Next the door bell rang and he met his buyer and let him in. They made an exchange. The pharmacist looked at all the cash. A year's salary in his hands. This was easy. They both stood when the doorbell rang. His buyer walked behind him. When he opened the door the flashing lights blinded him to his deeds, making drug doing, a big wrong. That was the second sting of the night with one to go. Valeria Dave got the report in a text. One to go …

The party goers on the dock listened to the music. The fireworks would begin any moment. Dave and Margarite went to the boat and ate another brownie. Valeria Dave thanked Margarite for her help tonight. He asked her if he could check in on her from time to time. Maybe they could even go to get supper every now and then. He said they both needed family as they had none. She liked that. She said yes. She missed her grandpa. "And Dave, you are like family," she said. Then they joined the crowd and sat in their seats waiting for the light show. They were so close to the event. Suddenly the first firework went sky high and it did not disappoint. It was practically above their heads. Only the river separated them, and just half of it. Colors of red and blue were dotted across the night sky with white bursts that kept going, all they way down to the river. Lots of oohs and aahs set the mood.

CHAPTER 36

"Ylove the fireworks!" Xochiquetzal yelled, then giggled.

Xochi sat on Rachel's lap and clapped. She thought she was going to be scared but the little girl seemed extremely happy sitting with the group. Maybe the melancholy would come tomorrow or later this week when everything died down and regular life set in. Henry, Jose, and Patrick all sat together like a pact. Bonding had been occurring for some time now with boating, exploring an island, illegally boarding a Coast Guard boat, sailing on the ocean, and finally, a picnic with fireworks. Yeah. They loved it. Patrick wished Seth had come but knew he would see him tomorrow, the next day and the next day after that. Jose kept saying how much fun he was on the sailboat, especially when he showed him the shark finder. The two older boys could not wait to get out on the ocean and spot the sharks with their names.

"Rachel, do you have a moment?" Valeria Dave asked her. The fireworks were almost over.

"Yes. Sure. Let me thank you for this lovely evening on the water. Thanks. Fantastic is all I can say. I am sorry Seth missed this. He would have loved it."

"I am sure he loves the rest right now. A little quiet time to settle his mind and thoughts probably helps. I want to thank you for saving my life. You reacted well out on the ocean in a boat. Lifesaving maneuvers are what you performed."

"Not sure it was that but you're welcome." He offered his hand and she shook it. "I wasn't sure about you when I met you but you are a good guy."

He smiled. His charm poured out. She finally had a good feeling about him. She also decided not to judge everyone by their looks.

"Wait here, I have something for you and Seth." In a moment he returned. Wrapped in foil he presented her with a pan of brownies. "These are adult brownies, for you two when you want to relax."

"Great. I always wanted to try college brownies. Thank you."

Earlier, around the six o'clock hour, Scarlet and Jessie prepared for the evening. Dressed in some of their finest clothing, this was going to be a special night. Scarlet had received great news earlier in the day that her own cancer had seemed to recede into remission from tests performed last week. She had one of those long-term cancers that drags the system from time to time but doesn't kill you outright. Still, she felt blessed and expressed this to Jessie-her longtime partner.

He felt the same. Time became more precious, so they acknowledged their love to each other. He bought her a diamond engagement ring. He felt she would say yes. And if she did not, then it would be a friendship ring. He won either way when she told him last week, she loved him and wanted her life to be with him and that they should do more fun things together. Travel, shop, dine, explore, make music and be happy! He could not wait to pop the question tonight and toast with champagne. He was setting the table with fine China when she came out from her bedroom and asked him to zip up her long royal blue satin dress.

"My, my, my dear, you are looking mighty pretty. I would say gorgeous is a better word."

"Jessie, oh dear, thank you. Please zip this dress up and then I will put our order in for room service. They said the lobsters would take about one hour to prepare."

"I suppose they have to go and catch them," he chuckled. "I have appetizers, music and drinks."

"That will occupy us for a while."

"We will have appetizers, drinks, dance some, listen to a couple of your best performances, then eat lobster with sides, biscuits to die for, followed by dessert, more music, then later champagne, chocolate and fireworks."

"Don't forget my special dessert I made," Scarlet reminded him.

"I will not. It comes with a special surprise of my own." He hinted, knowing she would never figure out the tip.

"Oh Jessie, I will have to have your special surprise for breakfast, I think. My stomach will not handle all this. Maybe if we dance until midnight, or go for another downtown, waterfront stroll tomorrow morning you can make room. We still have all that lunch food as well."

"That is a great idea. I am in."

After he set the table with plates, silver, water goblets, wine glasses and dessert plates he made a centerpiece with flowers, crystals, ribbons and gently inserted a diamond and gold ring amongst the display. Later he would make a small plate of petals, crystals, ring, and ribbons and serve it to her with her beautiful dessert. Then he would pop the question. Would she be surprised?

Scarlet ordered the dinner for tonight over the phone from her kitchen. She ordered two lobsters with butter and lemon, special herb biscuits, red skinned potato salad, fried okra, and collard greens. These items made it more like a picnic, even if they were having the best item on the menu. The dinner included pineapple coleslaw and corn casserole or jalapeno cornbread. She told them to send it all as they could use the sides for lunch tomorrow. She ordered two cheeseburgers with buns on the side for the lunch, forgetting she had many hotdogs. Maybe she was losing her mind. Everything was set, now for the fun.

Jessie walked out of his bedroom dressed in a black tuxedo. She rarely saw him out of his white suite and trousers. Sometimes he wore khaki suits or shorts with short sleeved plaid shirts and a hat. He looked like a new man all dressed up. He even had on shiny black shoes and his hair was slicked back. Scarlet went up and touched his hair, then stared at him eye to eye.

"Well, we are a pair. Look at us."

"I know, darling. Look at you with your hair all swept up and a few curls dangling, your makeup is like you are back on stage in Europe, and the dress is stunning all blue and shiny. It makes my eyes want to weep."

"Oh sweetie. Grab my black velvet shawl from the closet and let us go get a drink while they catch our lobster."

The couple strolled with hands held through the lobby and out to the bar which overlooked the bay and waterfront. They ordered martinis and sat down at the bar. There was a piano player playing lightly patriotic all-American tunes. The front entrance, hallway and lounge area to the back was exquisitely upscale, decorated for the clientele which inhabited the building. One felt safe and secure from the outside world, a feeling that Scarlet thought everyone should experience. She did her best for those less fortunate, either from beginnings, bad luck, or injustices. She believed in hard work but she also realized not everybody was built the same. Some people work hard naturally while others tag along, or just are not inclined to save the world, make it better or whatnot. They just live, do not bother anyone, move on or just are. That hadn't been her but while she had breath, she wanted to instill some fortitude into the boys at her ranch, those staying on her plantation, if you will. She understood some people did not like that word, but for her, she had mastered the old and brought new life into an old way of doing things. People liked her, understood her plan, recognized her privately and this made her smile. Jessie too, even if he did look like a butler, or a waiter. His life had been filled with grace. He had been with Scarlet since the beginning, traveled much of the world, seen her through two marriages, the children and still here he was spending his days with Scarlet. He was her business partner, friend, lover, and soon to be husband, he hoped. They finished their drinks, danced a couple numbers, tipped the piano man, walked outside onto the flowered courtyard, and then walked back to the elevator.

Once upstairs in the high-rise Scarlet went around and turned on the lights. Jesse displayed the appetizers of shrimp and oysters on the half shell. He poured them iced water and checked his watch. Dinner should be here any minute. He turned on his playlist to quietly play in the background. Scarlet opened all the curtains that faced the bay and towards Sarasota and Bradenton to allow the fireworks which came later to light up the rooms.

Her cell phone rang. It was Seth. She answered and he said, "Happy Fourth of July, honey."

"Happy Fourth of July to you, too."

"I know we talked earlier but I was thinking about you tonight, you and Jessie. I wanted to invite you over to my place tomorrow. Sit on the beach, be mellow, watch the waves as time passes by."

"I love that idea. I will have to ask my boss," she said and laughed.

"Your boss? You do not have a boss."

"I made him a partner in my ventures."

"Yes. Great idea. He is the quiet type, observing everything, missing nothing."

"Tell him I said congrats. Hope to see you both tomorrow afternoon."

Then the doorbell rang and Jessie went to open it. The lobster arrived; caught, cooked and ready to eat. The server set the food to their table arranging it nicely. Scarlet poured chilled white wine into the herringbone patterned glasses. Both sat down and began eating after a short prayer of thanks to God, country, and each other. Lobster with butter and lemon, potatoes, collards with ham, coleslaw with pineapple, herb biscuits, okra, and jalapeno cornbread. They took extra small helpings describing their feast almost like Thanksgiving. They somehow knew, each of them, tonight was extra special. Halfway through, Scarlet poured them a little more white wine and toasted her glass to Jessies. "Thank you for becoming my partner. I am happy. I know you will do a wonderful job supporting me and bringing new ideas to this venture."

"You are exceptional. Somehow, you convinced the US government to let you do what you do. That itself is amazing."

"They knew they were not winning the war on drugs. I am a small helper with big ideas. Turning around the youth is my biggest priority. Putting faith in them-getting them through the idle ages of 17-24 is the best idea, yet. It works. I am proving it. Persons that never had someone behind them, loving them, caring for them, telling them what is right or wrong are secretly yearning for it. Cheers."

They savored this special dinner with their own private thoughts.

Jessie told her to get her dessert ready and he would bring all the dishes to the kitchen, clear the table and do them in the morning. "Sounds like a great idea. Do you want champagne with the wireworks?"

"I do," he said. He looked up. He hoped she would say those words soon.

The couple in love sat out on the balcony watching the fireworks sipping champagne. Life did not get any better than this. No crowds. Full kitchen and bar. Music. And a super light show. Wait. There was something better. Jessie excused himself and said he would be right back. He removed his jacket to not be so formal. He gathered the crystals, flower petals, the ring and a ribbon and placed it on the small dessert dish. He made two helpings of her special dessert.

He set down the plates and handed her the plate with the ribbon. "A gift for you."

Scarlet picked up the red ribbon and saw the crystals and a ring. She looked up to Jessie. Then she picked up the ring and held it close to her.

"Will you marry me?"

"Yes."

CHAPTER 37

The two undercover cops sat idle in their vehicles. They had lost the mafia looking guy from the storage units. They had one last idea to check out the rental car and see if they could ID him. Both agreed they better try or they looked like incompetent undercover cops tonight. They drove together to a rental place right before closing time of 6 pm. One of them flashed their badge for extra clout and asked about who had rented a brand new large black SUV.

"Sure, we only have two of those. Let me check." She looked on her computer and found the renters. "One of the guys rented it for two weeks. Probably going on vacation. The other guy rented it for the weekend."

"Now, can you give me an ID or an address for those?"

"Ah, yes, you are a policeman, so sure. No harm, I suppose." She put the ID up and address of the first. He was 28 years old, lived locally, and probably was going on a family vacation with the little ones. The next ID was a slightly older, distinguished looking gentleman, who lived in Miami.

"Miami?" The two guys asked in unison. One of the cops wrote down his name, address, age, and features. "Did he happen to say where he was staying?" The pair needed some luck.

"Let me ask Julie in back as she checked him in earlier." The attendant went back and asked her coworker about the handsome man from earlier. She thought she would say The Ritz or something like that but she said he was staying near the airport in Sarasota. He even left a business card with Julie. She thought maybe he was flirting with her. Maybe he was maybe he was not. But she took it. He was told he could even return the car there. Perfect he said. He planned to do just that. She told the police guys the info and handed them the card and then they were gone.

They found the hotel and went to his room. To their surprise they found the drugs laid out on one of the beds. In shock they scoured the room in disbelief. "What now?"

"I am not sure but we have to call this in. He might just be out for dinner and coming back."

"You are right. That is it. We need to wait down in the bar or somewhere nearby and act like travelers."

"Good idea. I like that."

"Let me check his clothes, I'll put a tag, a tracer on something in case he bolts out of here on a plane, or something."

"Man, you watch too much TV. This is Sarasota, nothing big time happens around this sleepy little village." They both laughed.

"Miami."

Quickly, they exited and went to the bar after changing shirts to sporty polo tops, they bought in the gift shop along with baseball type caps. They ordered beers and fit right in.

They waited, played on their phones, and made the decision to not call in just yet. Something told them the loose ends were waiting to be exposed or still in the works.

The businessman who drove into the storage facility and back out again was interesting to the man in the black new SUV. He took his plates and called a friend, found an address, and followed him to some steak house where apparently, he was meeting his girlfriend or wife. He was not sure. Mr. SUV decided to eat dinner as well. After dinner he returned to his hotel by the airport, changed clothes in his room and took a shuttle to the airport. His private helicopter pilot was ready and waiting. The two cops in the bar saw him leave with the clothes on they had tagged. Hopefully, this would be successful. They waited. Shortly after they watched on their phone as he flew away towards the ocean. Both looked at each other and decided now would be an appropriate time to call it in. The time was nine thirty at night. Scarlet received the news at ten thirty and called Valeria.

"Valeria, the unit called me with news. One guy got away, the good-looking guy in the black SUV. Well, not exactly."

"Which is it? Tell me more, Scarlet."

"He's being traced out into the ocean."

"The ocean? He cannot sell drugs to dolphins or sharks now, can he?"

"Obviously, he is not a low man on the totem pole. Must be a big shot, maybe a new cartel."

"The guys did good with the tracer; else we'd be nowhere."

"We better lay low as he may have special optics and surveillance measures."

"Good idea. Wait why we find out who he is. We have an address and ID stats."

"Scarlet, you said the next part of Operation Lexi was going after the sources."

"What shall we call this next plan?" she asked him.

He paused, reflected and came up with a new name. "Operation Xochi, after a little girl that's in our arms safe from killers, namely the drug lords."

"Operation Xochi (ShoChee). Sounds pretty, too pretty for this mess. At least the drugs are on the bed in the hotel room. No one will be harmed."

"Let us take the rest of the night off. We got two of three out of an original four and maybe a lead towards the source. We should not blow it."

"Sounds good. Will you be coming to Seth's on the beach?"

"Yes. I will. Margarite may come too. Are you?"

"Yes. I have a good surprise for you."

"I love good surprises."

The helicopter sped towards the ocean and beyond to a waiting yacht far from shore. One could barely see the lights, just a twinkle or two, from shore. Izan Mendoza was a rich man and needed no drugs to make a buck. Once he landed, he disengaged from the helicopter safely and walked to the ships captains' quarters to thank him for waiting for him. Beautiful music was playing overhead. Moonflower by Carlos Santana played overhead. He immediately relaxed. His business was complete. The sky had been filled with fireworks and the enormous amount of them distracted his pilot for awhile until they were out over the sea. Now all was fine. They were winding down.

He chuckled to himself from the activities of earlier in the day. He was sure he had them running around wondering who he was. He poured himself a night cap and retreated to his chambers. This was the first real cruise he had taken since he ordered the yacht back in 2020 during Covid, when the world shut down and products were difficult to obtain. By 2021 the yacht was finished and he took ownership. For the very first cruise he took his entire extended family out of Miami and went on a two-week excursion. This trip he was by himself with a few paying guests aboard. In the morning he was going fishing, sunning himself, enjoying lunch, maybe read a book, take a nap, and prepare for dinner. Tomorrow night there might even be a poker game aboard his yacht he was told.

He was out fishing when a Coast Guard boat came by to check on his yacht. Routine they said. Absolutely routine in these waters to check maintenance and the like for safety of your passengers. His yacht passed. *Victorious* always passed inspections. She had a great team working aboard this priceless princess. She was around 280 feet long and held a helicopter with a helipad, a sporting 40-foot yacht for fishing deep seas on the back deck, two Jacuzzis, a pool, five decks, and a crew of 24 plus the Captain and First Mate.

The dining table outside sat ten people. Outdoor seating was available with comfortable cushions and a tent like tarp placed over head so one would not sunburn or get too heated. When he returned from fishing the cook told him he would make it for dinner if he liked. Sounded perfect he told him. Onto a dip in the pool, stretch on the lounge chair, eat lunch, then read a book in the shade, followed by a nap. Such pleasure. He loved the sea. And the sea loved his boat.

Later that night after dinner a poker game was started. It began at nine thirty indoors.

Meanwhile, the Coast Guardsman that boarded the boat was approached by a couple under cover guys later that day. They just asked questions, nothing was up, just investigating a late-night helicopter trip over the fireworks and wanted to make sure everything was good. He told them he was not aboard his yacht and that he was fishing on another boat and tonight he had a poker game with his guests. Sounds like just a rich guy the Coast Guardsman surmised. He smiled at the guys. They reported back to their unit guy and now the work was done. Over. The unit reported back to them that the next phase had started and they did good work. They were invited to be on the next operation. They would receive notice in a few days. They were told to take a few days off-so they did.

At nine thirty a poker game began in the middle lounge of the yacht. Decorated beautifully, the interior was first class from the wood floors to the fine details of the bar area, curtains and certain unique artwork displays. The table shone with holders for drinks and tray areas for cigars. A deck waitress brought them drinks, snacks, cigars, cigarettes, vapes, and anything else they might want. Even with all the fancy things this was down to earth playing and for quite small change. No one was going to lose their shirt tonight. Izan did not play like that. He had other things on his mind anyway and was not into concentrating a whole lot tonight. He was just happy to be on his boat and enjoying the company of guests. He would worry about tomorrow tomorrow, or even the day after.

After a few hours Izan cashed in his chips and politely excused himself. He was off to bed. He ended up by a few hundred dollars. His poker game was getting better he told himself.

Two days later the guys that busted the pharmacist at his home were called to a hotel at the airport. It seemed like part of their sting being the same drugs they had busted someone else for. On the way over they contemplated what they were going to find. The manager led them through the hallway towards a room. He let them inside and said, "A cleaning lady found this room just like it is-she reported it to me and we saved it for you. Nothing has been touched whatsoever."

"Perfect, thank you. We will be about an hour in here and then we will be gone." He flashed his badge and the boss left.

"What in the hell blazes is this?" He threw his hand over the bed where the drugs were laid out next to a note. The drugs took up three quarters of the bed.

His partner went to the note with gloves on and read it out loud. "To whom this may concern, your drugs you sold are cartel drugs but you know that. I'm sick of kids dying for taking a Percocet for pain, a Vyvanse to study for exams, and anything else experimental. I took these off the street for you. They are laced with fentanyl and will kill many people. This load alone reeks of a million lives and millions of dollars. Who am I? A concerned citizen. When you find me, we will talk about how to solve this problem."

"What on earth? The arrogance of this horseshit tells me

its cartel." He was fast to display his discontent.

"Not so fast. Why would a guy buy the drugs, expose himself and seem to know so much, all at once?"

"Yeah. Keep talking."

"This is for the next operation. This is not our business. They have a plan and probably are already working on who this guy is."

"I say. You win. Sounds like a plan. We might even be selected to be on that next operation knowing we did the right thing here."

"Now you are talking. It pays very well. We do a good job and get paid well. Happiness."

The guys took pictures, a few fingerprints, then wrapped up the drugs and called their unit guy. He called Scarlet to inform her of the bust and return of her own drugs. They would hold these drugs at the station until further notice. She told him Operation Xochi had just begun. She thanked him. A meeting was called for next Wednesday on how to proceed.

CHAPTER 38

Seth's guests arrived at eleven o'clock for a day at the beach. He himself had slept in until nine, and today, he felt fine. Rachel walked in with Xochi, Patrick, Henry, and his mom carrying their towels, toys, and coolers. Seth had plenty of beach chairs, water bottles, food, sunscreen, music and smiles. He was feeling great! The ocean was calm today but the kids still received the ocean rules. No kids on the beach or in the ocean without one adult present. Did everyone understand? Yes, we do they said. Next question was who is coming to watch us because we are ready?

Henry's mom offered to do the first duty. Rachel reassured her she will be down on the beach soon and for a long time. She would relieve her. She just had to check the paper first. She laid it out on the counter and scoured the headlines looking for the drug bust. The beachgoers left hastily ready for the beach and ocean action.

"Page three halfway down." Seth had seen it already. Operation Lexi complete was not mentioned. The police department stated they would continue working for the public. Rachel kept reading. No one has died here in our county since the young girl named Lexi. Vigilance is paying off and continued education to the kids who are most vulnerable was in play.

"I still don't understand: why the poisoning of regular drugs, who is behind it, why evil has gone global?" Rachel questioned.

"Because that was the next step. Squeeze us until we are beyond dry post pandemic, ultimately worn out, drugged, poisoned, killed by a weird virus, untested vaccine, or a pill with extras, then come at us or pull us into war, pollute our water, kill our whales, float balloons in our airspace, etc. Who knows? We must be more offensive in taking care of our own. The border is wide open on purpose, someone wants to take the United States down and we are letting them walk right in."

"Seth, that is the most dystopian thing I have ever heard you say. Did you mean it?"

"In training you must think worse than the other guys so there are no surprises. Sorry."

"And with that … we are on vacation for a couple days. You need a frozen Margarita for the beach. Let us make a pitcher!" Rachel would have one or two then watch all the kids with Seth's help. She had always heard kids take a good nap after being in the ocean and soaking up sun.

Her and Seth packed up the food cooler with snacks, sandwiches, and lemonade, then made a drink cooler with frozen blended margaritas. They put their sunscreen on, washed their hands, picked up more chairs and headed outside. Seth left a note on the front door for the rest of his visitors to call his number.

"What a gorgeous day!" Rachel exclaimed and went and gave Seth a big fat kiss.

"My, I like that. Hey, I have missed you. Did I tell you that?" Seth asked when the couple paused on the walkway to the beach.

"We have so much to discuss but it will have to wait until tomorrow when things are quieter. I do not return to work until next Friday. I have a week off."

The sunshine was bright, the beach was white and a summer breeze whistled by every now and then.

"Well, look at that." She pointed with her eyes as her hands were full.

Seth looked up and out to sea. He was not sure but it looked like a big yacht. He had never seen one so big offshore from his cottage. He supposed they rarely traveled this close in. He estimated it to be about four miles offshore sailing south. Though it was not sailing it was motoring he told himself.

"What a beautiful sight. Some billionaire cruising down to the Keys on his yacht."

"Lucky him. I would like to be aboard that ship. It is as big as a cruise ship but private."

"Dream Rachel, use your imagination."

"After I have a margarita." She walked on down to where Henry's mom was sitting and made her and Seth's place on the beach for the day. Henry and Patrick were using skim boards at the water's edge. How nice. Good for them. At least the sharks cannot bite where the waves break.

"Margarita?" She poured a cup for Henry's mom and gave it to her. Then she pulled out a sandwich for herself and enjoyed the view with the margarita. People were walking hand in hand. One was carrying a baby who wore a big hat, while others watched little kids play endlessly building sand castles or moats, even throwing nerf balls.

Seth handed out sandwiches to the boys even though they did not want to stop surfing. They sat for about ten minutes, then it was back to the ocean. Xochi had sunscreen on and a hat and Seth put an umbrella up for her that hung over her chair. She liked the sand and made a little castle with people in it. Seth poured a second drink for him and Rachel. By the time they finished it the large yacht had traveled farther south almost out of view. He wondered if he could track yachts like sharks. He thought about it. Of course, radar would pick up all their systems, but could you track a singular vessel that large? Well, duh? Of course, why not? He had never done it, he was not sure if his tracking methods would do it. He wanted to know where that ship was going. Like airplanes in the sky anything can be followed nowadays.

"Time to get wet. What do you think?"

"Sure. Xochi, do you want to go swimming?"

"Rachel, I can but want to float. I float."

"Then let's float, we can swim tomorrow."

She came running over to her. She was ready for the big ocean. Normally, Xochi was not afraid of anything. Maybe because the boys seemed so natural around the water and on their skim boards and she was not, she felt she could not play with them. She held Rachel's hand and they entered in. It was just right, not cold, nor warm. Seth joined them and took Xochi's other hand. They waded out until it was waist deep and Xochi floated. She tasted the salt water and wiped her mouth. She smiled and enjoyed herself. For quite a while the threesome lingered and enjoyed the buoyancy of floating and the saltiness of the ocean make them feel lighter and fresher with little waves to relax them. Nothing bothered them.

After a while she asked Seth a question. "Are there sharks out here near us?"

"Xochi, not really."

"You should check with your shark finder on your phone," the little girl remembered.

"Great idea. But we might not want to know. Rachel, do you want to know where the sharks are?" Rachel rolled her eyes at Seth. He was shutting down her time in the ocean. Yep.

"Absolutely not. In fact, I am going in. Once I think about them, I am out."

"Me too," said the little girl.

Around three o'clock Scarlet and Jessie showed up. She said they would be up on Seth's back porch. He said the back door was unlocked. They set there things inside, poured a drink and sat outside watching the kids and the ocean. Pretty soon the gang from the beach was wiped out and came walking up the path. It was time to get out of the sun, rehydrate and relax.

Seth was making ribs today, he set about lighting his grille and preparing that part of dinner. He had picked up side dishes, prepped corn on the cob, sliced tomatoes and strawberries, and put Rachel in charge of making cupcakes. While he was browning his ribs Scarlet and Jessie walked over to chat with him.

"Guess what?"

"What?" Seth looked at Scarlet and she showed him her ring. "No? Really?"

"Really." Jessie said and smiled so big.

He high fived Jessie and hugged him, then turned to one of his favorite people of all, and kissed her on the cheek, followed by a big hug. "I am so happy for you two. I have known you for five years now. I am just delighted. Such a blessing."

"Thank you. I know you mean it. I would like you to be my best man," said Jessie and shocked all three of them.

"Yes, of course."

"You are getting a good man. He takes such great care of you. He sees to everything. That is love." He spoke right to Scarlet.

"I found out yesterday I am in remission. I just cannot believe my good fortune. And now you have succeeded in our venture with even more to come. God's looking out for us."

Seth looked over at Rachel. For a glimpse of a second, he thought maybe they would be blessed as well. What a great day. He continued cooking, looking around feeling like the man of the house. Today he was.

"Congratulations on the remission and the engagement."

Blossom showed up and Rachel was happy to see him. She introduced him to all the kids and he looked shocked. "You guys were carefree, like birds when I was here, not even two months ago."

"Oh, I know. Let me introduce you to our new kiddie clan," she joked.

Valeria Dave called and told Seth he needed a rain check for today's visit. He was going to visit Margarite and her aunt and take them out for dinner. Seth told them to come swimming maybe tomorrow and that he had lots of food. Dave said they would come. Perfect.

Dinner was fabulous, filling and fun with a table full of guests. Seth did not know it could be this much fun to entertain. Where has he been all his life he asked himself. He served the cupcakes and proposed a toast to Scarlet and Jessie. Right at that moment she invited everyone to her ranch in Georgia for a late September wedding when it was cooler and things were harvested. She especially wanted Seth and Rachel to come and meet up with her other employees. They would love to they said and planned on it. Could they bring the kids?

"That would be fine, there are many things to do." They said their goodbyes and departed.

That evening Xochi went to bed and the boys played a game in a bedroom while Blossom sang a couple of songs outside on the back porch. He departed and said he would see them at the ranch in a couple of months. He had a date tonight he let slip so he had to go.

"Ooh, okay." And off he went.

Seth and Rachel were listening to music very much old-time music.

"So little snowbird ..." Seth looked at Rachel, "take me with ...." Rachel finished his words.

They ended that with a long, romantic kiss as she sat upon his lap outside in the night air with gentle breezes that came from above the night ocean.

The next morning when Seth was having coffee a familiar face showed up at his back door. He went and let him in.

"Coffee?"

"For sure."

"I expected you later today. Something is up, I can tell," issued Seth. "I've been doing this too long and I'm a bit warped."

Valeria Dave looked serious for a few moments then flashed his warm smile. "Sorry, I could not make it yesterday. You have got me on your side, partner, and guess what?"

"I can't guess."

"Operation Xochi is up. We are going for the sources. You are the expert; I am the muscle but I have cartel experience."

CHAPTER 39

Two months later at Scarlet's ranch, Palmetto Stars, in southern Georgia her invited guests arrived and settled in for a few days of rest, relaxation and her and Jessie's wedding. Seventeen guests came using ten of the twelve bedrooms on both floors of the massive plantation style home. Scarlet hired extra cooks and cleaners for this event. She had an outdoor tent assembled out back. A small band would play on Saturday night and a guitar player would entertain guests tonight at a welcome gathering. Barbeque headlined the menu tonight with a more formal dinner set for Saturday, the special event being the wedding reception. She had planned this immediately after getting engaged on July Fourth.

Guests mingled and found their seats outside under the large tent after ordering drinks at the outside bar. They listened to country music, and island music with a few oldies via the guitar player. The kids had a table of their own watched over by the parents nearby.

Scarlet informed her special crew, her undercover agents, about a meeting in the morning in her office. She had something special she wanted them to hear. It would take about an hour at most.

Once they all arrived in the room Scarlet shut the door. James and Megan were sitting, as well as Seth and Rachel. Introduced to the others was a congresswoman from Georgia named Kim, an older lady who had recovered from cancer, and Jessie. Scarlet began by telling them she was going to read a testimony given to her by a judge from a case that recently finished and a judgement had been handed down. Some of the group just looked around at each other not knowing what she was talking about. She went on to explain that this was an anonymous case and everyone would understand once she read the judges words. She had captivated everyone.

"Because of our work this has been made possible."

She picked up the paper and began to read …

"I am the judge presiding over this anonymous case before us and this shall be the testimony of such said anonymous person. The voice will be disguised and played before the jury in this trial against opposing parties. Because of the nature of secrecy very few persons will be allowed the contents thus protecting anonymous. Do you understand as well?"

"Yes."

"Then go ahead with anything you want to tell me. Start from the beginning."

"Thank you. I did not put things together until somewhere in the middle of it happening. However, certain things may have passed me by. I have felt threatened or like someone was after me for quite some time. I recall being home one summer and I pulled up in the driveway at my parent's home. There was an old small car parked in the driveway I did not recognize it. I walked in with sunglasses on and saw my parents sitting at the kitchen table with two young guys. My mother introduced them to me as the sister from Atlanta. They were IA (Intelligence Agency) agents interviewing them. I picked up my sunglasses, and frankly, didn't want anything to do with the conversation. I left and walked down into the basement.

In retrospect, my parents were not advised, and should have had a lawyer with them. Maybe that was the middle of the end, I do not know. I myself felt like my phone had been tapped and someone was following me. How would I know this? I would not. I figured it out in retrospect. While my brother was on the lamb doing his own research is when I was followed. That made sense. But it continued, on and on. I felt terrorized, tortured and waterboarded, psychologically. How is this possible you might ask? Was I paranoid? I have never been paranoid or had any mental condition. I am steady as they say. I felt confused about my brother's constant law struggles. He could not catch a break. I felt terrorized due to the following of myself in stores and such. The torture came on the internet. I was not physically harmed, ever, but before I figured out my phones wiretapping, I thought some social medias were trying to help me with writing and many people seemed helpful. I wanted to write a book. So I found connections through social medias. I navigated the internet. But in the end, they navigated me and harassed me. Information would be provided on one site only to be said that was wrong on another. Okay, I get it. Trolls. Differences. No problems. I swear though, someone or something was playing head games with me. It felt like maybe the site was hacked and someone else was coming through to mess with me.

I saw on the news that intelligence operatives took over some social medias. Could this be happening to me I asked myself? Was it the dark web? I would not know. I began to distrust the computer and social media sites. Who would go to that length to mess you up? I did not know. I wrote several books. My husband and I experienced medical trauma and our relationship ended, sexually. I began to read R rated material like Outlander, the tv show. A woman wrote it and it is a beautiful show, though for a mature audience. I entered a contest for writing and wrote a story for a contest in a heavy R rated content. I laughed about this. It felt funny. But it got me writing. That was a good thing. But I think it got the cops called on me, you know. Someone once told me the internet is sixty percent porn. I quickly changed to a regular (R or G) rating after my first book and began to write a second book. My story was beautiful. That is why I continued.

But shortly after my brother was sent to federal prison for five years, I suspected they were watching me and maybe even trying to get me. They were looking to win his case and send him to jail, to get rid of him. His rap sheet is a mile long and there is no violence whatsoever. They took my personal medical case and tormented me, repeatedly. They followed me on vacation and put a black jeep next to me with my last name on it on a placard on the dash. I was beyond frazzled with shaky nerves. This was torture. The black jeep opens in my first book. I had a black jeep in real life and my last name is not Smith or Jones. It is uncommon. What on earth? This torture and waterboarding must be by bad people or professionals. I had not done anything wrong. I obey laws. This is how we treat American citizens?" I questioned.

"The water boarding continued online with things that only I would know. I did not really understand. Was this AI? Was it the IA, smart intelligence operatives using high tech surveillance maneuvers that could make you go mad? I figured out twice when my phone was tapped, a female each time next to me, years apart, and finally, the last time at the phone shop. What should take one hour took over two and a half hours and she was sitting there with no mask on while everyone else had to wear a mask. I feel like they were downloading my content. I know. This sounds very paranoid. But the pursuit of my brother convinced me anything was possible. Might have been, might not have been. One time I was using a site that artists use. I loved that site. The person who made it married a nurse, I felt hey, that is good. It has the rating like Outlander, the series of eight books or so made into a series for television.

Most of the content was fine. But one evening it went to the gutter. This is difficult. The memory of it I cannot get out of my head. I am just going to say it. This is not the way I talk or what I look at. It is demeaning. And if this is what the stalkers are doing to people, then, I do not agree with it and they should be caught.

Your Honor, may I write this down for you to read. I just do not want to say it out loud."

"The witness will now write down in her words and hand the paper to me."

I am sorry, your honor. It is vile. It is extreme sexual activity that I was not searching for. Someone intimidated me on purpose. I am sure of it. Here goes …This naked guy, who I could still recognize, fucked this girl anally. Then he fucked her in the mouth and continued turning her. What on earth had I just seen? She had pigtails. I do not know her age but maybe sixteen or eighteen. Then I became frantic, shocked, and wholly paranoid that cops were going to show up at my door the next day. I did not seek that out at all. Judge, our kids might be seeing this awful material. It was not normal. I suppose they could have been actors. Me, I just thought they were after me. Ludicrous. I hope I can forget this ordeal and that other people are not shown explicit material like I saw. And I hope girls are not exploited to make sexual material by perverts and bad men. Thank you for allowing me to write it and you reading it.

"Over these years I continued to write novels, G or R rated. That my own government would seek to destroy me as a person did unnerve my soul. Who could it be? I thought since they were after my brother maybe I was a target. I do not know for sure who did this. I made a list going back to incidents that did not seem right. It amounted to a page and a half on yellow office paper.

I tried to write about it as it made for a good surveillance novel, which I later turned into a series. The internet should be used for good, not bad. I had heard of bad actors loading kid porn and getting arrested, but placing it on my computer and watching me seems ridiculous when our medical condition had destroyed our lives. Possibly, they got off on this. They had an extra special case to enjoy.

I had heard that persons can watch you over the phone, most likely law officials. I seriously believe it was my brother and his foes that ignited my demise and nerves from these horror tactics. I may sound like a lunatic. But I promise you I am not. I am a sound nurse, mother, and wife. I continued writing thinking that someone, a good reporter would find the story about my brother, research it, and get the bad guys. I hope they get them and the perpetrators rot in hell.

They knew personal things about me, judge, and it was like ten years of a policeman behind you in a car on a highway. Everyone thinks that is unnerving. I am still waiting for a great reporter to get to the bottom of this story for my brother, myself, and our future on the internet.

In the end if an adult was terrorized with images, like myself, can you imagine how a child would feel? We do not want porn normalized and seen by children."

"Thank you, Anonymous. There is a reporter, an undercover investigative journalist who, unbeknownst at the time, was hired by the IA (Investigative Agency) to get to the truth. I will be getting her testimony after you give me the page and a half of items. Continue."

"Okay."

Three weeks later ...

"Anonymous."

"Yes?"

"I have news for you."

"Go ahead."

"The jury heard your testimony, then the investigative reporters, and have decided the case against persons working in the government and other nefarious souls. The jury found them guilty on twenty-seven counts, or matters of yours described."

"No … really? Oh … my … gosh. Oh."

"The court has awarded you 4.6 million dollars for your suffering, terrorizing, torturing and waterboarding style of surveillance which lasted over ten years. That it went on for nearly that long was evil, unnecessary, distasteful, disgusting, and rather destroys the trust of the US government. I apologize for their behavior. You are to be commended for the persistence and fortitude knowing someone powerful was at your back over these years.

Sincerely, I wish you success and for you that your bad memories fade. You are doing a great service for children and the future of the internet."

"Oh, judge, thank you. I am sorry. I am crying. I cannot help it. I was scared for so long."

"Just breath. It is over. Lawmakers will need to deal with the internet."

Scarlet laid the transcript paper on her desk. Her eyes welled up. Seth and Rachel had confused looks of disbelief. James and Megan smiled. Done. Yes. Kim the congresswoman began clapping. She stood. They all clapped.

Well done was said to Scarlet. Truth. Justice. Liberty.

The wedding …

A small and intimate wedding was held late Saturday afternoon outside in front of the tent on the lawn. Seth waited at the altar with Jessie while Scarlet walked the red carpet. Blossom walked with her followed by little Xochi dropping flower petals along the way. The wedding party and party goers enjoyed a first-class celebration under the tent beneath a starlight sky.

Music played, champagne flowed and a fancy cake was cut. Dancing ensued. Toasts were made. Jessie announced a honeymoon next week aboard a fancy yacht named Victorious.

The crowd applauded.

Jessie kissed his bride.

THE HURRICANE

A hurricane had formed in the Atlantic, and watchful weather forecasters were trying to predict the route it would take. It looked like it may evade most of the Caribbean and even the Keys of Florida. That was good for the honeymooners, but Seth and Rachel were back in Sarasota. *Where would landfall occur?*

Caroline Clemens is currently writing book number four in the Coastal Crime Thriller aka Southern Surveillance series. The next title is aptly named *Tequila Sunrise,* and a hurricane is coming... Get ready.

FURTHER READING

Into the Vines
Brie's Story
Someday
The Pilot Log
Kiss Ride
String the Cranberries
Maiden Voyage-A Lighthouse Tale
Chocolate For Lilly
Three King Mackerel and a Mahi Mahi
Magenta Fleurs

Learn More at:

carolineclemens.com

twitter.com/KimTroikeUSA
facebook.com/clemensnovels